The
GRUMP
NEXT
DOOR

New York Times Bestselling Author

KENDALL RYAN

love,
Kendall

About the Book

One guest house. One week. One slow-burn disaster waiting to happen.

Dean Whitaker has zero interest in weddings, fairy lights, or the perky woman currently turning his guest house into a scented-candle crime scene. He's a divorce attorney. He thrives on prenups, logic, and not getting glitter on his suits.

Poppy Monroe is a wedding planner with a checklist for everything—except how to survive living next door to a hot, brooding, tightly wound lawyer—aka the groom's brother.

They're opposites in every way—except for the undeniable chemistry neither of them wants to talk about.

Their mission: survive one week of wedding chaos.

Her vibe: sunshine and glitter pens.

His vibe: whiskey and restraint.

Opposites attract. Then they combust.

1

STILL SMILING

Poppy

"You're fired."

I'm doing seventy-five on the throughway, wrestling a rental car that smells like beef jerky and bad decisions, when my entire life implodes through the Bluetooth speaker.

"Wait, what?" I swerve slightly. The car behind me honks. "Miranda, the Goldman wedding was perfect—"

"Perfect?" My now-former boss laughs, but it's a laugh that makes my stomach drop. "You let the mother of the bride's Pomeranian eat half the cake."

"That was—"

"You seated the groom's mistress at the family table."

"I didn't know she was—"

"And you told the bride's father to, and I quote, 'shove his suggestions up his trust fund.'"

Okay. That one I did do.

"Miranda, please. I have the Lin wedding next weekend. I can't—"

"It's nothing personal, Poppy. I'm sure you'll

land on your feet." The line goes dead.

I stare at the road, hands white-knuckling the steering wheel. My chest feels too tight. Like someone's sitting on it. Like I can't—

No.

No.

I slam my finger on the redial button. Nothing. I call again. Straight to voicemail.

"No."

The word comes out raw. Broken.

I've been at Coleman Events for three years. Three *years* of sixteen-hour days and bridezilla tantrums and eating lunch out of Tupperware in bathroom stalls because there's never time to actually sit down. Three years of building my reputation, my client list, my entire future.

And now it's gone.

My phone buzzes. For one stupid second, I think maybe Miranda's calling back. Maybe she's—

I laugh. Or maybe it's a sob. Hard to tell when your whole life is combusting at seventy-five miles per hour.

Because here's the thing Miranda doesn't know—I already told Ivy I'd be her planner. Already signed the contract. With my name. Not Coleman Events. She wanted me, *personally*, and I promised her of course it would be me. I figured Miranda would understand the technicality.

Now things are different. Which means I'm

about to show up at this estate to plan a wedding I'm no longer authorized to plan, for a client who thinks I still have a job, without a team, or a clue about what the hell I'm doing.

I should have known today was going to go off the rails. My flight was delayed two hours, I spilled matcha all over my blazer, and the bridesmaid group chat had already imploded *twice* before I boarded. But I force a *smile* because this week matters. No—it doesn't just matter. It's everything.

Deep breaths, Poppy.

Except the rental car smells like beef jerky and broken dreams.

I breathe anyway.

This isn't what I reserved. Not even close. What I reserved was a sleek, all-electric, whisper-quiet SUV that would glide into the Hudson Valley like a glossy, capable adult woman. What I got was a suspiciously sticky Subaru hatchback with a cracked Bluetooth screen and a backseat full of unidentified crumbs.

Still smiling.

I crank down the windows, because the air freshener smells like meat. I tell myself it's fine.

It's fine. Being fired could even turn out to be a good thing.

Right? *Right?!*

My phone rings again. It's CeCe. My best friend, moral support system, and the only person I've ever met who's better at dealing with bridal parties than I am.

"Did you know?" I demand.

"Poppy—"

"Did. You. Know?"

A pause. "She called me ten minutes ago. And offered me your job."

My stomach drops through the floorboard. "And?"

"I told her to get bent, obviously." Relief floods through me. "Did you tell Ivy?" she asks immediately.

"Tell her what? That I'm unemployed? That I'm about to show up at her wedding with no team, no resources, and no backup?" My laugh sounds unhinged. "Yeah, I'll just text her real quick. 'Hey girl! Fun update—your wedding might be a disaster!'"

"Poppy—"

"I can't lose this wedding, CeCe. I can't." My voice cracks. "This was supposed to be *it*. The one that launched everything."

"So what's the plan?"

I glance at my shoes. Eight-hundred-dollar-Louboutins that took me three months to pay off. The red soles that scream *I belong here* when everything else about me whispers *fake*.

"Fake it till I make it," I say. "What else is there?"

"With what team? Poppy, this is insane—"

"I'll figure it out." The words come out harder than I mean them to.

CeCe's quiet for a second, which is slightly unsettling, because of all the things CeCe is, quiet has never been one of them.

"Are you okay?"

"That depends," I say. "If you count being fired,

a crappy rental car, a matcha incident, a group chat implosion…" I tell her everything. By the time I get to the linen mix-up and a bizarre email about live butterflies, CeCe is openly laughing.

"This is going to be *your* story wedding," she says. "The one you tell future clients to prove you can handle anything."

Always looking on the bright side, this one.

"I was kind of hoping that story wouldn't begin with me being canned."

CeCe makes a noise of encouragement. "You've got this. You're a freaking ninja with a clipboard. You once ran a beach wedding during a hurricane and still managed to keep the flower girl's curls intact."

"True." I smirk.

"You're a professional. A magician. A beacon of calm under pressure. And also… slightly terrifying when pushed."

My smile stretches, real this time. "You're just saying that because I once made a cake designer cry."

"You're my hero," she says. "Now go charm the pants off the Hudson Valley. Call me tonight and tell me all about your mysterious grump of a property owner."

Oh. I'd almost forgotten about that.

I'll be staying in the guest house of the groom's brother. Dean Whitaker. A Manhattan divorce attorney who owns the estate and according to my clients, tolerates weddings the way people tolerate dental work. We haven't spoken yet, but I've seen the emails. Short. Direct. Zero emojis. He probably irons his socks and uses phrases like *per my last message*.

In my head, he's uptight, stiff, probably wears loafers and looks perpetually disappointed. The kind of guy who thinks kombucha is a gateway drug and prefers his coffee black, his shoes polished, and his interactions with people limited.

It's fine. I've dealt with difficult venue managers before. People who think wedding planners are frivolous or invasive or too much.

Dean Whitaker has no idea who he's dealing with.

The GPS chirps that my exit is in two miles. Two miles until I have to walk into this situation and pretend everything's fine. Pretend I'm still Poppy Monroe, wedding planner extraordinaire, not Poppy Monroe, unemployed disaster who's about to commit fraud.

I glance down at my shoes again. Image is everything in this business. Fake it 'til you make it. Smile 'til your face cracks.

Speaking of which.

I catch my reflection in the rearview mirror and practice. Bright smile. Professional. Capable. Not at all like someone whose entire world just collapsed.

"Hi! I'm Poppy Monroe, your wedding planner! Everything's perfect! I definitely have a job! And a plan! And my life together!"

Shit.

My phone buzzes again. I ignore it.

Then again. And again.

I finally glance down at it.

Six missed calls. Twelve texts from various vendors. One from my landlord about next month's rent.

Cool. Cool. Cool.

I take the exit too fast. The tires squeal a little. Whatever. Add it to the rental company's list of grievances.

The scenery changes from highway to postcard—rolling hills, stone walls, trees that look like they were placed by a set designer. It's gorgeous. Peaceful. The exact opposite of how I feel.

I roll my shoulders back and take in the scenery of where I'll be spending the next ten days. Towering trees and winding roads lined with wildflowers. The hills ripple gold and green in the late afternoon light, and for a moment, I pretend I'm headed to a wellness retreat. One where no one's texting me about linen shortages or whether the girlfriend of a groomsman is allergic to all seven major food groups.

The peace lasts exactly eight seconds before my phone buzzes again.

UNKNOWN NUMBER:

Hey just fyi we might need to reassign bridesmaids. Caroline and Zoe are in a feud. Again. No clue why.

Maybe over a dress? Or like... someone's ex?

I don't respond.

Because if I respond, I will scream.

The GPS chirps, "You have arrived at your destination."

I pull up the long gravel driveway and my breath catches a little.

Because—despite everything—*it's stunning*.

The estate sits atop of a soft, sloping hill, framed by tall oaks and wild hydrangea. The main house is older but elegant, all crisp white trim and classic shutters, with ivy crawling up one side like something out of a Nancy Meyers movie. There's a detached guest house just beyond a stretch of manicured lawn, the exact right amount of rustic charm.

For a second, I just sit there. Engine running. Staring.

I could leave. Turn around. Drive back to the city and figure out a different life. One that doesn't involve pretending everything's fine when it's all falling apart.

But then I think about Ivy's texts. Her excitement. The contract with my name on it.

This wedding is happening. It has to.

Because if I pull this off—if I can somehow execute the wedding of the year without a team, without resources, without anything but sheer determination and whatever's in my emergency kit—then maybe I don't need Miranda. Maybe I can do this on my own.

Maybe.

I kill the engine, check my face one more time, and open the car door.

Time to fake it like my life depends on it.

Because it basically does.

I step out of the car, smooth my dress, and immediately plant one Louboutin directly into something wet and squishy.

Still smiling.

Absolutely still smiling.

Even if it freaking kills me.

I look down.

"Oh no."

It's… not mud. It's something wetter. More offensive. And deeply unwelcome. Something that was, at one point, probably alive or at least partially digested.

I gag once. Just a little.

But I'm prepared. I'm nothing if not prepared. I yank a biodegradable wipe from my bag and crouch down on the stone path, balancing on one foot like a deranged flamingo as I try to salvage my dignity—and my shoes.

Which is exactly when I hear a voice.

"Can I help you?"

Deep. Male. Annoyed. Very much not the kind of voice that says *welcome*.

I look up—and nearly lose my balance.

Standing in the doorway of the main house is a man. Tall, broad-shouldered, and absurdly good-looking in the kind of way that makes you briefly forget how sentences work.

His dark hair is neatly combed but already threatening to fall out of place. A five o'clock shadow clings to his sharp jaw like it's made a permanent home there. A jawline that makes you reconsider your position on marriage. His eyes—gray? green? something stormy—are striking enough to make me momentarily forget that my foot is still covered in… something.

He's wearing khakis and a crisp white dress

shirt with the sleeves rolled to his forearms, the kind of casual-office look that he somehow manages to make look intimidating.

This has to be Dean.

The grump. The groom's brother. The anti-wedding energy Ivy warned me about.

And the universe, in its infinite sense of humor, has made him *hot*.

He is, objectively, alarmingly attractive. And unfortunately, I'm crouched in front of his house, one foot in the air, my designer shoe covered in shit, my entire life in shambles, trying not to cry.

Cool. This is going great.

So I smile. Bright. Professional. Unbothered. "Hi! I'm Poppy Monroe. Wedding planner for the Lin-Whitaker event next weekend?"

He doesn't smile back. He just looks at me. "I assumed you'd arrive earlier."

"I would've," I say, still crouched, still wiping, "but my flight was delayed, and the rental car situation was… character-building."

His eyes flick to my foot, then back to my face.

I grin, apologetic. "Sorry, I seem to have found a small… welcome gift on the lawn."

He doesn't smile. Not even a polite flicker. "You'll be staying in the carriage house. It's unlocked."

"Perfect." I rise to my full height and pretend my left shoe isn't squelching slightly. "Looking forward to settling in."

He gestures, vaguely. "Try not to track anything inside."

And just like that, the hotness dies a swift and

fiery death.

I paste on a tight smile, because if I don't, I might commit murder.

Ivy Lin is one of the biggest influencers on the planet and her wedding will be plastered all over social media. It'll be the most beautiful wedding anyone's ever seen, and it will launch my business into the stratosphere. I'll be able to hire assistants and wedding planners to work for me. They will be the ones stepping in dog shit on grumpy extended family's properties.

Deep breath.

I yank my rolling luggage from the trunk and I'm halfway up the stone path to the front door when I pause and look around, taking it in—not just as a guest, but as a planner.

The estate is stately but not showy, with symmetrical windows, pale green shutters, and a wraparound porch that could be dressed up with string lights and late-summer florals. There's a quiet elegance to it, like it knows it's beautiful and doesn't need to try too hard. There's even an old wooden bench under the front window that's practically *begging* for welcome drinks or a seating chart display.

It's going to be the perfect wedding.

It has to be.

I have a week and half to make it look like I have my shit together. A week and a half to figure out how to plan the best wedding anyone's ever seen.

Should be fine.

Everything's fine.

2

ONE WEEK OF HELL

Dean

She looks like a walking disruption.

I'm barely three seconds into meeting her, and I already know—she's going to be a problem.

Not just because she showed up late and immediately stepped in something, or because she's now tracking it toward my porch with an unsettling amount of optimism.

It's the smile.

It's too bright. Too practiced. A smile that says *I'm here to take over, now get out of my way.*

I shut the front door behind me and let out a slow, measured breath. The kind I only ever use during depositions or family holidays.

The quiet inside is a relief.

I walk through the living room—cool wood floors, built-in shelves, the soft creak of a house older than I am—and place my laptop and case files on the dining room table. Everything's tidy. Controlled. I know where every pen in this house lives.

I like it that way.

I loosen the top button of my shirt since I feel like I'm slowly being strangled.

My phone buzzes.

I don't answer.

I walk to the window and watch her. She's standing by the rental car, phone to her ear, gesturing with one hand and juggling a leather tote, and a garment bag in the other.

She's... energetic. Distractingly so.

I turn away before she catches me watching.

I grab my laptop and open my email—only to immediately regret it.

Subject line: URGENT - Partner Case Motion Response

My phone rings again before I can even finish reading.

I sigh, pinch the bridge of my nose, and answer. "Whitaker."

"Where the hell have you been?" Gideon's voice barrels through the line, sharp and impatient. "I've called twice."

"I stepped away for a minute," I say. "I'm at home."

"You're off-site?"

"I'm working remotely."

"Well, un-remote yourself. Feldstein just moved up the deadline. He wants a revised motion *tonight.*"

Of course he does.

Because this week—the one week I'm hosting a wedding on my property—is the exact week my future is being decided. If I land this case and close this client, I'm in. Name on the wall. Grant, Feldstein & Whitaker.

If I don't… well. That isn't really an option.

I rake a hand through my hair and stare at the files on the table. My jaw tightens.

"I'll send it by nine."

"Make it eight," Gideon snaps.

I look out the window again.

She's laughing now. Still on the phone, still unpacking, like none of this touches her. Like my week isn't unraveling by the minute.

Her smile is blinding.

My eye twitches.

"Why aren't you in the office, anyway?" Gideon asks.

"I told you—I'm hosting the wedding here this week. For Mason. My brother."

A pause.

"Right. The influencer circus."

I say nothing.

Because I'm already regretting it.

Agreeing to let my younger brother throw a wedding on my property was… not my best decision. But Mason asked. And he never asks for anything. After years of being the carefree screw-up, he's finally settling down—*and* marrying someone who makes him want to be better. I respect that.

Mason always was the golden one.

Not in the achievement sense—that was me. I was the straight-A student, the debate team captain, the one who graduated law school at twenty-four and never looked back. But Mason? He was the one people gravitated to. The one who smiled easy, laughed loud, made everything look effortless.

We grew up in a house where silence was prized and emotions were… edited. I learned early how to shrink myself into something palatable. Mason never did. He was chaos with a guitar and a crooked grin, and somehow, he always got away with it.

So when he asked me for a favor—for the first time in years—I said yes.

Letting him and Ivy host their wedding here, I was told, would be simple. Was told that she'd be here for one week, ten days tops. I'd keep my distance. Let the planner do her job.

I didn't know the planner would be a woman with a megawatt smile and legs that go on for miles.

"Eight. And don't screw it up," Gideon barks. "This client is your ticket."

I hang up without saying goodbye.

Because he's right.

This client—the founder of a media empire currently going through a scorched-earth divorce—is high profile, high maintenance, and watching every move I make. If I win this, I'll be the youngest name partner in the firm's history. If I lose… I won't.

But I don't lose. I've spent years making sure of it.

And I do *not* have time for wedding guests, or table linens, or the bossy wedding planner currently invading my space.

I have a deadline, my little brother's wedding looming, and a stranger in the guest house.

This week is going to be hell.

• • •

The scratching starts just after six.

Two short huffs, one long.

Then a pause—just long enough to make me think she's given up—before the snuffling starts again, lower to the ground, like she's trying to inhale her way under the door.

I exhale through my nose and open it.

Muffin waddles inside with all the self-importance of someone who pays rent.

She does not.

She's wearing the thunder vest again, which probably means someone in the neighborhood used a leaf blower today. Her toenails click against the hardwood as she trots toward me. She's small, but overweight. Like a beige throw pillow that occasionally farts.

"You weren't invited," I say.

She sneezes once and flops dramatically onto the rug, letting out a long, performative groan, panting like she's run a marathon. She hasn't.

I close the door behind her.

"I thought you were staying with Nadine this week."

Muffin belongs to Nadine, the woman who lives two doors down and treats HOA violations like war crimes. Somehow, despite our mutual disdain for the human race, Nadine and I have reached a silent truce over her dog.

Which is to say—we share custody of Muffin now.

Against my will.

She spends more time on my porch than she

does at her actual home, and I've stopped pretending to care. Mostly because she has separation anxiety, anxiety-anxiety, and a complicated relationship with the weather. Also, Nadine swears her calming CBD biscuits "work better in Dean's energy field."

I don't have an energy field.

I have caffeine, high blood pressure, and a growing suspicion that Muffin likes me better than she likes her actual owner. Not that I've pointed any of this out to Nadine.

Muffin grunts.

I retrieve the biscuits from the kitchen cabinet where I keep them next to the protein powder. I break one in half and hold it out like a peace offering.

"You know she's going to ruin everything, right?" I say, lowering myself into the armchair across from her. "Bright clothes. Big ideas. Probably labels things just for fun."

Muffin only blinks. She's chronically… unbothered. It's possibly one of the things I like most about her.

"I give it two days before she tries to put string lights on the carriage house. Or—God forbid—a chalkboard welcome sign."

She lets out a snore that sounds suspiciously like agreement.

I toss the other half of the biscuit into her food bowl and return to the files on the table.

"Who smiles that much after stepping in God-knows-what?"

Muffin doesn't respond, but one eyelid twitches.

"You're not helping," I mutter.

Muffin huffs again, rolls onto her side, and begins to softly wheeze.

It's deeply unprofessional. And oddly comforting.

3

THE NORTH LAWN NEGOTIATION

Poppy

The guest house is… charming.

That's what I decide to call it because "a little haunted but in a quaint way" doesn't look great in the client notes.

It's tucked behind the main house, partially hidden by hydrangeas, with weathered white siding, green shutters, and a front porch that creaks when I shift my weight. Inside, the floors are scuffed, the windows are sticky, and there's a faint smell of old wood and lemon cleaner that reminds me of my grandmother's attic.

But the bones are good.

There's a wide farmhouse sink, built-in shelves filled with mismatched books, and a faded patchwork quilt folded neatly at the end of the bed. It could be magical with a little work—fresh paint, some flowers, and a scented candle or two.

I drop my bags by the door and do a quick mental inventory.

To-do list for the week:

- Set up layout walk-through with Ivy and Mason.

- Reconfirm all vendor arrival times.

- Schedule the final dress fitting.

- Final menu approval.

- Avoid strangling the groom's brother.

My phone buzzes. I glance at a text from Ivy.

IVY:

Just posted the final countdown! I'm getting MARRIED!

I open her social media page and click through to her story. She's in her kitchen, smiling big at the camera and surrounded by giant balloons.

The thing about Ivy is she's not your typical influencer. She started out documenting her grandmother's recipes before dementia took them away—hand-pulled noodles, wontons with exactly thirteen folds, the secret to perfect Mapo tofu. Real stories about food, family, and the stuff that gets lost between generations.

Now she has over thirteen million followers who tune in for *Cooking with Nǎi Nai*, even though her grandmother hasn't cooked in two years. She uses her platform to spotlight immigrant-owned restaurants, does fundraisers for Alzheimer's research, and somehow makes meal prep look like meditation. She's not just an influencer; she's someone who turned grief into community. And she's a lovely person, inside and out.

Which is why this wedding matters. It's not just about the perfect photos or the viral moments. It's about honoring the love story her followers have been rooting for since Mason first appeared in the background of her cooking videos, stealing dumplings and making her laugh.

I can't mess this up.

It's why I came out here early—this matters to me. It has to be perfect, not just for Ivy and Mason, but for me and my career.

I'm halfway through checking my phone when I hear a soft *snort* from the doorway.

I turn.

And there, standing just outside the screen door, is possibly the roundest dog I've ever seen.

She's got short legs, shaggy fur, ears that stick out like fuzzy triangles, and some kind of vest velcroed snugly around her middle like a canine corset. Her face is part gremlin, part angel, and her entire vibe screams "emotional support animal with zero training and strong opinions."

"Hi there," I whisper, crouching slowly. "Do you live here?"

She snorts again, waddles closer, and rests her chin dramatically on the step.

I crack the door open.

"You're not supposed to be here, are you?"

She blinks at me.

"Well, join the club."

I reach out and give her a tentative scratch behind the ears. She melts instantly into a puddle of fluff and wheezing sighs, tail thumping once, then stopping as if that was too much effort.

"You're perfect," I tell her. "There's no way he's as grumpy as he acts if he owns *you.*"

She sneezes directly on my shoe.

I grab my planner, sit on the edge of the bed,

and flip to today's tab. The sun slants warm through the window, and for the first time since the airport, I feel like I can breathe.

The venue is beautiful, the clients are sweet, the dog situation is adorable, and I've survived worse than a prickly property owner. I've got this.

I smile down at the color-coded schedule.

And that's when my phone buzzes.

IVY:

> Are you at the estate?? We have a MA-JOR problem. Mason just told me HIS BROTHER is refusing to let us use the north lawn.

I blink.

The north lawn.

The one we mapped out together on Zoom. The one with the best light for photos. The one where the ceremony arch is supposed to go.

The one I just assumed was a done deal.

I glance out the window.

Dean Whitaker is back on his porch, a glass in one hand, reading something with his sleeves still rolled up like a catalog model for emotionally unavailable men.

I look down at the dog, still snoring at my feet.

"You and I are going to have to have a word with your human."

I march.

No deep breaths. No calming affirmations. No "maybe he has a good reason" inner monologue.

I just march. Possibly because I've had the day from hell, possibly because I'm ready to go full-Karen over someone taking Ivy's dream wedding spot.

Across the lawn, down the gravel path, back to the front porch of the man currently threatening to derail an entire wedding over a patch of grass.

He's sitting in one of the porch chairs now, a glass of something dark in his hand, and a look on his face that says he's been waiting for me to snap since the moment I arrived.

Well. Here I am.

"Hi," I say, too brightly. "Do you have a minute?"

He sets the glass down with infuriating calm. "I'm guessing this isn't a social call."

"Not unless you consider ceremony sabotage a social call."

His brow lifts. "Sabotage?"

"Don't play dumb," I snap, climbing the steps. "The north lawn is the ceremony site. It's in all the planning documents. Ivy approved it. Mason approved it. I approved it."

"I didn't approve it."

I blink.

"You didn't object when I mentioned it in the walk-through notes."

"I don't recall those notes including the phrase 'please trample my lawn with folding chairs'."

"Oh, I'm sorry," I say sweetly. "Did you want to host a wedding without any actual wedding things happening?"

He doesn't flinch. "There are other parts of the property."

"Not like that one. The light, the view—"

"—the sprinklers, the slope, the two massive

tree roots that'll trip someone's grandmother."

I stare at him.

He just stares back, calm and unreadable, like we're in court and he's waiting for me to present a better argument.

I take a breath, composing myself.

"This is really important to Ivy," I say, softening. "It's her dream spot. And it works. It works for the photos, for the acoustics, for the entire flow of the ceremony, from the parking to the—"

"No."

It's not harsh. Not loud. Just… final.

"Why?" I demand.

"Because I said so."

"Oh, well *that's* reasonable."

He stands slowly, and for the first time, I realize how tall he is. Broad-shouldered and serious, his dark eyes cutting through me.

I steady myself by drawing a slow breath.

But Dean isn't done. "I've already upped my liability insurance for the property. If someone eats it on that slope, I'm not footing the ER bill. Liability's a little more complicated than 'but the view is nice'."

My hands are shaking.

He crosses his arms. "I'm not risking a twisted ankle and a three-year legal battle because someone wants a golden hour glow. If Ivy wants scenic, she can take a picture. My premiums say no."

"Wow." I take a step back, suddenly aware of how close we're standing. "Great speech. I hope they don't invite you to give one at the reception."

"I didn't want this wedding here," he says, low

and even. "But Mason asked, so I agreed. What I didn't agree to is a stranger showing up and acting like she owns the place."

My pulse spikes.

"I'm not trying to own anything. I'm trying to do my job."

"Then do it somewhere else."

I blink, the pressure of the whole event suddenly rising behind my ribs.

And I snap.

"If you're so worried about your liability insurance, maybe you should keep a better eye on your dog."

His brows draw together. "My dog?"

"She let herself into the guest house and is currently napping under the bed."

He blinks once. "That's not my dog."

I stare at him. "She seemed pretty at home."

"She visits," he corrects. "Frequently. And without invitation."

"Oh."

He shrugs. "She prefers my rug to her actual home. I've given up arguing."

I open my mouth. Close it.

Because that doesn't even make sense.

He's trying to tell me a ten-pound dog has broken in? Staked her claim? And there's nothing he can do about it?

There's a brief silence in which I have to reckon with the fact that I've just yelled at a man about a dog that isn't his, after already yelling at him about grass.

We're off to a great start.

"I'll tell Ivy," I mutter.

"I'm sure you will."

I don't say goodbye.

I spin on my heel, march back to the guest house, and only when I've slammed the door and dramatically flopped on the bed do I dial CeCe.

She answers on the first ring. "Oh no. What happened now?"

I stare at the ceiling. "He's hot and horrible."

"Be more specific."

"The groom's brother—Dean. He's giving… *brooding CEO thunderstorm* energy."

"Pssh," CeCe makes a noise. "That's nothing you can't handle."

I hope she's right.

4

EVERYTHING IS UNDER CONTROL (IT ISN'T)

Dean

I'm about to close my laptop when something catches my eye through the window.

She's still out there, sitting on the guest house steps in the dark. Not on her phone. Just… sitting. With her head in her hands.

I should go to bed. I should mind my own business. I should definitely not care that a woman who tracked dog shit through my life is having a moment.

But Muffin's already waddling toward the door, whining.

"You're not going out there," I tell her.

She scratches at the door, insistent.

"Fine. But we're not talking to her."

I open the door. Muffin shoots out like a furry missile, straight toward Poppy.

Traitor.

I follow because apparently, I make excellent decisions at 11 p.m.

The moonlight catches her as I approach, and I have to remind myself why this is a bad idea. She's the kind of pretty that few men can resist—large blue eyes fringed with dark lashes and a mouth that lifts into a smile easily and often—though not tonight. Silky golden hair falls past her shoulders, catching the light even in darkness. Curves made for a man's hands.

A dangerous combination for sure. Good thing I've always been good at locking down anything resembling a wayward emotion.

She doesn't look up when Muffin reaches her. She automatically reaches down to pet her, and that's when I see it.

Her hand is shaking.

"You okay?" The words spill out before I can stop them.

She jumps and quickly wipes her face. "Geez. You scared me."

"Sorry. Muffin insisted."

"Right. The dog made you come check on me." But there's no bite to it. She sounds… tired. Defeated, even. Nothing like the woman who marched up my driveway this afternoon in eight-hundred-dollar shoes with unshakeable confidence.

I should leave. This isn't my problem. She's not my problem.

Instead, I notice the papers scattered beside her—vendor contracts, seating charts, all covered in notes in three different colors of ink.

"That's a lot of detail work for someone with a full team," I say.

She freezes.

Just for a second. But I catch it—the telltale stillness of someone whose lie has been spotted.

"My team's… handling other things," she says carefully.

It's a lie. I know lies; I catalog them for a living. The slight hesitation, the way her fingers tighten on the papers, the forced casual tone—all of it screams deception.

"Right." I glance at the papers again and spot it—a bank statement sticking out from under a contract. Multiple overdraft fees. Final notice stamps. A financial disaster that would send someone running to a faraway estate to pull off a society wedding on their own come hell or high water.

Damn.

She follows my gaze and quickly shoves the papers into a folder, but it's too late. I've already seen the truth she's trying so hard to hide.

"I should—" She stands too fast and stumbles slightly.

I catch her elbow, steadying her. The contact sends heat crawling up my forearm, and I'm suddenly aware of how soft her skin is, how she smells like something floral and expensive, and how easy it would be to pull her closer instead of letting go.

Once she's steady, I release my hold and shove my hands in my pockets where they can't betray me.

She looks up at me then, those large eyes wide and vulnerable in the moonlight, and I know I'm in trouble. Because behind all that beauty is something worse—someone real. Someone struggling. Someone who's trying so damn hard to keep it together that she's sitting alone in the dark, shaking.

This week just got complicated in a way I

didn't budget for.

• • •

The conference room is glass-walled and quiet, save for the rhythmic tap of my pen against the edge of my legal pad.

Across the table, two junior associates shift uncomfortably in their seats. One of them clears his throat; the other blinks too much. I don't bother learning their names until they give me a reason to.

"I'm going to say this once," I begin, setting the pen down. "This client is our white whale. He's angry, powerful, and rich enough to weaponize that anger in any jurisdiction he chooses. If we don't control the narrative—immediately—he will. And we will be the ones holding a bag full of unpaid invoices and NDAs."

The blinking one nods, scribbling furiously. The other one suggests reconvening after lunch.

It's already 2:10.

I haven't eaten. Again.

The tension behind my eyes has blossomed into a full-scale headache, pulsing behind my left temple like a second heartbeat. I should care. I don't. I've gone twelve hours on less.

We wrap up the meeting. I hand off notes to my paralegal, ignore the now-cold coffee someone left at my desk, and scroll through a backlog of client emails and calendar alerts—then I see a text from my brother.

MASON:

Bro, we need to talk. Call me.

I stare at it for exactly three seconds before exhaling slowly through my nose and getting up from my chair.

The hallway outside is glossy and sterile, gray floors, frosted glass, hushed voices. My domain.

I step into a small side office, close the door behind me, and call.

He answers immediately.

"Mase—what's the problem?"

"You told Poppy she couldn't use the north lawn?"

I pinch the bridge of my nose. Poppy? Oh yeah, the wedding planner from hell. "The slope is dangerous, Mason. The roots are exposed. I'm not risking a lawsuit because your fiancée likes the lighting."

"She doesn't just *like* it, man. She's been dreaming about that ceremony spot for months. It's not about lighting—it's about her."

"I said no."

There's a pause on the other end. "You always do that."

"Do what?"

"Act like you're doing everyone a favor just by showing up. Like saying yes to this wedding means you can say no to every other detail without question."

I sit on the edge of the desk, my headache pulsing harder now. "I let you use the estate, Mason. I cleared my schedule. I didn't even charge you."

"I didn't ask for that."

"No—you just asked for everything else."

The silence stretches long enough that I almost

think he's going to hang up.

Then, softer, he says, "You know this isn't about the lawn, right?"

I close my eyes.

"Yeah," I say quietly. "I know."

And I do. It's about the fact that I always put work first. That I don't show up unless I'm needed. That I'm halfway through a name-partner-making case while he's planning a wedding, and it feels like we live on different planets.

But I can't be the guy who's sentimental. That's never been my role.

"I'll see what I can do," I say.

Mason exhales. "Thank you."

"I said I'll *see.*"

"Still a win."

He hangs up before I can argue.

I sit there for a long minute, staring at my reflection in the dark glass of the window.

Then I get up and go back to work.

Because that's what I do.

By five, my head is pounding, my inbox resembles a war zone, and my assistant informs me she's ordering dinner because I forgot that food is a thing humans need to function.

Again.

I should have known the day was going to be bad when the printer in the copy room started smoking, or when the two junior associates nearly tanked a brief with a formatting error, or when Feldstein chewed me out on speakerphone in front of a client.

So when I finally arrive home and spot the

enormous cardboard box sitting on my front porch, nearly blocking my path to the door, my first reaction is not curiosity—it's suspicion.

The label reads, RUSTIC BLISS EVENTS.

Of course it does.

I step closer, and there it is in black blocky print: "Ceremony Arch – Assembly Required."

Fantastic.

I unlock the door, toe it open, and manage to carry the box inside, slamming it a little harder than necessary against the wall by the entry.

Muffin lifts her head from the rug and yawns, unimpressed.

"You could've warned me," I mutter.

She flops back down.

I kick off my shoes, drop my bag by the couch, and head to the kitchen, where a brown paper bag waits on the counter. Thai, judging by the smell.

Thanks, Carly.

My assistant had dinner delivered.

I grab a fork and shovel half the container into my mouth before I even pour a drink. It's barely warm. I don't care.

After a few minutes, I exhale, finally slowing down enough to register my own exhaustion.

The day from hell.

Feldstein moved up the timeline on the revised motion. A key witness canceled last minute. And the client—the one who could make or break my future at the firm—sent a four-word email that simply said, "Your strategy better work."

No pressure.

I wash my hands, pour two fingers of whiskey,

and walk toward the window.

Outside, the light is starting to change. The estate is quiet.

Too quiet.

Except for the giant cardboard reminder that this place doesn't belong to me this week.

I glance at Muffin.

She blinks.

I head for the back door, whiskey in hand.

It's time to take a walk.

Not to change my mind, but to verify what I already know—the north lawn is a logistical nightmare.

The sun is just starting to dip as I head back out.

I tell myself I'm checking the drainage slope and sprinkler layout. I tell myself I'm being thorough, responsible, and cautious. I tell myself this has nothing to do with Mason's phone call.

Damn, Mason.

Muffin trails behind me like a heat-seeking meatloaf.

We round the hedges near the edge of the north lawn, and I stop.

I don't want to admit it, but… yeah. It's beautiful.

The way the trees frame the view. The light filtering through the leaves. That soft hush of wind right before sunset. It *feels* like a wedding spot.

If someone believed in such things as weddings.

A giant waste of money—says the man who spends his days drafting prenups or strategizing nasty divorces.

Still, my jaw tightens. The slope isn't terrible, but it's not ideal. The tree roots could trip someone if they're not careful. And I don't love the idea of guests trampling over this part of the grounds.

But would it really be that hard to level the chairs? Move the arch over a few feet?

I exhale slowly and rake a hand through my hair.

"Am I insane?" I mutter.

Muffin huffs once and sits at my feet.

I look down at her.

"You get that this isn't about the lawn, right?" I murmur. "It's about boundaries. Structure. Not letting people walk all over me because they smile pretty and carry clipboards."

She tilts her head.

"She shows up late, tracks mud into the house, rearranges the porch chairs, and now she wants the lawn too."

I crouch next to the dog and rub behind her ears.

"She's chaos in lipstick. You know that, right?"

Muffin blinks and leans her whole weight against my side.

"And she brought four bags," I add. "Who packs *four* bags?"

Muffin's got nothing.

"She said you fell asleep under her bed, you little traitor."

"You really can't blame her for that."

The voice behind me makes me go still.

I stand slowly, turn, and find Poppy halfway

down the path, arms crossed and expression un-readable. She's wearing a soft blue dress—nothing flashy. It's simple and casual, but it moves with her, swaying just enough to distract me. It's paired with floral-printed designer tennis shoes. Her hair is down today, and I realize how long it is—nearly reaching her elbows and golden when it catches the light.

"She packs four bags," she continues, "because she's running a 300-person event on her own, with backup supplies for every possible disaster scenario. Including, apparently, one grumpy man."

I lift a brow.

She steps forward, then kneels to scratch Muffin's chin.

"Hi again," she says softly.

Muffin lets out a contented groan, as if she's been waiting all day for this exact moment.

I shove my hands in my pockets. "You spying on me now?"

"You were muttering to a dog about my luggage. Kind of hard to miss."

I glance away, my jaw ticking.

"I wasn't—"

She stands. "Look, I know you're just trying to protect the property, and that this week is probably the last thing you want. But I'm not here to ruin your house. I'm here to give Mason and Ivy the wedding they've dreamed about."

Her voice softens slightly. "I think they deserve that."

I study her for a moment.

Then I nod—once, short and clipped. "I'll figure something out."

She blinks. "Wait, really?"

"Don't get excited. It's not a yes."

"But it's not a no."

I give her a firm look. "It's a conditional maybe."

Just as Poppy opens her mouth to say something else—something smug, probably—we hear it.

"Muffin? Muuuuuffinnn?"

I close my eyes.

Poppy tilts her head. "Friend of yours?"

Over the hedge comes the unmistakable sound of Velcro sandals slapping against the ground. Moments later, Nadine emerges on the path, visor cocked to one side and wearing what I can only assume are orthopedic walking shoes.

She stops when she sees us.

"Oh." She glances between me and Poppy, her tone already loaded with meaning. "Well. Isn't this cozy."

"Nadine," I say tightly.

"Muffin wandered off again," she says, heading closer. "You know how she gets. Separation anxiety, gut sensitivity—all the things."

Muffin, traitorous as ever, lets out a happy grunt from where she's now firmly planted on Poppy's feet.

Nadine squints. "She likes you."

"She's perfect," Poppy says with a warm smile, bending down to scratch Muffin's ears. "We bonded."

"Oh, I can tell," Nadine replies, as if that's not

a compliment. She turns back to me. "This one's new."

I grit my teeth. "This is Poppy Monroe. She's the wedding planner."

Poppy extends her hand, radiating sunshine and professionalism. "Hi! Nice to meet you."

Nadine ignores the handshake entirely.

"She doesn't look like a wedding planner," she remarks.

I lift an eyebrow. "What *does* a wedding planner look like, Nadine?"

"Less… California," she replies, adjusting her visor as if she's just delivered a critical diagnosis. "You know. Less leggy, more librarian."

Poppy smiles politely, but her grip on Muffin tightens slightly.

"Anyway," Nadine continues, already pulling out her phone. "If Muffin's going to be over here all the time—and she *is*, let's be honest—you should really brush her out. She gets mats, especially when she's emotional."

"I'll pencil it in," I mutter.

"Oh, and I hope she didn't interrupt anything." Nadine gives a little wave, already turning back toward the hedge. "Although judging by the tension in the air, I'd say *someone* just got told no."

Poppy blinks. "Excuse me?"

Nadine is already halfway gone. "Good night, kids!"

She disappears, orthopedic shoes thudding down the path like a drumbeat of doom.

I stare after her, my jaw clenched.

Next to me, Poppy stifles a laugh. Barely.

"She's a lot," she says.
"That's rich," I mutter.
Muffin lets out a sigh.
And Poppy?
She *smiles again.*
And I hate how much I don't hate it.

5

THE FLOWER WITCH
WILL SEE YOU NOW

Poppy

The town feels like it stepped straight out of a Hallmark movie—if Hallmark movies featured better coffee and more women in athleisure who clearly do Pilates before 7 a.m.

The main street is cobblestoned, which is objectively rude to anyone wearing sandals with no arch support. However, I forgive it because every storefront is a delight. There are painted shutters, flower boxes, and hand-lettered chalkboard signs proclaiming things like *Life's short, buy the croissant*—which I gladly do.

I tackle my to-do list—confirm the final headcount with the caterer, swing by the florist—who happens to be my aunt Gloria—to check on the last-minute boutonnières Ivy added, and bribe the bakery into making two extra gluten-free cupcakes that weren't in the original order. (I call it strategic planning; CeCe calls it wedding sorcery.)

Next, I pop into a tiny gift shop that smells like eucalyptus, where I find the prettiest sun-dried linen throw blankets I've ever seen. I don't need them, but I buy two.

By the time I settle onto a bench outside the general store, cappuccino in one hand and local honey sticks in the other, I feel like I've finally exhaled.

I call CeCe.

She answers with a dramatic sigh. "Did you survive?"

"Barely. But I'm on the upswing."

"Has he glared at you again today?"

"He monologued to a dog about my luggage."

"This man sounds dangerously unwell."

"That's not even the weirdest part. His neighbor—Nadine?—showed up looking for the dog, wearing what I'm pretty sure were orthopedic wedges and harboring a personal vendetta against joy."

"I cannot wait to meet her."

"You're going to love this town," I say, stretching my legs out in front of me. "It's sunshine, quirky little shops, and people who all know each other's coffee orders."

I could honestly live here—if my entire life weren't back in California.

CeCe sighs dreamily. "I knew I should've come early."

"You'll be here in a few days, just in time for peak chaos."

"And then it's off to Italy for you," she says.

I grin into my coffee lid. Even if I can't afford it right now, the plane ticket is booked, and so is my rental. "Portofino," I remind her.

"Try to sound less smug when you say it."

It's going to be my post-wedding decompression trip—sun, pasta, and absolutely no one needing a seating chart from me. It's my first real break in over three years.

Just me, a journal, a few sundresses, and the Italian coast. No clients. No deadlines.

I can hardly wait.

"Ugh, I hate you."

"No, you don't."

"Not today. But if you send me another picture of a cappuccino next to your color-coded planner, that could change."

I glance down at the photo I just took—a quiet little street, pink hydrangeas, a linen blanket folded just so, and peeking out of my bag like it's auditioning for a lifestyle shoot.

"I don't know," I say softly. "This place is so… easy. I kind of wish I had more time."

CeCe is quiet for a moment. "Yeah. But you need a reset. Italy will be good for you. And if the Hudson Valley just happens to throw in some brooding lawyer eye candy while you're there… that's not a crime."

"He is *not* eye candy."

"Uh-huh."

• • •

The next town over is smaller but just as charming.

I park in front of a little white cottage with a lavender mailbox. I haven't seen my aunt Gloria in more than a year, but we always pick up right where we left off.

Gloria never planned to become a florist.

She was a fashion editor in Manhattan for twenty-five years—glamorous, sharp-tongued, and always three seasons ahead of everyone else. Then one day, she walked out of a Condé Nast meeting, took a train upstate, bought a little white cottage with peeling shutters, and started filling vases with whatever she could yank out of the soil.

She says it was burnout. I think it was freedom.

Now she's the Hudson Valley's unofficial flower witch—part artist, part chaos agent, part therapist with pruning shears. Her arrangements are wild, emotional, and deeply impractical—"Like me," she once said with a wink. She creates them when she feels like it, for clients she finds interesting.

And, apparently, for me.

Well, for Ivy. But only because I asked.

"I'll do it," she'd said when I called. "But I have two conditions. No burlap and no one tells me where to put the peonies."

Deal.

So now, here I am, pulling into the gravel driveway of her wildly unofficial floral "studio."

A wind chime made of silver teaspoons dances in the breeze.

I step out of the car and inhale.

The smell hits me instantly—roses, soil, something herbal and expensive—Gloria.

The screen door is ajar, and Billie Holiday is playing somewhere inside.

I follow the sound through the jungle of blooms and vines, brushing past a hanging fern that tries to block my way.

Gloria stands in the middle of the room, inspecting an arrangement of delphiniums.

She's wearing billowy chartreuse pants, a black tank top adorned with sequined bees marching across the chest, and what I'm pretty sure is a velvet turban. Her lipstick is coral, and her nails are lavender. Her whole vibe says, *I retired from the fashion world, but I'm still judging your hemline.*

"Darling!" she cries when she sees me. "You're early. And glowing! Did you fall in love with the town already? I told you you'd love it."

"I do love it." I laugh, hugging her. "Almost all of it. Except for the grumpy, emotionally unavailable lawyer whose guest house I'm staying in."

"Most lawyers are emotionally constipated," she says, waving a hand as if this is nothing new.

She smells like sandalwood and fresh-cut stems—always vaguely expensive, always vaguely mystical. She pulls back and scans me, her eyes narrowing.

"You've lost weight."

"I haven't."

"Well, you *look* like someone who's been surviving on adrenaline and chai lattes, so either way, we're getting lunch. I made quinoa. Don't argue."

"Yes, Chef."

She leads me through the chaos to a tiny kitchen where plants hang from the ceiling and a disco ball dangles in the corner as if it's completely normal.

I drop my bag and sigh—the sort of sigh you can only have in the presence of someone who's known you your whole life and never once asked you to tone it down.

"You okay, poppet?" she asks, spooning quinoa into hand-thrown bowls. "You've got that 'I'm fine but don't ask me twice' look."

"I'm okay," I say. "It's just… a lot. The wedding. The clients. The venue."

"And the lawyer."

I pause. "He's… impossible."

"But handsome?"

I groan. "Annoyingly so."

"Delicious and difficult. Like a croissant with a god complex."

She pours me a glass of sparkling water infused with hibiscus. I take a sip. It's tart, floral, and a little fizzy—annoyingly perfect, like everything Gloria touches.

"He's Ivy's fiancé's brother. Dean Whitaker."

Gloria blinks. "Wait. Whitaker, Whitaker?" She taps her temple, thinking. "The Manhattan divorce attorney?"

"You know him?"

"I know of him," she says, already intrigued. "Big-deal firm. High-profile cases. Always looks mildly annoyed in press photos."

I shouldn't be surprised. Aunt Gloria knows everyone. She never had kids and has maintained quite the rolodex. Plus, she's managed to keep up with everything Manhattan, despite moving away years ago.

"That sounds like him."

Gloria laughs. "And?"

"And he's hosting the wedding at his estate."

"Okay…"

"And he hates that we're there."

She hums and begins gently arranging a spray of sweet peas. "Ah. One of *those* types."

"Totally type-A. Cold. Condescending. Uses phrases like 'liability risk' and 'revisit the terms of use.'"

"He sounds delightful."

"He monologued to a dog about how chaotic I am."

"Was he wrong?"

I squint at her. "Whose side are you on?"

"The dog's," she says. "Always."

I shake my head and finish my drink. "He's impossible. Every time I make progress, he throws up another boundary. And the worst part is… I think he's doing it to protect himself. Like, genuinely."

Gloria's hands still over the arrangement.

"Ah," she says quietly. "So he's not just a cold bastard. He's a wounded cold bastard."

I groan. "Don't make this romantic. It's not romantic."

"Of course not," she replies, her tone far too agreeable. "Just a wedding planner living in a guest house across the lawn from a handsome grump with a power complex and haunted eyes. Nothing to see here."

I throw a sprig of rosemary at her.

She catches it midair and tucks it into the arrangement. "Well, if things escalate, I expect to be the first to know."

"They won't."

"They might."

"They won't."

She winks. "I'll just keep some extra peonies

on hand. In case of emergency."

I roll my eyes and eat my quinoa.

After lunch, Gloria gestures toward a long, butcher paper–covered table behind her. "You brought the mood board, didn't you?"

I dig into my bag and pull out a crisp portfolio, sliding it across the table like it's a sacred artifact. "Printed *and* laminated. You're welcome."

We move to the stools at the larger table, and she fans through the pages, nodding slowly, her many bracelets jangling with each turn. "Okay. This I like. Very soft. Very romantic. Like a Jane Austen heroine on her third mimosa."

"Ivy's big on whimsy. She described it as 'cottagecore meets cool-girl editorial,' which I think roughly translates to wildflowers, but make them expensive."

Gloria snorts. "Translation: she wants it to look effortless but not *actually* be effortless."

"Exactly."

"Don't we all," she says wistfully. "Basically, that's the story of my life."

We move to the greenhouse side by side, pulling bundles of Gerbera daisies, ranunculus, and feverfew from buckets. Gloria works intuitively, her fingers flying. I work with a ruler, a clipboard, and a very specific plan.

And somehow, it always balances out.

"What's the plan for the ceremony install?" she asks, jotting some notes to herself.

"Ivy wants a full floral arch—heavy on texture but still airy. Sage, dusty rose, pale peach. I was thinking of adding local wild clematis if we can get it—"

"Already ordered."

I pause, smiling. "You're the best."

"I know."

We continue working in silence for a minute, comfortable and happy. The sun shifts through the trees outside the window, scattering light across the flowers.

Gloria ties off a bouquet with a ribbon and holds it up. "You know," she says, studying it, "for all the stress and last-minute nonsense, this wedding's going to be beautiful."

I nod, suddenly and unexpectedly a little emotional. "Yeah. It is."

• • •

By the time I pull back into the driveway, the sun has dipped just low enough to tint the sky pink and gold. It's that fleeting hour when everything looks romantic, soft, and slightly filtered.

Which is probably why it takes me a full five seconds to realize there's a goat on the porch.

A real one.

Just… standing there. Like he lives here. Okay, the dog was one thing… but Dean has a goat? I'm having a hard time picturing that.

I climb out of the car and eye the goat.

He's scruffy, charcoal gray with darker markings around his eyes, giving him a vaguely villainous look. Like a goat that once got cast as the bad guy in a children's cartoon and never quite let go of the role.

He's chewing something.

I squint.

No. Not something.

My linen table runner!

"Excuse me!" I shout, darting closer as if I'm about to perform a citizen's arrest.

The goat—unbothered, unimpressed, and possibly entertained—does not stop chewing.

"Oh no no no," I mutter, walking faster. "Hi. Hello. That's… not yours."

He flicks an ear and continues chewing.

I freeze at the foot of the porch, doing the kind of frantic mental math that only panic can induce.

Goat. Porch. Chewing. No one else around.

And then it hits me.

"Oh no."

Is this *my* goat?

I pull out my phone and scroll through my email until I find it—the message I sent to a small local farm down the road—Shelby's Heritage Hooves. I'd attached a carefully curated mood board. Subject line: "A Rustic-Chic Reception Idea."

I read it now like it's a confession note.

I think it could be magical to have a couple of small goats wandering the cocktail lawn—very curated natural energy. The photo ops would be incredible. Plus, the bride is a chef and very farm-to-table. Let me know if this is something you'd consider!

She never replied. Never confirmed.

And yet.

I look at the goat, who is now trying to wedge his face into one of the porch planters.

"Did she just… drop you off?"

He sneezes dramatically and resumes eating a flower.

"This is not happening." I run a hand down my face. "You're my goat. I manifested a goat."

He knocks over the planter with his hoof.

They were supposed to be a couple of them, and they were supposed to be *cute*, *mini* goats.

I crouch, careful not to spook him. "Okay. I can fix this. Maybe you're temporary. Maybe you're just visiting. A loaner goat."

He headbutts the side of my tote bag.

"No? Not a loaner? Just… casually committing to chaos, are we?"

He makes a low, satisfied noise and sits in the middle of the porch like a guest waiting for dinner.

I stare at him.

"I cannot believe I accidentally ordered a goat."

6

GEORGE

Dean

All I want is ten quiet minutes.

Ten minutes to loosen my tie, take off my shoes, and maybe—if the universe is feeling generous—drink something that isn't luke-warm coffee from a travel mug that's been living in my car since Monday.

Instead, I pull into the driveway and immediately slam on the brakes.

There's a goat in the driveway.

A goat.

Standing like some sort of smug, four-legged patrol. Head high. Beard twitching. Creepy yellow eyes locked on me as if this is *his* property now.

And just behind him, chaos.

Poppy is in the middle of the lawn—barefoot, muddy, one arm streaked with what I hope is dirt—holding a broom. Her hair is half up, half frizz, her sundress clinging to one side of her thigh like it lost a fight with a sprinkler, and she is *yelling*.

At the goat.

Which is currently standing on top of a folding chair.

I park. Slowly. Like I'm defusing a bomb.

I get out and take three steps before my brain catches up with what my eyes are seeing.

The entire back garden is trashed.

One flower arrangement is overturned. There's ribbon in the bushes. A bucket has been kicked over and is now floating in the pond. And smack in the middle of the patio—

Goat poop.

Because, of course.

"What," I say flatly, "is happening?"

Poppy spins toward me, cheeks flushed, hair plastered to her forehead, and a wild gleam in her eye.

"I can explain."

"You'd better."

"There was a misunderstanding with a goat farm," she says breathlessly. "It was supposed to be… charming."

The goat hops down from the chair and immediately starts chewing on the hem of her dress.

"Charming," I repeat.

"Yes." She yanks the hem of her dress from the goat.

I gesture to the wreckage. "This is charming?"

"I didn't know he was coming! He just— showed up. And now he won't leave."

"Have you tried asking him nicely?"

She shoots me a death glare. "He ignores boundaries."

"So do you."

She throws up her hands. "Okay, you know what? That's fair. But it's not like I can just *un-goat* the situation."

The goat chooses this moment to leap onto a wicker loveseat and knock over an entire tray of welcome gift bags. One lands in the mud. Another lands in what is definitely not mud.

Poppy groans and grabs her forehead.

I stare at the sky.

"Of course," I mutter. "Of course this is how today ends. Of course I come home to find a farm animal desecrating my lawn."

I step around a suspicious pile and look at her again.

She's out of breath, covered in dirt, one strap of her dress falling off her shoulder.

And she's laughing.

Low at first, then louder—an uncontrollable, slightly hysterical laugh that bubbles out of her like she's finally cracked.

"I'm sorry," she gasps. "It's not funny. It's absolutely *not* funny."

The goat bleats.

She laughs harder.

I cross my arms. "This wedding is going to kill me."

She snorts. "You? I'm the one who just got headbutted into a flower bucket."

I blink. "You what?"

She gestures to her soaked dress. "Fell backward. Knocked over the whole thing. Hosed myself off. It's been a day."

She's still laughing. And now, despite myself, I feel it too—that twitch at the edge of my mouth, a laugh that I try to bite back, even though I already know I won't succeed.

Because somehow, this ridiculous mess? This feral goat, the mud, and this woman who showed up and turned my house into a set for an SNL skit?

It's the most alive this place has felt in years—a small, annoying part of my brain supplies.

Even if I hate it. Even if I don't have time for it.

Poppy exhales, hands on her hips, eyes turned toward the wreckage. Her hair is stuck to her neck in damp curls. She's exhausted. Covered in grass.

"Have you eaten?" I ask.

She turns her head slowly. "What?"

I gesture vaguely toward the house. "I've got sandwiches. From this place in town that doesn't screw them up."

She blinks like I just offered her a diamond necklace.

"You're offering me food?"

I sigh. "I'm not trying to poison you. It's just a sandwich."

"And you're not going to follow it up with a list of venue restrictions or goat-related fines?"

"I can't promise that."

She smiles, small and real.

"Give me five minutes," she says, already heading toward the guest cottage.

Five minutes later, I knock once on the guest cottage door, holding a brown paper bag and two bottles of sparkling water under my arm. The goat is nowhere to be seen, which is either a good sign or the start of a horror movie.

The door creaks open.

She's changed. A cotton sweatshirt, shorts, hair

pulled up, face still flushed. She looks… softer. Less feral. But only just.

"You really brought me dinner?" she asks.

"It's a sandwich."

She opens the door wider. "Come in before George eats you."

"George?" I ask, stepping through the door.

"It's what I'm calling the goat now."

I nod like it makes perfect sense.

Inside, it's cozy and smells faintly like vanilla, her, and the lemon cleaner I used before she arrived. Her things are neatly stacked—her planner, an emergency sewing kit, a notebook covered in sticky tabs. There's a floral-print mug on the windowsill and a playlist humming softly from her phone. A couple of candles are burning on the coffee table. I've never seen this place appear quite so lived in.

I'm not sure how I feel about that.

I pass her the bag.

"Roasted turkey with smoked gouda," I say. "I had a backup."

"Dean," she says, her voice mock-serious. "Are you… being *nice* to me?"

"I'm legally required to offer aid in a crisis."

She snorts, unwraps the sandwich, and takes a bite. She moans. "Dear God."

I nod, acknowledging that yes, Fatty's sandwiches are the bomb.

We sit on opposite ends of the couch. Not touching. Not talking for a long minute.

Just… eating.

It's the first quiet moment since she arrived.

The first time I've felt like maybe this wedding won't actually kill me.

And then—

CRASH.

Something hits the window.

We both bolt upright.

"Was that…?" she whispers.

"Sounded like a tray."

I move toward the window and pull back the curtain. George is on my patio table. But this time… he's not alone.

George stands on the table, and Muffin is there too, at the base, staring up at him like a fuzzy, thunder-vested war general. One paw raised. Silent. Unmoving.

George munches on a stick.

Muffin growls—a low, slow, threatening little rumble that suggests she's finally had enough.

"Is this happening?"

Poppy appears beside me and gasps. "Are they—are they *having a standoff?*"

"Looks like it."

George flicks an ear, hops in a slow circle, and makes direct eye contact with the dog. Muffin stays rooted, gaze locked, vibrating with judgment and ten pounds of CBD-powered restraint.

"I think she's about to snap," I whisper.

"She's trying to protect her turf."

"I respect that."

We watch in silent horror as George casually hops down from the table.

Muffin *launches*.

Everything erupts. There's barking. Bleating. A

flying potted plant.

Poppy groans and covers her eyes. "This is a nightmare."

I reach for the door. "No," I say. "This is Tuesday."

Only Tuesday?

I breathe. In through the nose. Out through the mouth.

The goat isn't the only trespasser. There's something else skittering across my carefully pruned life—bright, relentless, and wearing floral-print sneakers. I'm just not sure whether Poppy Monroe is here to ruin my lawn or whatever's left of my sanity.

• • •

The house is finally quiet.

Which is saying something, considering that two hours ago there was goat poop on my patio and my lawn was torn half to shreds by a demented goat.

I'm showered. And Muffin is curled up beside me in bed. I don't remember when she graduated from porch dog to bedtime snuggler. But here we are.

The Amazon box with her brush arrived today—soft-bristle, detangling, the whole nine. I open it and peel away the packaging like it's sacred. Because apparently, I'm that guy now.

"Okay," I mutter, settling in. "You ready?"

Muffin sighs. A big, dramatic exhale, but she doesn't move. I take that as consent.

I start brushing. Slow, careful strokes. Avoiding the sensitive spot behind her back leg where she always flinches.

"Can't have you getting matted," I murmur. "You've got standards to uphold."

The finest mutt this side of the Hudson River.

She grunts, snuggles in deeper, and lets me keep going.

For a while, we sit in silence. Just the soft bristle of the brush working through tangled fur and the occasional snore.

And then—because no one else is here—I say it out loud.

"She's a disaster."

Muffin opens one eye.

"Poppy," I clarify. "She's chaos. Loud. Messy. Overly enthusiastic. Probably responsible for at least two dozen zoning violations."

Muffin blinks once. Noncommittal.

"And she talks with her hands. Constantly. Like she's conducting an invisible orchestra."

Silence.

I narrow my eyes. "I don't care how pretty she is."

Muffin blinks again. Slightly slower this time.

"Don't give me that look. I know you noticed."

I pause the brushing.

"She's infuriating," I say, more to the room than the dog. "Always humming. Always smiling. Stealing my lawn with flower buckets and a vision. Lighting candles in the guest house."

Muffin yawns.

I go back to brushing.

"And now she's got a goat."

Another long pause.

"A *goat*, Muffin."

She doesn't respond.

I lean back against the headboard and exhale. "George is a complete and total dick."

That, she agrees with. A low growl rumbles in her chest.

"See? Finally, something we see eye to eye on."

She sighs again and shifts closer.

And even though I won't admit it—to her, or myself—I keep brushing long after I need to.

7

ONE GUEST HOUSE. ONE GOAT. ONE EMOTIONALLY CONSTIPATED LAWYER. LET THE GAMES BEGIN.

Poppy

It's a perfect afternoon.

Sunny. Warm. Birds chirping. I stand just off the north lawn with my clipboard in one hand and a measuring tape in the other, trying to visualize where the ceremony arch will go—once we've confirmed it won't topple downhill and take someone's aunt with it.

Muffin snoozes nearby in a patch of sun, her thunder vest gone now, tongue lolling out like she's been through some things.

She has. We both have.

I'm in the middle of taking notes about chair spacing when I hear the telltale slap of orthopedic sandals on flagstone.

"Thought I'd find you out here," Nadine announces, as if she lives in a BBC murder mystery and I'm her prime suspect.

I turn to her. She's holding a Tupperware container like a bribe and wearing a lemon-print visor that somehow makes her look *more* judgmental than usual. The shirt is linen. The energy is hostile.

"Hi," I say, cheerful and professional because I've planned enough weddings to know that small-town neighbors often wield more power than local officials. "What a gorgeous day."

"Debatable," she replies, already extending the container. "Lemon bars. Low-sugar. No gluten. Practically health food."

I take them because I've been raised right and also because I'm not sure what happens if you say no to Nadine.

"Thank you."

Muffin lifts her head, watches Nadine approach, then slowly stands and walks over to me.

Then—dramatic as a soap opera exit—she sits directly at my feet and leans her entire weight into my leg.

Nadine squints. "Interesting."

"Is it?"

"She usually doesn't pick sides until at least day four."

"I didn't realize there were sides."

"There are always sides," Nadine says with conviction. "And she's not subtle."

Muffin lets out a soft sigh and settles in.

Nadine leans down and pets Muffin lovingly. "Oh good, Dean did brush you out."

I highly doubt that—I can't picture Dean being so soft, gentle, and nurturing with a dog, but whatever.

She does look somewhat more groomed than usual, though it could just be because I'm used to her wearing that little vest.

"So," Nadine says, eyeing my clipboard, "big wedding. Big vision. Big mess waiting to happen."

Gee, thanks.

"Hopefully not the last one," I say with a smile that's 90% teeth.

She hums, clearly unconvinced. "And Dean agreed to all this?"

"He did."

"Willingly?"

I pause. "It's his brother's wedding."

"Oh, I know. I just never thought he'd go for it. The Dean I know doesn't even allow solar-powered garden lights."

That… checks out. He's not one for frills.

She folds her arms and glances toward the main house. "He used to live in the city, you know. Sleek little apartment. All concrete and cold air, with furniture out of a minimalist catalog."

"I can picture it."

"This place?" she continues, gesturing to the estate like it's an accusation. "He bought it from a client. Nasty divorce. They just needed out. He got a screamin' deal."

"I… didn't know that."

"Oh, honey. Most people don't. He came out here to 'reset.' Said it was temporary, that he planned to flip it and make a nice profit. That was three years ago."

I look down at Muffin, who's still glued to my leg like she's making a statement. I brush my hand over her soft little head.

"So now he lives here," I say.

Nadine narrows her eyes. "He exists here.

That's different. He still commutes to the city a few times a week. Ninety minutes each way."

Before I can respond, she checks her watch and snaps the lid back onto the lemon bars.

"Well. I'll leave you to it. Muffin has therapy at three. Acupuncture. And I need to confirm the appointment."

She gives me one final once-over, like she's still trying to decide if I'm a threat, a liability, or a tragic lifestyle blogger.

And then she's gone.

Muffin stays.

I busy myself with the work ahead. Dean has commuted to the city for work today, so the property is quiet. There's so much to do. This weekend, I'm throwing one of the most important weddings of my career—one that could make or break me.

Ivy Lin is an influencer with over thirteen million followers, and she and Mason arrive in a couple of days, so I need everything to look perfect. A yard crew is patching up the destruction caused by George yesterday, and I've still got a lot to do— vendors to call and magic to make happen.

It starts quietly, like all great disasters do.

One minute, I'm organizing a crate of glassware on the back patio. Muffin is curled up nearby in a rare moment of zen, the sun filtering through the trees, and I'm feeling—dare I say it?—slightly in control.

And then I hear it.

The soft clunk of hooves on wood.

Followed by a metallic rattle.

Followed by the unmistakable sound of something headbutting an innocent, helpless table.

I turn slowly.

George is standing triumphantly on the porch railing, one hoof planted on a crate of candles, the other on my clipboard. He looks like a king surveying his domain. He lets out a sharp bleat, eyes wild, beard twitching.

And then he *leaps*.

Straight off the porch. Lands hard. Charges.

Right at Muffin.

Muffin—peaceful, aging, full of trauma and chicken-based treats—screams.

She doesn't bark. She *screams*.

Then she runs.

She shoots past me like a cannonball, ears flapping. George is right behind her, hooves clacking, head lowered like this is the final round of a medieval jousting match.

"Oh no, no, no," I shout, dropping a box of napkin rings. "GEORGE!"

They barrel down the lawn.

Around the floral arch-in-progress.

Through a cluster of folding chairs.

Past the beverage station.

And then—miracle of miracles—a car pulls into the driveway.

A black SUV.

Dean's car.

He steps out, fresh from the city, still in a suit. Tie straight. Shirt crisp. Eyes tired.

And then he sees it.

A goat. Chasing his dog. His neighbor's dog?

Across his property. Through a wedding venue.

His expression doesn't change at first—just a slight twitch at the corner of his mouth, like his soul is trying to exit through his teeth.

He sets his briefcase down. Removes his jacket. Rolls up his sleeves. And walks toward the chaos like he's approaching a hostage negotiation.

"George!" I shout, running to catch up. "Stop! I swear to God if you eat another charger cable—"

Dean intercepts them on the side lawn.

He moves fast, to his credit. I'll give him that. But George is… well, *George*.

Dean lunges for him once. Misses.

Lunges again.

Grabs him by the collar.

And just as he gets a grip—George twists, jerks, and drags Dean three feet across the grass like a man-shaped sled.

Dean digs in his heels.

"Poppy," he says through gritted teeth, "call off your goat."

"He's not my goat!"

"You manifested him!"

"That's not legally binding!"

Muffin circles back, clearly confused, then decides she's had enough and flops down in the shade.

Dean is holding George by the collar, breathing hard.

His white shirt is smeared with mud across one shoulder, his tie hangs loose, he's missing one shoe, and there's a chunk of grass stuck to his sock. He's breathing through his nose like someone counting to ten, and he has *definitely* reached eight.

I wipe tears from the corner of my eyes, still

chuckling. "You… you okay over there?"

His glare could melt titanium. "Do I look okay?"

"Honestly?" I bite back another laugh. "You look like a Calvin Klein ad shot in rural hell."

George sneezes. Again.

Dean exhales like it physically hurts. "I have three hours of work to do. Two meetings. One urgent client request. And this"—he gestures to George, to the grass stains, to *everything*—"was not on the agenda."

"Well, neither was the goat," I say, bristling a little. "I didn't ask for this."

"You didn't *not* ask for it."

I stiffen. "Excuse me?"

"You emailed a farm and sent them a Pinterest board titled 'Rustic Dreams.'"

"First of all, it was *Rustic-Chic Reception Inspiration,* and second of all, I never heard back! This isn't my fault."

George tugs at the collar and lets out a loud, goat-y sigh.

Dean looks like he might combust.

"I came home to find my dog traumatized, my lawn destroyed, and *myself* being used as a human sled by a very angry farm animal."

"Okay, that part *was* kind of funny—"

"It was *humiliating.*"

"If it helps, you looked very professional doing it!"

His jaw tightens. "It doesn't. I don't have time for this," he says. "I have a career. A motion due by midnight. A senior partner breathing down my neck."

"So maybe don't pick now to wrestle live-stock?" I snap, then immediately regret it.

His eyes narrow. "This is not what I signed up for."

I cross my arms, heart hammering. "You think I did?"

We stand there, glaring, the lawn between us muddy and ruined, George the Goat standing perfectly still like he's awaiting judgment.

Dean shakes his head slowly. "This wedding is a circus."

His words sting because he's right. I've always prided myself on my work, but this is not my best. And I hate that.

"I'll get rid of George," I say, my voice small.

"Please do," he snaps, finally releasing the collar and wiping his hand across the front of his dress pants with disgust.

And with that, he stomps up to the house.

8

THIS WEEK IS GOING TO KILL ME

Dean

I should be working.

There's a brief due at midnight, an entire section of a case I need to rewrite, and an email from Gideon marked URGENT in all caps that I haven't opened yet because I value my blood pressure.

Instead, I'm sitting at the dining room table in a clean T-shirt and sweatpants, freshly showered, staring blankly at my laptop screen while the cursor blinks as if it's mocking me.

No matter how hard I try to concentrate, my brain keeps circling back to—

Goats.

Mud.

And Poppy Monroe.

Poppy Monroe, who laughed so hard she doubled over while I was being dragged across my own lawn like a cartoon character.

I scrub a hand through my hair.

She's infuriating.

All sunlight and chaos, big ideas, and that *damn* clipboard she waves around as if she's so important. And now she's got Muffin choosing her side. Again. Considering the little beast is nowhere to be found.

I open a document, stare at the screen, type two words, and delete them both.

A soft *thump* outside the window draws my attention. I glance up.

Muffin.

Trotting across the lawn like she owns the place.

A moment later, there's a light scratch at the door.

I don't move.

Another scratch.

I sigh, push back my chair, and open the door.

She barrels past me without even pretending to wait for an invitation, waddles over to her designated spot on the rug, and flops down with a grunt.

"Make yourself at home," I mutter, shutting the door behind her.

She stretches. Smiles, probably. I don't know. Her eyes are smug. I sit back down and glare at my laptop as if I can will it into submission.

"Still nothing," I say after a beat. "Because apparently my entire frontal lobe has been hijacked by a wedding planner and a goat."

Muffin yawns.

I fold my arms. "I don't care how much Mason's paying her—whatever she's charging, it's too much."

The dog lifts her head and blinks slowly.

"She's disorganized. Unprofessional."

Muffin licks her paw.

"And she's taking over everything. My lawn. My porch. My dog."

Muffin thumps her tail once and then curls up tighter, as if she's heard enough.

I lean back, stare at the ceiling, and sigh. "Sure, she's cute. In a hyper-organized, ruins-your-life-with-a-smile kind of way."

"But she's not my type," I say into the silence.

The silence doesn't agree. I lean back again, stare at the ceiling, and scrub a hand over my face.

This week is supposed to be about focus. Work. Strategy. Partnership. Locking in Feldstein's client. Closing the deal. Becoming the youngest named partner in the firm's history.

That's it. That's the whole plan. No distractions. No detours. Just delivering the best motion of my life and collecting the brass ring.

Instead?

I'm chasing down goats and arguing with a woman who's taken over my property.

Muffin sighs from the rug.

I open a new tab and click onto Reddit. I don't even know why I do it.

Okay, I know exactly why I do it. I just want to see if anyone else on earth has lived through something like this.

I click into the "Am I the Asshole" subreddit.

My fingers hover over the keyboard.

Then I start typing.

And I let it all pour out—unedited, unfiltered.

Posted to r/AmItheAsshole

username: RestingBriefFace

Am I the Asshole for wanting to evict a wedding planner from my guest house who's turning my property into a three-ring circus (even though I technically agreed to host the event)?

I (36M) *agreed—against my better judgment—*to let my younger brother (30M) and his fiancée (28F) host their wedding on my property. His fiancée hired a wedding planner (29F) who has taken over my guest house, my yard, and possibly my will to live…

It's a large estate I own in upstate NY. It has a carriage house/guest house out back that is now, unfortunately, occupied by this woman—the wedding planner.

And she's… a lot. Energetic, constantly smiling. Basically, a total type-A. On steroids.

She moved in a few days ago to "oversee operations on-site." Since then:

My dog (who belongs to my elderly neighbor but spends 80% of her life at my house) now seems to prefer her.

A goat showed up and never left. His name is George. No one knows where he came from. Apparently, he's "a vibe."

She's been burning scented candles

in the guest house; it now smells like a vanilla crime scene.

She sings while she works. Sometimes to the goat.

I work in a high-pressure legal job. I have meetings. Deadlines. I used to have peace. Now there's goat poop on my driveway and a woman who makes color-coded seating charts is practically everywhere I look.

She's not doing anything *wrong* per se. She's just... everywhere. On my lawn. On my porch. In my brain. And the week's only just begun.

I'm working remotely while trying to close a high-profile legal case that could determine the rest of my career. I need focus. Quiet. Zero distractions. I'm getting none of that.

So: Would I be the asshole for asking her to relocate?

I stare at it for a second.
Hesitate.
I read it back three times, and consider deleting it. Then I remember getting dragged across my own lawn by George.
I hit *submit* before I can change my mind.
It's anonymous. No one will ever know. Just a quick vent to the internet. A digital scream into the void, if you will.

Muffin blinks up at me.

"What? Don't judge me." I toss her a baby carrot from my plate.

She ignores it.

Typical.

I close the laptop and stretch. Muffin lifts her head as if to say *finally*.

"Come on," I mutter, rising from my chair. "Let's go ruin a bush."

We step outside into the cooler night air. The lawn is quiet. The catering table has been reassembled. George is nowhere to be seen. Small mercies.

And then I see her.

Poppy.

Still out there.

She's barefoot now, walking slowly across the lawn with a clipboard and a roll of twine in one hand, a mug in the other. She's squinting up at the arch as if she's imagining it fully built and fully blooming. There's a pen tucked behind her ear and smudges of something—probably mud or goat-related trauma—on her jeans.

She doesn't see me.

She's focused. Quiet. The exact opposite of how she seems in the daytime.

Muffin trots over to her without hesitation and plops down at her feet.

Poppy glances down, smiles softly, and reaches to scratch behind Muffin's ears.

"Hi, sweetheart," Poppy coos at her.

I stand there, watching, for a second too long.

And just like that—guilt. It creeps in before I can shut the door on it. Because yeah, she's a huge pain in my ass but… she's also trying. Working late. Fixing the things that go wrong. Carrying more weight than anyone sees. All for my brother and Ivy.

I exhale through my nose and head back inside, ignoring the discomfort sitting in my chest.

I grab a glass of water, return to the dining room table, and open my laptop.

My Reddit post has blown up.

There are already over 400 comments.

I scroll for a second.

ThrowawayWife27:

Dude. She sounds like sunshine and goats are cute. You sound like you need a nap.

I frown.

That's… an aggressive take.

BreadOnPurpose:

You let her *move* in, *run a* wedding, and burn scented candles. You're not the asshole. You're married.

lemonlawyer:

Not the Asshole. You are allowed to not live in a rom-com. That said… is she single?

CozyChaosQueen:

She sings to the goat?! I LOVE HER. Invite me to this wedding.

legalbeagle96:

OP left out whether he's developed feelings. I feel like the goat knows.

salty_but_sweet:

You're the asshole—if you kick her out before at least ONE unresolved sexual tension argument over cake forks.

lilmuffy96:

Wait. Is this the guy with the thunder vest dog? I've been following that saga on r/dogfree. Small world.

BagelDad:

As someone who has literally been pooped on by a goat at a winery wedding, I feel you. But also? You're totally gonna fall in love with her.

NotMyMothersDaughter:

OP, be honest: have you *ever* bought a woman flowers? You sound a little high-strung. Let the goat soften you.

gayunclesrevenge:

Sir, you are not asking if you're the asshole. You're asking if it's okay to be in love with a woman who smells like vanilla and organizes for a living. Yes. It's okay.

I groan.
This is why we don't trust the internet.

I click through a few more, scanning responses filled with goat puns, wildly incorrect assumptions, and at least one person suggesting I'm repressing deep romantic feelings I'm afraid to confront.

Okay, *first of* all—no.

Second of all… hell no.

Muffin settles in under the table, totally unfazed. Typical.

twoglassrosé:

Plot twist: the goat is the officiant and you're the groom. I've seen this movie before.

saltyfrombirth:

You listed "sings while she works" like it's a crime. Sir, this is not a villain origin story. This is *foreplay.*

"I'm not the villain here," I say to no one.

cottagecore_cynic:

This is the enemies-to-lovers goat-inclusive wedding novel I didn't know I needed.

passiveaggressiveduck:

You could've just said "I'm in love with a chaos goddess," but no. We had to *get here* via goat poop and candle rage.

Judgybutjustified:

Bro. You said she's not doing anything

wrong. You invited her. She's working. You're just annoyed she's not boring. You're the asshole.

lawyerdad22:

This is *absolutely* a "grumpy introvert meets cheery extrovert" situation, and I would like a weekly update, thanks.

goatsarepeopletoo:

George did nothing wrong. Team Goat.

I close the tab.

I need to get back to work. The internet is full of unqualified opinions from people who have no concept of nuance, legal precedent, or human decency.

Ridiculous. I shouldn't have bothered.

9

CHAMPAGNE AND CHAOS

Poppy

By morning, the lawn is pristine, the goat is nowhere to be seen, and I've already reorganized the seating chart twice.

Everything looks fine.

Which is exactly why I don't trust it.

I walk up the path toward the main house, armed with two printed vendor schedules and a backup roll of washi tape. The plan is to check in with Dean, confirm the delivery window for the lighting crew, and *not* let him get under my skin.

Easy. Totally doable.

I knock lightly on the front door, expecting to hear him bark something like *"What now?"*

Instead, I hear… nothing.

His SUV is here, parked right where he left it last night.

I knock again and step inside.

"Hey, I have a quick—"

I stop. Blink.

Muffin is lying belly-up in the middle of Dean's sleek, overly serious office rug—legs in the air, paws twitching as if she's dreaming of world domination. And Dean is crouched beside her, mid-rub, giving her a tender, slow-motion belly scratch.

She is, clearly, living her best life.

"…uh. I'll come back," I say.

Dean looks up.

"She broke into my house again."

I tilt my head. "She's like ten pounds. I'm pretty sure she can't *break* anything."

"She wheezed until I opened the door. It was either let her in or get sued for emotional distress."

He stands, brushing dog hair off his perfectly pressed slacks. Muffin wheezes louder, like she's personally offended by the lack of follow-through.

"Do I smell… salmon?" I ask.

He sighs like this is the weight he must bear. "CBD-infused smoked salmon treats. Nadine says they mellow her chakras."

I blink. "You're trying to calm Muffin's chakras?"

"She took them. I was… tricked."

"Uh-huh."

He adjusts his shirt collar, then smooths his hair even though it doesn't need it. There's something odd about him this morning—stiffer than usual. Like he's trying *too hard* to be casual, which—fun fact—makes him *weirder*.

"Are you okay?" I ask.

"I'm fine."

That was fast. Too fast. Definitely not fine.

I give him a long, slow once-over. His sleeves are rolled up neatly. His jaw is tight. His eyes are doing that *I'm fine but also having a quiet existential crisis* thing.

Dean Whitaker is acting weird.

And I don't know why.

But I do know I'm going to find out.

He's still frowning when I sit down across from him and pull out my clipboard.

"Okay, since I'm here and Muffin has had her chakra realignment for the day, can we run through a few quick things?"

He hesitates.

I raise an eyebrow. "Unless you have a goat therapy session scheduled next?"

That earns me a look—classic Dean. Flat and withering, but the corner of his mouth twitches as if he's fighting off an eye roll.

"Fine," he mutters. "What now?"

"Power access," I say, flipping a page. "The band's arriving Friday for rehearsal, and I need to ensure we have an outdoor power source they can tap into. Preferably something that isn't also powering your security cameras and outdoor lighting."

He exhales and leans back in his chair. "Fine. There's an outdoor breaker panel on the west side of the house. I'll unlock it."

"Perfect. AV needs a staging area for the speakers and cables. I was thinking to the right of the arch, but I wanted to check with you first."

"That's fine—just keep them off the flowerbeds. George's mishap with the tulip massacre is already costing me an arm and a leg."

I scribble a note. "Done. Next, cords."

His brows lift. "Cords?"

"Yes, as in—what are people tripping over? Where are we routing the wires? How do we keep your liability insurance intact?"

His eye twitches slightly, and I call that a win.

"We'll need access to the garage for a few cable covers," I add sweetly. "Unless you'd prefer your guests to surf their way across live wires in heels."

"Is electrocution part of the theme?"

"It is now."

He exhales sharply. That *almost* sounded like a laugh.

I'm about to move on when I remember the big one.

"Oh! And where do you want the luxury porta-potties?"

He goes still. "The *what?*"

"The luxury porta-potties," I repeat cheerfully. "Climate-controlled. Bluetooth-enabled. Ivy picked them out. They arrive Friday."

Dean looks genuinely rattled.

"Why are they Bluetooth-enabled?"

"I didn't ask. I was too busy wondering if they also have voice activation and mood lighting."

He glares at me.

"You can't have 300 people traipsing inside your house to use the restroom. It's better this way."

He scrubs a hand over his face. "I cannot believe I let them talk me into this."

"You let *her* talk you into this," I say gently.

His expression softens for a fraction of a second. "Yeah. I did."

We sit in silence for a moment, both of us realizing that this week has been even more unhinged than we anticipated.

I nudge my clipboard toward him. "So, where

do you want them?"

He doesn't respond right away. He just looks at me—really looks—and I feel it like a static charge.

"You're enjoying this," he says.

"Am I?"

His gaze drops to my mouth, just for a second.

I smile. "I mean… I could put them right in front of the house if you'd like."

"Try it," he says, his voice low. "See what happens."

Muffin groans from under the desk, tired of being around whatever this is.

This tension between us—it's undeniable.

I grin, stand, and tap my pen against the clipboard. "Think about it. I'll be back later. Oh, by the way, George is supposed to be picked up after lunch."

"Finally," he mutters. "That's the best news I've heard all week."

• • •

It's 1:47 p.m.

George was supposed to be picked up after lunch.

It is currently… *after lunch.*

He is still here.

Not just here, but perched like a bearded overlord on top of a folding table, chewing aggressively on a discarded ribbon spool and ignoring every single one of my increasingly desperate bribes.

"This is getting ridiculous," I mutter, shaking a small bucket of grain the farm left behind. "Come on, George. Be cool."

George snorts.

I lower the bucket and glance across the lawn toward the house. Dean is pacing, his tie half-undone, sleeves rolled up, and eyes fixed on his phone as if he can will the goat removal team into existence. He's muttering under his breath. I catch the word *lawsuit.*

Muffin, for the record, is hiding somewhere inside. She wants *no* part of this. Smart girl.

"I called them again," Dean calls out, looking up. "Still no answer."

"Maybe they got stuck in traffic," I offer weakly.

"Or maybe this is a prank and I now own livestock."

"Could be worse," I say. "You could own two."

Dean shoots me a look that could curdle milk.

And that's when it happens.

A car pulls into the driveway. At first, I think—finally. The goat farm. George is saved. We're saved. But it's not a pickup truck. It's a sleek SUV with tinted windows.

The door opens.

Ivy climbs out in the cutest yellow sundress, big sunglasses, and a perfect messy bun that definitely took a professional forty-five minutes to create.

Mason gets out next, guitar case in one hand, coffee in the other, grinning like he's arriving at summer camp.

"Surprise!" Ivy calls, waving.

Dean and I both freeze.

"Oh no," I whisper.

Dean mutters something I won't repeat in polite company and immediately starts walking toward them.

Too late. George leaps from the table, hits the grass with a thunk, and bolts in a half-circle—directly toward Ivy.

Mason yelps. Ivy shrieks. Dean sprints.

And I'm left holding a grain bucket, wondering if this wedding has an exorcism package I forgot to check off.

Two minutes later, George is finally wrangled—barely—and tied to the porch post with a length of garden twine I truly hope will hold. Because if not—heaven help us all.

Ivy fans herself with a sample program, visibly rattled but holding it together in that cool-girl influencer way.

Mason, bless him, is laughing. Of course he is.

"Was that… a goat?" Ivy asks, pulling off her sunglasses.

Dean adjusts his collar. "He's being picked up. Allegedly."

I step forward, clipboard in hand, ready to salvage what I can. "You're early! We thought you were coming tomorrow."

"I wanted to see the space, and I couldn't wait," Ivy admits. "Mason said you had everything under control."

Dean looks at me. "Define control."

I ignore him. "Let me show you around."

Mason grins.

Dean closes his eyes briefly, as if negotiating with the universe.

I lean in. "Hey," I whisper, "remember how relieved you were when I said George was getting picked up?"

Dean doesn't respond, just glares.

George lets out a triumphant bleat behind us, as if he knows *exactly* what he's done.

Once George is secured, there's a pause. A silence.

Dean runs a hand through his hair and mutters, "Well. You're here now."

I glance at Ivy and Mason, then back at him.

He sighs. "How about a toast? I think I've got a bottle of champagne in the wine fridge."

Ivy perks up. Mason immediately says, "Yes. Thank you."

I'm about to politely excuse myself—because surely this is a family thing, and I'm still faintly goat-scented—when Dean turns to me.

"Poppy?"

My head lifts. "Me?"

He nods. "You're part of the chaos. Might as well raise a glass to it."

For reasons I don't fully understand, that one sentence shifts something in my chest. I follow them inside.

Dean's house is not what I expected.

It's warm, quiet, and lived-in without being cluttered. Built-ins along the walls are filled with books and records. Soft leather couches invite relaxation. Framed black-and-white photographs, likely expensive, adorn the walls. Everything smells faintly of cedar, soap, and something citrusy that I *refuse* to find attractive.

Until now, I've only seen the entryway. The guest house felt like a cozy Airbnb, but this feels like *him.*

There's a piano in the corner. Of course there is. A dark upright with stacked sheet music beside it and a brass lamp perched on top, suggesting it's used regularly.

Dean disappears into the kitchen and returns with four crystal champagne flutes.

Ivy pops the cork with a grin and pours, the fizz filling the silence.

We gather in the living room—Mason on the couch, Ivy curled beside him, Dean standing near the window with one hand in his pocket and a glass in the other. I perch on the edge of a leather chair, pretending not to notice how the cushions sink just enough to throw me off balance.

"To the bride and groom," Dean says, raising his glass.

We all echo the toast.

I sip. It's cold, fizzy, and delicious.

Now that the adrenaline from their surprise arrival has worn off, I finally get a moment to *look* at Ivy and Mason properly.

They're infuriatingly perfect.

Ivy, sipping from her glass, tucks a tendril of hair behind one ear, her skin practically glowing. She makes "bridal" look effortless—like it's always been part of her DNA.

And Mason? He's tall, nearly as tall as Dean, but scruffy, with sun-streaked curls shoved under a backward baseball cap. He's dressed in a T-shirt, and his jeans are ripped at the knees in that *"on purpose"* kind of way. Ivy is polished and sweet, while Mason exudes charming boyish energy. They are adorable together.

I take another sip and feel Dean's eyes on me.

So I focus on my champagne.

The bubbles hit *immediately.*

And wow. Have I eaten today? Do goat-related cardio bursts burn more calories than I realized? Because *three sips* in, I'm feeling it—light, warm, and maybe slightly floaty.

Dean catches me looking at the piano.

"You play?" he asks, his tone casual.

I shake my head. "No. But I *pretend* I can every December when I try to learn Christmas carols and give up by New Year's Eve."

His mouth twitches. "Tragic."

"Tell me about it. I've been trying to conquer 'Jingle Bell Rock' since 2014."

Ivy watches us from the rim of her glass, her gaze sharp and knowing, but she doesn't say anything.

Yet.

Dean looks at me again—not a quick glance, not annoyance—just… looking. Like he's trying to figure something out and is annoyed that he can't.

I take another sip.

The room feels warmer now.

Mason's telling a story—something about how he proposed to Ivy and accidentally dropped the ring in a bowl of pasta. Ivy's groaning and laughing. The moment's easy. Unstaged.

I glance at Dean.

He's not laughing. Not really. But there's something there—a shift, the faintest tug at the corner of his mouth.

"You should try smiling more," I tease. "It's good for your blood pressure."

"Is that a medical opinion?"

"That's a 'your jaw is permanently clenched' opinion."

He exhales—a quiet little sound—but I sense there's something deep beneath his stony surface. He's like an iceberg.

I take another sip of champagne, my eyes on Dean. "Do you even like weddings?"

He huffs. "I like contracts. And prenups. And legal briefs."

"So that's a no."

He doesn't look at me when he replies, but I hear the shift in his voice. "I like the idea of someone believing in something that much."

I blink.

Then he actually *does* smile—small, lazy, and completely unexpected—and it hits me, all at once, how stupidly cute he is when he forgets to be annoyed with me.

Yep. Champagne's gone straight to my head.

"I'm just gonna—yeah," I murmur, standing a little too fast. "Get back to work."

I step outside into the afternoon sun, hoping the air will clear my head and maybe cool the flush rising up my neck. It doesn't.

Dean's smile—*real*, fleeting, totally unsanctioned—is still playing in my head.

Stupid smile.

Stupid face.

I shouldn't have had that glass of champagne.

I make it halfway across the lawn before I hear the door creak open behind me.

"Poppy," Ivy calls.

I stop, square my shoulders, and turn with a polite smile. "Hey."

She strolls over, champagne glass still in hand, her designer sandals somehow not sinking into the grass like mine did an hour ago.

When she reaches me, she loops her arm through mine as if we're old friends, rather than people who've only had three Zoom meetings and an email chain 87 messages deep.

"Okay," she says in a low, conspiratorial voice, glancing toward the house. "What's the deal?"

"With what?" I ask, even though I already know.

"With my future brother-in-law…"

"Dean?"

She smirks. "He's being weird."

"He's always weird."

"Weirder than usual," she replies. "Not in a bad way—just in a *has he always had that jawline and tension* kind of way."

I pause. "Did you just say jawline and tension?"

"I'm just saying." She raises her hands, mock-innocent. "If he weren't already family—"

"*Ivy.*"

She winks. "What? I'm just saying, that man is *not* indifferent to you."

"No, he's just…" I trail off, staring at nothing. "Stressed."

"Uh-huh." She sips her champagne. "And cute,

apparently."

"I never said that."

"You didn't have to."

I groan, tug my arm from hers, and head for the tent. "I have things to do."

"Don't worry," Ivy calls after me. "Your secret's safe with me. For now."

I don't look back, but I can feel her grin chasing me all the way across the lawn.

10

FOCUS

Dean

The elevator doors close with a soft hiss, and I immediately regret not taking the stairs.

Forty-three floors. Forty-three floors of thinking about vanilla and the way she laughs when George headbutts something expensive.

I check my phone. Three missed calls from Gideon. One text that reads, "WHERE ARE YOU?"

Perfect.

The elevator dings. Forty-third floor. I straighten my tie, roll my shoulders back, and remind myself why I'm here—partnership, legacy, the biggest case of my career.

Not as a wedding planner who smells like expensive candles and chaos.

I manage the elevator ride without once thinking about the way she smells and how I want to bury my face in her neck.

Well. Mostly.

I step into the familiar gray-and-glass hallway of Grant & Feldstein, nod to the receptionist, and head straight for my office.

"Whitaker!"

Gideon's voice cuts through the hallway before I even reach my door. He's standing outside the conference room, arms crossed, looking like a disappointed father whose kid just brought home a C-minus.

I stop. "Morning, Gideon."

"Is it? Because according to my watch, morning was three hours ago."

I glance at my phone. 9:47 a.m.

Shit.

"Traffic," I say.

"From where? Connecticut?"

Close enough. "I'm here now."

He steps closer, squinting like he's trying to diagnose me. "You look… off."

"I look tired."

"No, you look annoyed. More than usual. Which is saying something, because your baseline is already pretty hostile."

I unlock my office door. "I'm fine."

"You're not fine. You're wound tighter than a Swiss watch. What's going on?"

I dump my briefcase on the desk and power up my laptop. "Nothing's going on. I've got a motion to file and a client to close. Same as always."

Gideon doesn't move. He's still standing in my doorway like a human roadblock.

"When's the last time you took a vacation?"

Absurd. "I don't take vacations."

"When's the last time you got laid?"

I look up. "Excuse me?"

"You heard me. You're walking around like

someone who needs to either punch something or—"

"Gideon."

"—get naked with someone who—"

"Gideon."

He holds up his hands. "I'm just saying. Maybe delegate some of this workload. Take a long weekend. Get a massage. Find a nice woman who—"

An image flashes in my mind. Poppy. Her bare feet on the grass. Hair falling in her face as she laughs. The way she bit her bottom lip when she was thinking.

I clear my throat. "I'm fine."

"You just twitched."

"I didn't twitch."

"Your left eye twitched. Like a tell."

This is why I hate people.

I sit down, open my laptop, and start typing. "The Morrison brief needs to be filed by five. The deposition notes need to be organized. And I've got a conference call with opposing counsel at two."

Gideon leans against the doorframe. "Dean."

"What."

"You sure nothing's going on at home?"

Home.

Where she's probably reorganizing something. Singing to herself. Making lists in that careful handwriting. Where Muffin's probably following her around like a furry stalker, and George is... God, I hope George is gone by now.

"Nothing's going on."

"Because if there was—say, a woman—I'd understand why you're acting like someone stole your favorite pen."

I stop typing. "There's no woman."

"Uh-huh."

"There isn't."

"So you're just naturally this tense?"

I lean back in my chair and give him the look that usually makes junior associates apologize for breathing.

It doesn't work on Gideon.

Damn him.

"Okay," he says, clearly unconvinced. "Well, when you're done pretending you're not thinking about whoever she is, Feldstein wants to see you. Conference room. Now."

He walks away before I can argue.

I stare at my screen. The cursor blinks back at me, mocking.

There's no woman.

There's a wedding planner who's temporarily disrupting my life. There's a problem I need to solve. A distraction I need to eliminate.

That's it.

I save the document, grab my notepad, and head for the conference room.

Feldstein is already seated when I walk in. Expensive suit, silver hair, the kind of quiet authority that makes everyone else in the room feel like they're twelve years old.

"Dean. Sit."

I sit.

"The Morrison case. Where are we at?"

I straighten my shoulders. "The motion's drafted. Deposition's scheduled for Friday. Opposing counsel's getting desperate, so they're stalling on discovery."

"And you're confident we'll close this?"

"Yes."

He leans back, studying me. "Good. Because if we don't, there's going to be a conversation about your future here. And not the kind that ends with your name on the wall."

I nod. "Understood."

"I hope so. Because I've been watching you, Dean. You're good. Damn good. But good isn't enough anymore. I need brilliant. I need someone who can handle the pressure, close the deal, and never let personal shit interfere with business."

Personal shit.

Like goats. And vanilla candles. And the way she looked at me while she sipped that glass of champagne.

"There's no personal shit," I say.

"Glad to hear it. Because this client? He's worth eight figures. And if we land him, you're looking at partnership. Real partnership. Not just a promotion."

It's everything I've been working toward for over a decade.

He stands, smooths his tie, and heads for the door.

"Don't screw this up, Dean."

The door closes behind him with a soft click.

I sit there for a minute, staring at the conference table. Eight figures. Partnership. Everything I've worked for. Everything I've wanted.

I pull out my phone and check the time. It's just

past ten.

I wonder what she's doing right now. If she's fixed whatever George broke. If she's still barefoot on the lawn, making everything look effortless.

I wonder if she's thought about me at all.

Then I remember where I am. Who I am. What's at stake.

I put the phone away and get back to work.

By four o'clock, I've written sixteen pages of legalese, fielded twelve phone calls, and consumed enough coffee to power a small city.

I've also thought about Poppy exactly… let's call it zero times. Sure.

If you don't count the moment I caught myself wondering if she'd eaten lunch.

Or the time I imagined her reaction to Gideon's massage comment.

Okay, fine. I've thought about her more than zero times.

But not enough to matter. Not enough to interfere with work.

I'm in the middle of reviewing case precedent when my phone buzzes.

Text message.

Unknown number.

My stomach does something weird.

I open it.

POPPY:

George update: FINALLY picked up. Your lawn is safe. Also, Muffin misses you. She's been sitting by the front door for an hour.

A picture follows. Muffin, pressed against the

glass door, looking tragically abandoned. I stare at the photo longer than I should.

Then I type back:

Three dots appear. Disappear. Appear again.

POPPY:

DEAN:

POPPY:

I almost smile. Almost.

DEAN:

POPPY:

It's not okay. It's the opposite of okay. Because now she can text me whenever she wants, and I'll probably answer, and that's exactly the kind of personal shit Feldstein was talking about.

DEAN:

POPPY:

I put the phone down. Face down. Like that'll help.
It buzzes again.
I ignore it.
It buzzes again.
I flip it over.

POPPY:

Work. It's about work. I can answer work questions.

DEAN:

POPPY:

DEAN:

POPPY:

DEAN:

Of course she is.

This time I do smile. Just a little. And that's the problem.

I put the phone in my desk drawer and lock it.

I've got two hours to finish this motion. Two hours to prove I'm partnership material. Two hours to focus on what actually matters.

Not vanilla candles.

Not color-coded itineraries.

And definitely not the way she says my name like it's a challenge and a promise at the same time.

I open a new document and start typing.

The phone buzzes from inside the drawer.

I ignore it.

It buzzes again.

I keep typing.

The third buzz breaks me.

I unlock the drawer and check the message.

POPPY:

Your brother says you play piano. True or false?

I stare at the text.

Why does she want to know?

Why does it matter?

Why am I already typing back?

DEAN:

True.

POPPY:

What kind of music?

DEAN:

Classical mostly. Some jazz.

POPPY:

That's... actually really sexy.

I stop breathing.

Did she just—

My phone rings. Gideon's name is on the

screen.

I answer on the second ring, my voice rougher than it should be.

"What?"

"Feldstein wants to see you. Again. Now."

I clear my throat. "On my way."

I hang up, shove the phone back in the drawer, and head for the conference room.

But I can't stop thinking about that word.

Sexy.

She thinks I'm sexy.

And that's exactly the kind of personal shit that's going to ruin everything.

11

REINFORCEMENTS

Poppy

CeCe's laugh carries across Gloria's flower shop like wind chimes in a hurricane—bright, chaotic, and completely unstoppable. She flew in this morning, and I'm so glad she's here.

"So let me get this straight," she says, perched on a stool between buckets of peonies and what I'm pretty sure is artisanal moss. "You accidentally manifested a goat, the grumpy lawyer gave you his phone number, and you texted him about piano playing being sexy?"

I bury my face in my hands. "When you say it like that—"

"It sounds like you're halfway to jumping his bones."

"CeCe."

Gloria snorts from across the room, where she's arranging what looks like controlled chaos in a vase. "Jumping whose bones?"

"The emotionally constipated lawyer," CeCe supplies helpfully.

"Dean," I correct.

"Same thing," they say in unison.

I grab a stem of lavender and twirl it between my fingers. The smell is calming. I need calming. Because ever since I sent that text yesterday, my brain has been running a constant loop of what if he thinks I'm hitting on him, what if he doesn't think I'm hitting on him, and what if I was hitting on him without realizing it?

Spoiler alert: I was totally hitting on him.

"He hasn't texted back," I say.

CeCe raises an eyebrow. "Since when?"

"Since… yesterday afternoon."

"Honey. It's been less than twenty-four hours."

"That's like three years in text time."

Gloria abandons her arrangement and joins us, settling onto a velvet ottoman that definitely wasn't designed for flower shops but somehow works perfectly here.

"Show me the conversation," she commands.

I hesitate. "It's not that interesting."

"Bull. Hand it over."

I reluctantly pass my phone. Both women crowd around the screen like they're decoding ancient hieroglyphics.

"Oh my God," CeCe breathes. "Look at these response times."

"Immediate," Gloria observes. "Every single one."

"And he resigned himself to your color-coded itinerary."

"That's basically foreplay for control freaks."

I grab the phone back. "You guys are reading way too much into this."

"Are we though?" CeCe tilts her head. "Because from where I'm sitting, this looks like a man who's trying very hard not to be interested and failing spectacularly."

Gloria nods sagely. "The best ones always fight it the hardest."

"He's not fighting anything. He's just… Dean. Serious and professional and probably regretting ever letting Mason use his property."

"Uh-huh." CeCe doesn't sound convinced. "And that's why he hand-delivered you a sandwich after the goat incident?"

"That was basic human decency." And I now regret telling them that.

"Poppy, darling," Gloria says, her voice gentle but firm, "basic human decency doesn't involve gourmet turkey and smoked gouda from the area's most beloved deli."

I pause. "How do you know what kind of sandwich it was?"

"You described it. In detail. Twice."

Shit. I did, didn't I?

"Plus," CeCe adds, "you've mentioned his jawline at least four times since I got here this morning."

"I have not—"

"Sweetie, you have."

"I was being descriptive."

"You were being thirsty."

I throw a piece of baby's breath at her. She dodges it with dancer reflexes.

"Okay, fine," I admit. "Maybe I'm a little… aware of him."

"Aware," Gloria repeats, like I just said I'm a little aware of gravity.

"Physically aware."

"There it is," CeCe says triumphantly.

I groan and flop backward against a pile of burlap that smells like dirt and possibility. "This is such bad timing. I'm trying to run the biggest wedding of my career. I'm supposed to be focused. Professional."

"Who says you can't be professional and attracted to someone?"

"Me. Because I get weird when I like someone. Remember Jake?"

CeCe winces. "We don't talk about Jake."

"I reorganized his entire apartment on the second date." I pause, remembering back.

"To be fair, his apartment probably needed reorganizing."

"I color-coded his spice rack, CeCe."

"…Okay, that was a lot."

Gloria laughs, low and knowing. "Honey, some men like a woman who takes charge."

"And some men run screaming."

"The ones who run aren't worth keeping anyway."

I sit up, brushing burlap fibers off my dress. "Besides, it doesn't matter. After this weekend, I'm going to Italy. A week of pasta and wine and absolutely zero responsibility for other people's happiness."

"Italy," CeCe muses.

Only because it's already paid for. Before I can slide into doom and destruction, my phone buzzes.

All three of us freeze.

"Check it," CeCe whispers.

"What if it's just work?"

"What if it's not?"

I grab the phone with shaking hands.

DEAN:

Muffin broke into my house again. She's holding my office hostage.

The attached photo shows Muffin sprawled across Dean's desk, belly up, looking absolutely blissful.

"Oh my gosh," CeCe squeals. "He sent you a dog photo."

"That's…" Gloria studies the screen. "That's his office, isn't it? He's at work, and he stopped to take a picture of the dog and send it to you."

My stomach does something fluttery and inconvenient.

"It's just about Muffin."

"Honey," CeCe says gently, "men don't send unsolicited dog photos unless they're flirting."

I stare at the picture. Muffin looks ridiculously content, like she owns the place. And in the background, I can see the edge of Dean's laptop, some scattered papers, and a coffee mug that looks expensive.

It's intimate. Weirdly domestic.

I type back:

She knows a good office when she sees one.

Three dots appear immediately.

DEAN:
She's drooling on my case files.

POPPY:
That's her way of improving them.

DEAN:
My client might disagree.

POPPY:
Your client clearly has no appreciation for artistic collaboration.

DEAN:
Is that what we're calling it?

I bite my lip, suddenly hyperaware of CeCe and Gloria watching over my shoulder.

POPPY:
I'm calling it Muffin being Muffin.

DEAN:
Fair point. How's the wedding prep?

POPPY:
Controlled chaos. Your favorite kind.

DEAN:
I don't have a favorite kind of chaos.

The dots appear and disappear. They appear again.

Finally, he replies.

I stare at the screen.

"What does that mean?" I ask out loud.

"It means," CeCe says, "that he's thinking about you too."

"Or it means he lives there and will inevitably see me when he gets home."

"Or," Gloria interrupts, "it means he's looking forward to it."

I lock my phone and set it face down on the counter. "You guys are delusional."

"We're optimistic," CeCe corrects. "There's a difference."

"A small one."

"Speaking of which," CeCe says, suddenly standing and brushing off her jeans, "I brought supplies."

She walks over to her oversized tote bag and starts pulling out items like a magician's assistant: champagne, fancy face masks, a bag of gummy bears, and—

"Is that glitter?" I ask.

"Emergency glitter," she confirms. "In case your lawyer needs some joy forced into his life."

"Please don't glitter bomb Dean." Something

tells me he would *not* appreciate it.

"I make no promises."

Gloria claps her hands together. "Oh, this is going to be fun."

I look between them—CeCe with her mischievous grin, Gloria with her knowing eyes—and realize I'm either about to have the best week of my life or the most embarrassing.

Possibly both.

"Promise me," I say, "that you won't do anything that'll get me kicked off the property."

"We promise," they say together.

Too quickly.

Way too quickly.

My phone buzzes again. This time it's not Dean.

IVY:

Emergency! Mason's parents just decided to come a day early. They'll be here tomorrow morning and want to meet everyone involved in the wedding. Including you. And they're... particular.

I show the text to CeCe and Gloria.

"Well," CeCe says cheerfully, "looks like tomorrow just got interesting."

"Define particular," I mutter, already mentally rearranging my entire schedule.

My phone buzzes again.

IVY:

Also, they're bringing their two dogs. Hope that's okay!

I close my eyes.

"More dogs?" Gloria asks, reading over my shoulder.

"More dogs."

CeCe grins. "I'm definitely staying for this."

And suddenly, I have the horrible feeling that this wedding is about to become way more complicated than one slightly possessed goat and a grumpy lawyer who may or may not be flirting with me via dog photos.

But honestly?

I can't wait to see what happens next.

12

MORNING MAYHEM

Dean

I wake up to the sound of industrial drilling.

At six. Effing. A.M.

"What the—"

I shoot out of bed, nearly tripping over Muffin, who has somehow migrated from her dog bed to directly under my feet. She grunts at me as if this is my fault.

The drilling gets louder.

I yank on yesterday's jeans and storm downstairs, ready to commit whatever level of murder is legally defensible when someone attacks your morning with power tools.

I throw open the front door and—

What the hell?

My lawn looks like a war zone.

There are trucks everywhere. Three? Four? I stop counting when I see two men attempting to erect what appears to be a circus tent where my yard used to be.

"No," I say to no one. "Absolutely not."

"Oh good, you're up!"

I turn to find Poppy—because of course it's

Poppy—powerwalking across the lawn with a clipboard in one hand and what might be the world's largest coffee in the other. She's wearing jean shorts that should be illegal and a tank top that says "BRIDE'S BESTIE" in glitter.

"What," I gesture at the chaos, "the hell is this?"

She doesn't even slow down. "Tent installation. They were supposed to start at eight, but I got them here early. You're welcome."

"Are you insane? I'm welcome? For what?"

"For getting a jump on the day." She consults her clipboard. "We've got the tent up at seven, the lighting crew at nine, and—oh, the porta-potties arrive at noon."

I release a choked sound.

She finally looks at me. Really looks at me. And her step falters just slightly.

Right. No shirt. I forgot about the no-shirt thing.

Her eyes do a quick sweep—chest, abs, that V-thing I've been told is distracting—before snapping back to my face. There's a tiny flush creeping up her neck.

Good.

"Luxury porta-potties," she says, her voice only slightly higher. "Remember? Climate controlled. Very classy."

"Nothing about porta-potties is classy."

"These have chandeliers."

"That doesn't make it better."

A guy in a hard hat approaches. "Where do you want the second tent?"

"Second tent?" I practically growl.

Poppy doesn't miss a beat. "Northwest corner,

by the oak trees." She turns back to me. "Reception tent and ceremony tent. Standard backup in case of rain."

"Standard would be asking permission before turning my property into effing Coachella."

She tilts her head. "Did you want me to wake you at 4 a.m. to ask? Because I can do that tomorrow if you prefer."

I open my mouth, then close it.

Because what am I supposed to say? That I specifically told Mason he could use the property? That I agreed to this whole circus? That technically, she's doing exactly what she's supposed to do?

"Coffee?" she offers, holding out her cup.

"I don't share germs with chaos agents."

"Your loss." She takes a deliberate sip, and I definitely don't watch her lips wrap around the lid. "It's got cinnamon."

Another contractor approaches. This one's carrying what appears to be a small chandelier.

"For the luxury toilet?" I guess.

"See? You're learning."

I run a hand through my hair, probably making it stick up worse. "This is insane."

"This is a wedding."

"Same thing."

She studies me for a moment. "You really hate this, don't you?"

"What gave it away? The clenched jaw or the eye twitch?"

"Both, actually." She softens slightly. "Look, I promise we'll be as unobtrusive as possible. You'll barely know we're here."

A tent pole crashes to the ground with a sound like thunder.

We both look at it.

"Starting when?" I ask.

She bites her lip to keep from laughing, and I absolutely don't notice how that makes her mouth look.

"I'll buy you breakfast," she offers. "As an apology for the wake-up call."

"I don't eat breakfast."

She looks positively offended. "Everyone eats breakfast."

"I drink coffee and judge people. That's my breakfast."

"Well, I make excellent coffee and I'm extremely judgable, so…" She gestures at herself like she's presenting evidence.

Another crash—this time, it's a whole section of tent.

"Son of a—" One of the contractors starts swearing creatively.

Poppy winces. "I should probably—"

"The oak tree has a weak branch," I say. "On the north side. If they set up under it, it'll come down in the first strong wind."

She blinks at me. "Oh. Okay. Thanks for being helpful."

"I'm not being helpful. I'm preventing a lawsuit."

"Right. Very practical." But she's smiling now—the real kind, not the professional one. "Gary! Not under the oak! Move it six feet south!"

Gary gives her a thumbs-up.

She turns back to me. "Any other lawsuit-preventing advice?"

"The sprinklers go off at six-thirty."

"Shit. Really?"

"Every day."

She's already speed-walking toward the contractors. "Everyone move your equipment! Sprinklers in twenty!"

I should go inside. I should remove myself from this situation. I should definitely put on a shirt.

Instead, I follow her.

"Why are you like this?" I ask.

"Like what?" She's directing traffic now, pointing contractors away from the sprinkler zones with the efficiency of an air traffic controller.

"Aggressively cheerful. It's unsettling."

"Why are you aggressively grumpy? That's equally unsettling."

"I'm not grumpy. I'm realistic."

"You want to murder happiness itself."

"Happiness woke me up with a power drill."

She laughs—full-on laughs. "God, you're such a drama queen."

"I'm a drama queen? You rented chandeliers for toilets."

"Luxury toilets."

"That's not better!"

We're standing too close now. I don't know how it happened. One second we were walking, and the next we're toe-to-toe on my lawn, her looking up at me with those stupidly blue eyes, me looking down at her glitter shirt and trying not to think about what's underneath it.

"Dean?" she says.

"What?"

"The sprinklers."

And that's when the water hits.

It's like being attacked by a thousand tiny ice bullets. The sprinklers don't just turn on—they explode, sending jets of freezing water in every direction.

"Shit!" I try to shield her, but it's too late. We're both soaked in seconds.

She shrieks, then laughs, then shrieks again. "It's so cold!"

"I told you seven-thirty!"

"It's seven-twenty-one!"

Leave it to her to be precise.

We run for cover, her grabbing my arm to steady herself, me trying not to notice how her tank top is now basically see-through.

We make it to the porch, dripping and breathless.

She's still laughing. Hair plastered to her neck, mascara starting to run, her glitter shirt now a contender for a wet T-shirt contest.

"Your sprinklers are broken," she accuses.

"Your timing is terrible," I counter.

"Your lawn is a death trap."

"Your whole existence is a death trap."

She steps closer, still breathing hard. "Big words for a man in wet jeans."

"Big talk for a woman in see-through clothing."

Her eyes widen. She looks down. "Oh!"

"Here." I gesture vaguely at the door. "There are towels inside."

"I can't go in your house like this!"

"You also can't stand on my porch like that unless you want to give the contractors a show."

She crosses her arms over her chest, which only makes things worse—or better, depending on your perspective.

"This is your fault," she mutters.

"My fault? My sprinklers are on a timer. A consistent, predictable timer."

"You could have warned me sooner!"

"I did warn you!"

"Six seconds is not a warning!"

We're arguing about sprinklers, but there's something else happening. Something in the way she looks at me, water droplets catching on her eyelashes. Something in the way I can't stop noticing the goosebumps on her arms.

"Towels," I say roughly. "Inside. Now."

She nods, suddenly no longer arguing.

I hold the door open, and she ducks inside, careful not to brush against me.

Except she does—just barely. Wet skin against wet skin, and damn if that doesn't send heat straight through me despite the cold water.

"Dean?"

"Mm?"

"Your parents are in your living room."

I freeze. "What?"

"Your. Parents. Are. In. Your. Living. Room."

I push past her to see, and—yeah, there they are. My mother in her standard Connecticut casual, my father in golf clothes, both staring at us like we're a particularly interesting exhibit at the zoo.

Oh, and they've brought the dogs.

"Dean, sweetheart," my mother says, her voice dripping with false surprise. "We thought we'd drop by to discuss the wedding arrangements."

"At seven-thirty in the morning?"

"We were in the neighborhood."

"You live an hour away."

"Don't be dramatic." She turns her attention to Poppy, and her smile sharpens. "And you must be the wedding planner."

Poppy, to her credit, doesn't even flinch. She stands there, dripping on my hardwood floors like this is totally normal.

"Poppy Monroe," she says, extending a wet hand. "Lovely to meet you."

My mother looks at the hand like it might be contagious. "Indeed."

That's when the dogs make their move.

My parents have two Cavalier King Charles Spaniels—Bingley and Darcy—who are usually about as energetic as throw pillows.

Not today.

They launch themselves at Poppy like she's made of bacon, circling her legs and jumping, whining with joy.

"Oh!" She laughs, crouching down to pet them. "Hello, babies!"

Bingley—who has never liked anyone, including the people who feed him—immediately rolls over for belly rubs.

Darcy starts licking her face.

"Well," my father says. "That's new."

My mother's expression could cut glass.

"They're not usually so… enthusiastic."

"Dogs know good people," Poppy says, still petting them.

"Do they?" My mother's tone suggests she disagrees.

I grab towels from the hall closet and toss one to Poppy. "What are you really doing here?"

"We wanted to ensure everything is running smoothly." My mother eyes Poppy, who's now trying to towel off while two dogs compete for her attention. "Though it seems there have been some… complications."

"Sprinkler mishap," Poppy says cheerfully. "Nothing we can't handle."

"Mm." My mother turns to me. "Dean, darling, might we speak privately?"

"No."

The word comes out harsher than I intended.

Everyone looks at me.

"No," I repeat, softer but not by much. "Whatever you need to say about the wedding, you can say in front of Poppy. She's the planner."

My mother's lips thin. "Very well. We have concerns about the… scale of this event. The trucks outside, the tents. It seems excessive."

"It's a wedding," I say. "Not a barbecue."

Bingley whines, sensing the tension. He presses closer to Poppy, who absently strokes his head.

"I think," Poppy says carefully, "what Dean means is that Mason and Ivy have a very specific vision for their day. And as their planner, it's my job to execute that vision."

My mother turns her laser focus on her. "And

what are your qualifications, exactly?"

"Mom—"

"It's fine," Poppy interrupts. "I've been planning weddings for three years. I've handled events for ten to five hundred guests. I've worked with budgets from five thousand to half a million. And I've never had a dissatisfied client."

"How impressive," my mother says in a tone that suggests the opposite.

"We should go," my father intervenes. "Let you… dry off."

They move toward the door, but my mother pauses. "Dean, darling, do think about what we've said. And perhaps suggest to Mason that a smaller gathering—"

"Goodbye, Mom."

She sighs again, collects the dogs (who have to be physically dragged away from Poppy), and sweeps out.

The door closes.

Silence.

"So," Poppy says. "That was fun."

I laugh. I can't help it. It's either that or punch a wall.

"I'm sorry," I say.

"For what? The sprinklers? The surprise parent visit? The weird dog thing?"

"All of it."

She studies me, really looks at me for the first time since we came inside. I realize we're both still soaking wet, standing in my foyer, probably ruining the floors.

"Your parents seem… intense."

"That's one word for it."

"What's another?"

"Toxic. Controlling. Emotionally manipulative."

"Ah." She wraps the towel tighter around herself. "And they don't approve of Mason?"

"They don't like that Mason chose happiness over their version of success."

"And you?"

I shrug. "I chose their version. Look how well that turned out."

She's quiet for a moment. Then she says, "The dogs liked me."

"The dogs have good taste." It slips out before I can stop it. We both freeze.

"I should…" She gestures vaguely at her wet clothes.

"Right. Yes. You should."

But neither of us moves.

"Dean?"

"Yeah?"

"Thank you. For not letting them kick me out."

"I wasn't going to let them—"

"You stood up for me. To your parents. That was…" She bites her lip. "No one's done that before."

The admission hangs between us. Too honest. Too real for whatever this is supposed to be.

"Poppy—"

"I should really go change now."

"Right."

"Right."

She backs toward the door, still clutching the

towel. "I'll, um, make sure the contractors stay clear of the sprinklers."

"Good plan."

"And I'll keep the noise down." Her voice is softer now.

"Appreciated."

"And Dean?"

"Yeah?"

"Maybe put on a shirt? It's very… distracting. For the, um, contractors."

I stand there, dripping on my own floor, processing everything. My parents. The dogs. Poppy in a see-through shirt defending her qualifications while shaking inside.

She slips out before I can respond, leaving me standing in my foyer, soaked and somehow more confused than when I woke up.

The way she looked at me when I told my mother to stand down.

"Damn it," I mutter to the empty room.

Because I think I might be in trouble here. The kind of trouble that doesn't wash off with cold water.

Muffin chooses that moment to waddle in from wherever she's been hiding.

"Thanks for the backup," I tell her.

She snorts and heads for her food bowl.

My phone buzzes. Three texts from Mason.

MASON:

Mom just called.

WTF did you say to them???

Also, why did Mom mention you were half-naked with my wedding planner?

I stare at the texts.
Then I pour myself some coffee.
It's going to be a very long couple of days.

13

RISOTTO AND REVELATIONS

Poppy

Mason's text hits while I'm untangling myself from a vendor call about linens. Something about the wrong shade of ivory, which apparently matters more than world peace.

MASON:

> Dinner tonight? 7p.m.? Casual at the house.

> Ivy demands your presence.

> She insisted and she gets violent when people skip meals.

I stare at my disaster of a workspace — seating charts everywhere, three empty coffee cups forming a grief support group on the windowsill.

ME:

> I should work through dinner.

My stomach does this stupid flippy thing.

Great. Dinner with the happy couple and their brother who makes me forget basic motor functions whenever he does that thing with his sleeves. The thought alone short-circuits my focus.

I check the time. 5:47. Crap.

Not much time to make a dent in my to-do list, but still, I try my best.

An hour passes in what feels like the blink of an eye.

I grab the first clean thing I find—jeans with a hole in the knee and an oversized sweater that keeps falling off my shoulder. Hair goes up in a messy bun secured with the nearest writing implement (a pencil, because I'm classy like that).

The walk to the main house takes thirty seconds. Long enough to wonder what the hell I'm doing. Not long enough to come up with a good excuse to bail.

I knock once and walk in because apparently,

we're at that level of familiarity now.

"—just saying she's nice," Mason's voice drifts from the kitchen.

"I hadn't noticed." Dean. Dry as dust.

"Bullshit. I saw you watching her during the tent setup."

"I was watching my property value plummet."

"Through her tank top?"

"Mason—"

"What? She's hot. You're single. Math isn't your strong suit?"

I clear my throat, and both brothers freeze — Mason perched on the counter like an overgrown teenager, Dean at the stove with a wooden spoon and a murderous look.

"Hey." I hold up the wine I grabbed from my emergency stash. "Brought the good stuff."

Dean's face does this thing, part embarrassment, part amusement.

"Where's Ivy?" I ask, desperately needing another person in this room.

"Upstairs. Changing. She'll be down soon." Mason hops down, swipes the wine. "Come on, I'll give you the tour while Dean has his control issues in private."

"I don't have—"

But we're already leaving. I glance back to find Dean glaring at the risotto like it personally offended him.

The more I see of the house, the more I love. Mason narrates like a discount tour guide.

"Living room where Dean pretends to relax. Office where Dean actually lives. Piano nobody's touched since 2019.”

“Why’d he stop?”

Mason’s quiet for a beat. “Same reason he stopped doing a lot of things.”

Before I can ask what that means, Ivy appears at the top of the stairs in a sundress that probably cost more than my rent.

“Poppy! You came!”

She hugs me like we’re old friends. She smells expensive. I probably smell like stress and dry shampoo.

“Thanks for having me.”

“Please. You’re doing us a favor. Dean needs more human interaction that doesn’t involve billable hours.”

We head back to the kitchen where Dean’s now plating risotto with the focus of a bomb technician.

Cool.

“Smells amazing,” I offer.

He glances up. Does this quick scan—sweater, jeans, pencil in hair—and something flickers across his face.

“It’s just risotto.”

“Just risotto,” Mason scoffs. “That he’s been stirring for forty minutes.”

“It requires constant attention.”

“So does therapy, but here we are.”

Ivy smacks Mason’s arm. “Be nice.”

“I am nice. Dean’s the mean one.”

“I’m not mean. I’m selective with my enthusiasm.”

“That’s literally the definition of mean.”

I bite back a laugh.

Dean catches it, eyes narrowing. "Something amusing?"

"Nope. Just… you two. It's cute." I gesture between the brothers who couldn't be more opposite.

"We're not cute," they say in unison, which only proves my point.

We migrate to the dining room. Through some configuration I don't fully track, I end up next to Dean. Our knees bump under the table. He shifts away. I pretend not to notice.

The risotto is, annoyingly, perfect. Creamy and comforting with a hint of tangy parmesan and plenty of buttery goodness.

"Okay, this is stupid good," I admit after the first bite.

"It's just arborio rice and—"

"Take the compliment."

He pauses. "Thank you."

"See? Was that so hard?"

"Excruciating, actually." But he's almost smiling. This lazy, tiny thing at the corner of his mouth that makes my chest do weird stuff.

"So Poppy," Ivy says, pouring me a glass of white wine. "Tell us about Italy."

Safe topic. I grab it with both hands.

"I fly out Sunday after the wedding. A week in Portofino. Just me and carbs."

"Alone?" There's something in the way she asks it.

"That's the plan."

"No… special someone to take?"

I laugh. "My special someone is my passport."

"Relatable," Dean mutters.

Mason and Ivy exchange a look I don't like.

"What?"

"Nothing," Ivy says too quickly. "Just thinking Dean could use a vacation."

"I don't do vacations."

"You don't do fun," Mason corrects. "There's a difference."

Dinner continues. Stories get told. Ivy shares how they met (book club, his was the only male perspective, she was intrigued). Normal couple stuff that makes my chest tight with something I refuse to name.

"What about you?" Ivy asks. "Worst wedding disaster?"

This one?

I tell them about the beach officiant with food poisoning, the stoned maid of honor, writing her toast on her palm in Sharpie. Even Dean laughs— this low sound that does things to my spine.

"More wine?" he asks, already pouring.

Our fingers brush on the glass. Lightning shoots up my arm — quick, sharp, impossible to ignore. I swallow before I can embarrass myself and focus on my plate like it holds answers.

"So, Dean," Ivy says, and her tone makes my stomach drop. "Still single?"

The temperature plummets. Even the air feels different, brittle somehow.

"Yes." Dean doesn't look up from his plate. His fork scrapes once against the porcelain, deliberate.

"Really? Mom mentioned that woman from your firm—" Mason cuts in.

"Is married," he says flatly. "To her wife."

"Oh." Ivy deflates, shoulders slumping. "Well, there goes that."

Dean finally sets his fork down. "What?"

"Nothing." Ivy glances at Mason, then back at Dean. "Just thought maybe…"

His head tilts, just slightly. "Maybe what?"

"Maybe you'd finally let someone in?"

Dean goes still. Not frozen — still. Like something dangerous coiling up, waiting for the wrong move.

"I'm fine."

"Nobody said you weren't—"

"Then why the interrogation?"

His voice is quiet, but it lands heavy. Ivy winces. Mason opens his mouth, probably to defuse, but Dean's stare cuts him off before he can.

"It's not an interrogation," Ivy says softly. "It's concern."

"It's invasive."

"When's the last time you went on a date?" Mason tries, half teasing, half shielding.

"I date."

"Depositions don't count."

Dean exhales through his nose. "March."

Silence. The kind that hums. I feel the words like static in the room.

"March?" Ivy repeats, blinking. "It's August."

Dean's knife tenses in his grip. "Your point?"

Ivy's lips part, but nothing comes out.

"Dean—"

He stands abruptly. The chair legs scrape hard against the floor. "I should check on dessert."

And he's gone, the sound of retreating footsteps echoing down the hallway.

The table breathes again.

"Too far?" Ivy whispers.

"Little bit," Mason confirms, dragging a hand over his face.

I'm already on my feet. "I'll go."

"Poppy—"

"It's fine." I force a small smile. "I speak emotionally constipated."

The kitchen's dim except for the under-cabinet lights. They cast a soft, yellow glow over stainless steel and tension. Dean's at the counter, methodically slicing strawberries like they've wronged him.

"They mean well," I say, leaning against the doorway.

"They always do." He doesn't look up. "You don't have to—"

"I know."

I move closer, close enough to smell sugar and heat and something faintly citrus on him. Not close enough to make him retreat. I fold my arms, watching him massacre fruit.

"Being single isn't a disease," I offer.

"Tell that to coupled people."

"Fair point." I steal a strawberry slice from the cutting board, mostly to have something to do with my hands. "Though March is kind of a long—"

"Don't."

The knife pauses mid-air.

"Right. Shutting up."

More quiet slicing, aka fruit carnage. His jaw's doing that clenched thing again.

Then, without looking up, he says, "Her name was Rebecca."

I blink. "Okay…"

He sets the knife down, fingers braced on the counter. "She was an investment banker. We met at a conference. Dated for three months."

I wait. "What happened?"

"She wanted more."

"And you didn't?"

He finally looks at me. His eyes are tired—not in the physical sense, but in the way someone looks when they've stopped expecting to be understood.

"I wanted to want it," he says quietly. "Does that count?"

Something twists in my chest. The honest kind of ache.

"Yeah," I whisper. "It counts."

For a second, the air between us feels heavy, fragile. My chest squeezes. "Yeah. It counts."

"Do you know what it's like?" His voice drops. "To go through the motions? To sit across from someone beautiful and accomplished and feel… nothing?"

"Actually? Yeah."

He blinks.

"His name was Mitchell," I say. "He was a photographer. Sweet. Talented. Looked at me like I hung the moon."

"And?"

"And I felt like I was suffocating." I grab another strawberry. "Kept waiting to feel what everyone said I should feel. Never did."

"How long?"

"Eight months."

"Damn. I barely lasted three."

"Yeah, well. I'm an overachiever."

He huffs. Might be a laugh.

We stand there, surrounded by strawberry casualties and unspoken things.

"This is complicated," he says.

"What is?"

He gestures vaguely between us.

Oh.

"Everything's complicated," I say carefully. "Doesn't mean it's not worth—"

"DESSERT?" Mason yells from the dining room. "You guys get lost?"

The moment breaks. Dean grabs plates. I grab spoons. We don't talk about whatever just almost happened.

But back at the table, his thigh presses against mine.

And he doesn't move away.

14

BLURRED BOUNDARIES

Dean

She leaves right after dessert.

She makes excuses about vendors and early mornings. Hugs Ivy, fist-bumps Mason, and gives me this look I can't decipher.

"Thanks for dinner."

"It was just risotto."

"Well, it was the best *just risotto* I've ever had."

Then she's gone—back to the guest house, back to safe distances and professional boundaries.

Mason helps clear the plates while Ivy makes tea. It's a normal post-dinner ritual, except my mind won't stop replaying the conversation in the kitchen.

"So," Mason says, too casually. "Poppy seems nice."

"Don't."

"Don't what?"

"Whatever matchmaking scheme you're cooking up. Don't."

"I'm just saying—"

"She's leaving Sunday. Flying to Italy. Building her business. She doesn't need—" I gesture at myself. "This." Not to mention, she lives in California.

"This? You mean a stable, successful guy who cooks?"

"I mean an emotionally unavailable workaholic with trust issues."

Mason stops loading the dishwasher. "Is that really how you see yourself?"

"It's accurate."

"It's bullshit."

"Mason—"

"No. You know what? Forget this." He turns, genuinely angry. "You've been punishing yourself for six years. Six. Years."

"I'm not—"

"Emily left. It sucked. But she left because she was selfish, not because you're broken."

Her name hits like cold water. "Don't."

"Someone has to. You act like caring about someone is this massive character flaw—"

"Caring about someone got me a failed engagement and a mortgage on a house meant for a family I don't have."

The words hang there—too honest, too much.

Ivy appears in the doorway, tea forgotten, steam curling around her fingers.

"Dean…"

"I'm fine." The words come out sharper than I intend.

"You're not," Mason says quietly from behind her. "And that's okay. But Poppy—"

"She's temporary," I cut in. "Here for the week. Then gone."

Mason crosses his arms, leaning against the doorframe. "So?"

"So this conversation is pointless." My voice sounds tired even to me.

"She makes you smile," he says, stepping closer, "Maybe that means something. You're different around her. Softer. Less… weaponized."

I glare at him. "Weaponized?"

"Yeah. Most people get your courtroom version. She gets the off-duty one."

I scoff and release a sharpy exhale. "Great assessment, Dr. Phil. Are you done now?"

Mason's quiet for a moment, his eyes steady on mine. "She pulls you out of your head. You actually show up when she's around. You're not thinking ten steps ahead or judging everyone's life choices. You're just… there."

My stomach tightens. "I'm always 'there.'"

"Not like that. Not with anyone else."

He's smirking again, but there's something softer underneath—concern. Genuine concern from my little brother, the one I've spent years trying to take care of.

"I'm not saying marry her," he adds. "I'm saying maybe, just maybe, let yourself enjoy something for once."

I grab a dish towel and wipe the counter, even though it doesn't need it. "I enjoy plenty of things."

"Name one."

I keep wiping. The silence stretches until it starts to feel like pressure. "Arguing with you."

Mason snorts. "Besides that."

Nothing comes to mind. My throat feels tight.

Damnit.

"Exactly." He moves a little closer. "She's cool, man. You're… you. Just talk to her. Like a human. With feelings."

"I don't—"

"Have feelings? Bullshit." His voice is easy but sure. "I saw your face during dinner."

"What about my face?"

"You kept looking at her when you thought nobody noticed."

"I was being polite."

"You were being smitten."

I snort. "Nobody says *smitten* anymore."

"I just did." He heads for the stairs, casual as ever. "Text her."

"Why would I text her?"

He glances back once. "Because you want to."

He's gone before I can come up with a retort.

The kitchen feels different once he's gone—quieter, bigger somehow. The kind of quiet that presses at your ribs.

Ivy lingers, studying me over the rim of her mug. "He's right, you know."

"Not you too." I drop the towel and lean on the counter.

"She's good for you."

"You've known her four days."

"I've known you three years." Her smile is soft but certain. "I've never seen you like this."

"Like what?"

"Alive."

She crosses the room, kisses my cheek, and leaves.

The scent of her tea lingers—jasmine and honey, fading fast. I stare at the sink full of dishes, at the knife I never finished drying, at my phone sitting beside it, screen dark.

Mason's voice echoes back in my head. *Because you want to.*

I tell myself that I don't.

And I almost believe it.

I clean—methodically, mindlessly.

Definitely don't think about Poppy's hand on my shoulder or how she smells like vanilla and chaos, or the way she said *I wanted to want it* like she understood.

My phone sits on the counter—silent, judging.

I shouldn't text her. What would I even say? *Thanks for understanding my emotional damage. Want to grab coffee and discuss our mutual inability to feel normal human emotions?*

Yeah. Hard pass.

I finish the dishes, pour myself a whiskey, and sit at the piano for the first time in months.

My fingers remember the keys, even if my brain's forgotten the point. I play without thinking—muscle memory, background noise for an empty house.

Except—

There's a light on in the guest house.

I can see her through the window—laptop open, hair still up with that pencil. Working. Always working.

Like me—hiding behind tasks and deadlines because it's easier than admitting we're terrified of everything else.

I stare at the light across the lawn, at my life with its carefully maintained boundaries and color-coded loneliness.

Screw it.

I grab my phone, find her contact, and type and delete six different messages.

Finally, I land on one.

ME:
The strawberries survived. Barely.

I send it before I can think too hard.

Three dots appear immediately.

POPPY:
It was touch and go there for a minute.

ME:
They were plotting against me.

POPPY:
Paranoid much?

ME:
Prepared.

POPPY:
Right. Very different things.

Should I be concerned you're texting me at 11 p.m.?

Fair point.

I stare at the question, picturing a life where I played piano for more than background noise, where I cooked for someone besides myself, where Saturday mornings meant something other than billable hours.

POPPY:

Sometimes I think about starting over—maybe opening a gift shop or a restaurant.

ME:

Really?

POPPY:

Food brings people together. Weddings just show them where to sit.

ME:

That's... actually profound.

POPPY:

I have my moments.

ME:

Why don't you?

Three dots appear, disappear, then appear again.

POPPY:

Same reason you babysat your risotto.

Easier to control outcomes when you follow the recipe.

Damn. Called out via text at 11:17 p.m. Brutal.

ME:

I should let you sleep.

POPPY:
You should.

ME:
Early vendor meetings?

POPPY:
6 a.m. flower delivery.

ME:
Inhumane.

POPPY:
Necessary. Your lawn needs beauty.

ME:
My lawn needs hazard pay.

POPPY:
Drama queen.

ME:
Chaos agent.

POPPY:
Good night, Dean.

ME:
Night, Poppy.

I set the phone down. The light in the guest house stays on.

So does mine.

We're twenty feet and a lifetime apart, both working through the night because it's easier than admitting we're not built for normal.

But for the first time in six years, maybe that's okay.

Maybe broken recognizes broken.

Maybe that's enough.

For now.

15

DRESS DISASTER

Poppy

The scream pierces the morning at 7:43 a.m.

Not a cute little *oh no* scream. A full-on, horror-movie, someone's-been-murdered scream that makes me drop my coffee and sprint toward the main house in yesterday's sleep shorts and an oversized T-shirt without a bra.

I burst through the back door without knocking because, well, someone's dying.

"What happened? Who's hurt? Do we need—"

I stop.

Ivy's standing in the middle of the kitchen in her wedding dress. Or what used to be her wedding dress. Now it's…

"Is that… red wine?" I ask.

She nods, tears streaming down her face. "I was trying it on, and Mason brought me coffee, but then Muffin ran between my legs, and I tripped, and the coffee hit the wine bottle on the counter, and—"

"Breathe."

"IT'S RUINED."

The dress is screwed. Like, properly screwed. Red wine splattered across the entire left side, coffee stains down the front. She looks like a very expensive murder victim.

"The wedding's in two days," she whispers. "Two days, and I have no dress, and—"

"Hey." I grab her shoulders. "Look at me."

She does. Mascara is everywhere. Full raccoon mode.

"We're gonna fix this."

"How? It's vintage Vera Wang! My grandmother's veil goes with this specific dress! The alterations took six weeks!"

Mason appears in the doorway, looking like he might vomit. "I'm so sorry, babe, I didn't see Muffin, and—"

"Not helping," I tell him.

"Right. Shutting up."

"Where's Dean?"

"Office. Working."

Of course he is.

"Okay." I turn back to Ivy. "Take off the dress. Carefully."

"Why? It's ruined."

"Because I need to see the label and construction. Go."

She disappears upstairs. Mason hovers, wringing his hands.

"This is my fault," he says.

"Unless you trained Muffin to be a wine assassin, no, it's not."

"She's gonna hate me."

"She's gonna marry you. But first, I need coffee, my car keys, and about six hundred dollars in cash."

His eyes widen. "Uh—"

Dean appears in the doorway as if he was summoned. Hair perfect, shirt pressed, expression somewhere between annoyed and concerned.

"Why is everyone yelling?"

"Dress emergency," I say.

"Define emergency."

I gesture at the wine puddle, the coffee splatter, and Mason's guilty face.

"Ah." He takes in my appearance—sleep shorts, no bra, hair in yesterday's bun. His jaw tightens. "What do you need?"

"Prayers. Cash. Maybe a small miracle."

He pulls out his wallet and hands me a credit card. "Pin's 0827."

I stare at it. "You're just… giving me your credit card?"

"You're fixing this?"

"That's the plan."

"Then yes."

Our fingers brush during the exchange. Neither of us acknowledges it.

"Try not to make it worse."

"Your faith in me is touching."

An almost-smile. "Poppy?"

"Yeah?"

"Put on real clothes first."

I look down. Right. Basically naked in his kitchen. Cool.

"Give me five minutes."

• • •

Two hours later, I'm standing in a vintage shop

with the owner, a dress that might work, and a seamstress who thinks I'm insane.

"You want me to what?" She's sixty, German, and takes no shit.

"Recreate the bodice structure of the ruined dress on this one. Today."

"Impossible."

"I'll pay triple."

She pauses. "Show me the pictures again."

I pull up the photos I took of Ivy's destroyed dress. The seamstress—Greta—studies them like battle plans.

"The beading will be different," she warns.

"She won't care if you make it work."

"I'll need four hours minimum."

"You'll have three."

She snorts. "You remind me of me. Annoying."

"I get that a lot."

My phone buzzes.

DEAN:

Status?

ME:

Found a dress. Might work. Seamstress currently calling me names in German.

DEAN:

Promising.

ME:

How's Ivy?

That stops me. Two words. But the way he

just… believes I'll fix this. Like it's a fact.

Greta clears her throat. "Your boyfriend's texting can wait."

"He's not my—"

"Sure." She's already working, pins in her mouth. "Not boyfriend with the credit card and worried texts."

"It's complicated."

"Always is with the good ones."

• • •

Three hours and fourteen minutes later, I'm back at the estate with a garment bag and barely contained panic.

The kitchen's been transformed into what looks like a grief bakery. Cookies everywhere. Muffins. Is that a freaking pie?

"Stress baking?" I ask Mason.

"I made brownies," he says helplessly. "And scones. And… I think that's banana bread?"

"Wow."

Dean's at the sink, sleeves rolled up, washing dishes. Because of course he's the one handling the chaos cleanup.

"Where's Ivy?" I ask.

"Living room. Slightly drunk."

"Perfect. Don't let her come up for twenty minutes."

I head for the stairs, garment bag over my shoulder.

"Poppy."

I turn. Dean's watching me, dish towel in hand.

"Thank you," he says. Simple. Sincere.

"Thank her when it fits."

Upstairs, I spread the dress on the bed and hold my breath.

It's not the same. It can't be. But it's close. Ivory silk, similar silhouette, and Greta worked actual magic with the beading. Different pattern but same vibe. Romantic. Classic. Very Ivy.

I text Dean.

ME:

Send her up. Alone.

And maybe have tissues ready.

A minute later, Ivy appears in the doorway. Mascara fixed, buzz fading, hope warring with dread on her face.

"Close your eyes," I tell her.

"Poppy—"

"Trust me."

She does.

I help her into the dress, zip it carefully, adjust the shoulders.

"Okay. Look."

She opens her eyes. Stares at the mirror.

Silence.

"I know it's not the same," I start. "But Greta

matched the bodice structure, and the beading is actually—"

"It's perfect."

I blink. "It is?"

She turns, examining every angle. "It's… God, it's better than the original."

"You're drunk."

"Was drunk. Now I'm… How did you do this?"

"Vintage shop in Hudson. German seamstress who called me an asshole in three languages. Dean's credit card."

"Dean paid for this?"

Something warm unfolds inside me. "Yeah."

She stares at herself again, then at me. "Why?"

"Because it's your wedding. And the dress doesn't matter nearly as much as the marriage, but it also totally matters, and anyone who says otherwise is lying."

She hugs me. Hard. Like, might-crack-a-rib hard. "Thank you," she whispers. "Thank you, thank you, thank you."

"Okay, crying is bad for the alterations—"

"I don't care." She pulls back, mascara running again. "You saved my wedding."

"It's just a dress."

"No. It's not." She wipes her face she practically floats to the bathroom. "I have to show Mason. And Dean. And—Poppy?"

"Yeah?"

"You're officially family now. No takebacks."

Something warm blooms in my chest. "Thanks, Ivy."

I head downstairs, exhausted but victorious.

Dean's still at the sink. The kitchen's spotless. Mason's nowhere to be seen.

"Banished him to the porch," Dean says without turning. "He was about to start on croissants."

"Smart."

"Is she happy?"

"Ecstatic."

"Good." He turns, and there's something soft in his expression. "You did good."

"Just doing my job."

"No." He steps closer. "Your job was planning the wedding. This was… more."

We're standing too close. Again. Always ending up in each other's space like magnets with no sense of self-preservation.

"Dean—"

"The seamstress," he says. "How much?"

"Check your credit card statement."

He winces. "That bad?"

"Worth it though."

"Yeah," he agrees.

"Did you see Mason's face? He thought she'd hate him forever."

"She could never hate him." He's looking at me weird. Intense. "That's not how it works when you love someone."

"Speaking from experience?"

"Observation."

"Right." I need to move. Need space. Need to not think about how he smells like dish soap and expensive cologne. "I should—"

"Poppy."

"Yeah?"

"You're really good at this."

I freeze. "At what?"

"Taking care of people." He reaches out, tucks a stray hair behind my ear. His fingers linger. "Making things okay when they're falling apart."

"I—"

"POPPY!" Ivy's voice from upstairs. "THE ZIPPER'S STUCK!"

The moment breaks. Dean steps back. I run upstairs like the house is on fire.

But I can still feel where his fingers touched.

Still hear him saying *you're really good at this* like it meant something.

Like I meant something.

16

MIDNIGHT CONFESSIONS

Dean

It's 11:56 p.m. and I can't sleep.

Not because of work. Not because of the wedding chaos. But because there's a light bouncing around my backyard like a drunk firefly.

I watch from my bedroom window. Someone's out there with a headlamp, dragging string lights across my pergola. In the dark. Alone.

Three guesses who.

I pull on jeans and head outside barefoot, because apparently I make excellent decisions after midnight.

She's balanced on a ladder that's seen better days, headlamp crooked, muttering something that sounds suspiciously like "damn you, physics."

"You know it's midnight, right?"

She jerks. The ladder wobbles. I'm there before I think about it, hands on the sides, steadying.

"Geez." She looks down at me, one hand pressed to her chest. "Wear a bell or something."

"On my own property?"

"When you're sneaking up on people? Yes."

"I wasn't sneaking. You were distracted by

your war with gravity."

She adjusts the headlamp, which just makes her look like a deranged miner. "These lights won't hang themselves."

"They could. Tomorrow. When humans typically work."

"Tomorrow's packed. Florist at seven, caterer at eight, final sound check at—"

"So you're doing it now. At midnight. On a broken ladder."

"It's not broken. It's… vintage."

The ladder creaks ominously.

"Get down."

"No."

"Poppy."

"Dean."

"You're gonna fall and break your neck. Then I'll have to find a new wedding planner right before—"

"Your concern is touching."

"Get. Down."

She sighs but climbs down. The ladder immediately lists to one side.

"See? Vintage."

"Death trap." I grab the string of lights from her hands. "What are you even trying to do?"

"Soft perimeter lighting for the cocktail hour. Ivy wants *magical garden party* not *suburban barbecue*."

"At midnight?"

She shrugs. The movement makes her headlamp slide sideways. "I couldn't sleep."

I should go back inside. Should let her deal

with her insomnia and questionable ladder choices alone.

Instead, I say, "Hold this."

I pass her one end of the lights and grab the other. We work in silence, stringing them through the pergola beams. Her on one side, me on the other. Meeting in the middle.

"Why couldn't you sleep?" I ask.

"Brain won't shut off. You?"

"Same."

"What's keeping the great Dean Whitaker awake? Billable hours? Existential dread?"

"Poppy Monroe doing construction in my backyard."

She glances down from the ladder, her headlamp flickering like a dying star. "I'm hardly doing construction—shit." The clip slips from her fingers. "These clips are evil."

"Here." I reach up, fixing the strand before she can try again. Our fingers brush—a small thing, but my pulse kicks anyway. "You're shaking."

"It's cold."

It's August.

"When's the last time you ate?" I ask.

"Um. Lunch?"

"Which lunch?"

She winces. "The… yesterday kind?"

"Damn it, Poppy."

"I've been busy—"

"You've been stubborn." I finish the last clip and step back. "Come on."

"Where?"

"Kitchen. Food. Now."

"I don't need—"

I'm already walking away. After a beat, her footsteps follow.

"Bossy," she mutters.

Practical, not bossy. Someone has to make sure the wedding planner doesn't collapse in the middle of my property. It's a liability waiting to happen.

The kitchen is dim, the under-cabinet lights throwing soft shadows across the counters. I pull out leftovers. She perches on a barstool, headlamp still crooked, exhaustion written all over her face.

"You can take that off now."

"Oh. Right." She removes it, and her hair comes with it, falling around her shoulders in loose waves.

"Better?" she asks.

Worse, actually. Much worse.

I slide a plate across the counter. "Eat."

She eyes it suspiciously. "What is it?"

"Food. Eat it."

She takes one bite and groans softly. "Oh wow."

"It's just pasta."

"It's heaven," she says around another bite. "When did you make this?"

"Earlier. While you were running around playing fairy godmother."

"I wasn't—" She stops, smiles sheepishly. "Okay, maybe a little."

Silence settles—comfortable but full of static. She eats; I lean against the sink, watching her demolish the pasta like she's been starving for days. The sight stirs something protective in me I don't want to name.

"Why do you do that?" I ask.

She blinks up. "Do what?"

"Take care of everyone but yourself."

Her fork stills halfway to her mouth. "I take care of myself."

"When?"

She laughs once, short and breathy. "It's been a busy week."

"Why do I have a feeling it's always a busy week with you?"

Her fork lowers to the plate. There's a shift—the kind that changes the air. "Maybe because if I stop moving, I'll have to think about—" She stops. "Nothing. Forget it."

"Poppy."

"It's fine."

"It's not fine. You're stringing lights at midnight and forgetting to eat."

"So? You're feeding a stranger at midnight instead of sleeping."

"You're not a stranger."

The words come out too fast. Too true.

She looks at me for a long second, then says quietly, "No. I guess I'm not."

She pushes pasta around her plate, appetite fading. "This wedding… it's important."

"All weddings are important to you." I mean it as an observation, not an accusation.

"This one's different," she says.

"Why?"

She meets my gaze. There's something raw there—fear, maybe, or exhaustion. "Because if I mess this up…"

"You won't."

"You don't know that."

"I know you." My voice drops. "You'd die before letting Ivy down."

Her mouth twitches. "That's kind of the problem."

I move closer, leaning on the counter across from her. Close enough to catch the faint scent of vanilla shampoo and stress. "What aren't you telling me?"

"Nothing. I'm just… stressed. Normal wedding planner stuff."

"Bullshit."

She laughs—quick, brittle. "Can't get anything past you."

"Poppy."

She exhales, pacing. "What do you want me to say? That I'm in over my head? That I'm one bad vendor call away from a complete breakdown? That I haven't slept in three days because every time I close my eyes, I see all the ways this could go wrong?"

"Start with the truth."

"The truth?" She stops, hands on her hips. "The truth is I'm freaking terrified, okay? This wedding has to be perfect. It has to be. And I'm—"

She stops. Shakes her head.

"You're what?"

"Tired." She looks away. "I'm tired."

When she moves past me, I catch her arm—just enough to stop her. The warmth of her skin hits me first, then the tremor beneath it.

"That's not what you were going to say."

"Let it go, Dean."

"No."

Her voice lowers. "Why do you care?"

Because you make the house feel less empty. Because I see too much of myself in your exhaustion. Because I don't know how to stop.

"Because you're about to burn out on my property," I say instead, "and I don't want the liability."

That earns me a real laugh—soft, genuine. "There he is. Mr. Practical."

"Someone has to be."

We're standing too close now. Her arm's still in my hand, her pulse quick beneath my fingers.

"There's a leaf," I say, because my brain short-circuits.

"What?"

"In your hair. From the pergola."

"Oh."

I reach up, pluck it free. I should step back. I don't. The space between us feels thinner than air.

"Dean?"

"Mm?"

"You're still holding the leaf."

I look down. She's right—a dead leaf between my fingers, my hand inches from her face.

"You have pasta sauce," I say. "On your… just—"

I brush my thumb across the corner of her mouth. Warm skin. Soft breath.

She freezes. So do I.

The kitchen hums—refrigerator, maybe our heartbeats.

"This is complicated," she whispers.

"Everything with you is complicated."

"Is that bad?"

I should say yes. Should pull back. Should remember how temporary she is.

Instead, I shake my head. "No."

Her hand comes up, fingers tracing my collar—featherlight, curious. "You're always so put together."

"Occupational hazard."

"Even at midnight?"

"Especially at midnight."

She tugs lightly at my shirt. "Must be exhausting."

"You have no idea."

She's close enough now that her breath grazes my jaw. The world feels quieter, narrower. Just her, me, and a thousand things I shouldn't want.

"I should go," she says softly.

"Probably."

"Early morning."

"Right."

Neither of us moves.

"Dean?"

"Yeah?"

"Whatever happens with this wedding… thanks. For catching me. On the ladder. And… in other ways."

The words land somewhere behind my ribs.

"Just didn't want a lawsuit," I mumble, my voice low.

"Liar." Her fingers linger one beat longer. "You care."

"Don't let it get around."

"Your secret's safe." She steps back, small but decisive. "Along with mine."

"What secret?"

"The one where I'm not as put together as I pretend to be."

Before I can respond, she's gone—back across the lawn to the guest house.

Through the window, her light flicks on. Stays on.

She's keeping something from me. Something that doesn't fit the version of her everyone else sees.

And I'm going to find out what.

Because Poppy Monroe doesn't string lights at midnight unless she's running from something.

And whatever it is, she shouldn't have to face it alone.

17

TROUBLE IN A THREE-PIECE SUIT

Poppy

"**O**kay, but like—" I'm three glasses deep at some dive bar that smells like peanuts and bad decisions. "—his forearms are basically criminal."

CeCe screams. "I KNEW IT. I knew you were hot for lawyer boy!"

"I'm not hot for—"

"You literally just said his forearms are criminal," Ivy interrupts, sliding another shot across the sticky table. "That's textbook horny behavior."

We've commandeered a booth in the back corner. Mason and his groomsmen are destroying each other at darts, being loud and stupid and twenty-something. Dean went with them to "supervise," which probably means he's nursing a beer and cataloging everyone's poor decisions.

Gloria flags down the bartender for another round. "Sweetie, just admit you want to climb him like a tree."

"I don't want to—"

"Yesterday you froze mid-sentence when he looked your way," Ivy says. "Just stopped. Like someone unplugged you."

"There was a bee."

"Where?" CeCe demands.

"Near his… arms."

They all cackle. Even through the dim lighting, I can see CeCe's face turning red.

"Fine." I knock back the shot. It burns going down. "He's attractive. In an uptight, probably-color-codes-his-closet way."

"And?" Ivy prods.

"And he made me pasta. At midnight. Because I forgot to eat."

"MIDNIGHT PASTA?" CeCe shouts so loud I flinch. "That's basically a proposal!"

"It was leftovers—"

"He fed you. At midnight. In his kitchen." Gloria's using her therapist voice. I hate when she does that. "How did that make you feel?"

"Annoyed."

"Try again."

"Confused?"

"Getting warmer."

I thunk my head on the table. It's sticky. Everything here is sticky. "I don't know, okay? He's just… ugh."

"Ugh?" Ivy's grinning. "That's not an adjective."

"He does this thing. Where he looks at me. Like really looks. Like he's trying to solve me."

"And?"

"And I want him to." Crap. Did I say that out loud? "I mean—"

"Too late!" CeCe's practically vibrating. "You

admitted it!"

"I'm leaving Sunday." I stare at the ceiling, which is stained with water and questionable life choices. "Italy. Vacation. No Dean Whitaker and his stupid competent hands."

"Competent hands?" Gloria murmurs. "Interesting word choice."

"Have you seen his hands? They're like… architect hands."

"What the heck are architect hands?" Ivy asks.

"I don't know! Precise. Capable. Like they could build something or… or…"

"Or take you apart?" Gloria suggests with a wink.

"I hate all of you."

"No, you don't." CeCe grins. "You know what I think?"

"That I need water?"

"That you're scared."

That lands like a gut punch. "Of what?"

"Of wanting something real with someone who sees through your bullshit."

"I don't have—"

"Poppy." Her voice goes soft. "Babe. You haven't told him about Miranda."

The table goes quiet.

"That's different," I mutter.

"Is it?"

"Yes. Because that's business. This is…"

"What?" Gloria asks.

I grab Ivy's drink, steal it, and down half of it. "Complicated."

"The best things always are," Ivy says.

"That's bride brain talking."

"Or maybe I think you deserve someone who makes you midnight pasta and catches you when you fall."

"I wasn't falling—"

"Metaphorically, bitch."

We all laugh, but it's sharp around the edges.

"He's just so…" I wave vaguely.

"Hot?" CeCe supplies.

"Intense. Like, he does this jaw thing when he's thinking—"

"Oh my God, you're so gone," Ivy says.

"Can we stop—"

"You're the one going on and on."

"Because you got me drunk!"

"Because you needed to admit you want to—"

"HEY." Dean's voice cuts through our chaos.

We all freeze, even CeCe, with a glass halfway to her lips.

He's standing at the end of our booth, beer in one hand, looking amused and annoyed and—

Crap. His sleeves are rolled up.

I stare at the table, anything to avoid looking at those strong, veiny forearms.

"Mason's about to do something stupid with darts," he says. "Thought you'd want to watch."

"We're busy," Ivy says.

"Doing what?"

"Girl stuff," Gloria offers.

"Which involves yelling about my forearms?"

I want to die. I want the sticky floor to open up and swallow me whole.

"No one was yelling about—" I start.

"The whole bar heard you."

"That's CeCe's fault."

"Hey!" CeCe protests.

Dean's mouth twitches, almost a smile. "Come on. He's drunk enough to attempt trick shots."

"In a second," Ivy says.

He looks at me. Does the intense thing. "You good?"

"Peachy."

"She's drunk," CeCe announces.

"I noticed." He's still looking at me. "Water?"

"I'm fine."

"Sure you are." He heads to the bar, presumably to order a water I didn't ask for.

"Holy shit," CeCe whispers. "The tension."

"There's no—"

"He heard you talking about his arms and came over anyway," Gloria says. "That's… interesting."

"It's mortifying."

"It's foreplay," Ivy corrects.

"I'm starting to see what all the fuss is about," Gloria says, her gaze glued to Dean's tall frame at the bar.

I'm saved from responding by Dean, who hands me a water and Mason, who appears with a handful of darts and the confidence of someone six beers deep.

"LADIES!" He attempts a bow and nearly falls. "Watch this."

What follows is ten minutes of Mason trying to hit the board blindfolded while Dean stands nearby, radiating disapproval and occasionally stepping in to prevent property damage.

"Your future husband's an idiot," I tell Ivy.

"Yeah, but he's *my* idiot." She's got the dopey love face. "Look how happy he is."

She's right. Mason's grinning like a kid, completely comfortable in his skin. No pretense. No walls.

Must be nice.

Dean catches me watching and raises an eyebrow.

I look away.

"Okay," Gloria says, checking her phone. "I should head out. Early morning."

"Quitter," I say.

"Survivor." She kisses my head. "Don't do anything I wouldn't do."

"That leaves a lot of options."

"Exactly." She winks.

After she leaves, Ivy gets pulled into the dart game, and CeCe goes off to make a phone call. Suddenly, I'm alone in the booth with my questionable decisions and—

"Here."

Dean slides another glass of water across the table and sits down across from me.

"I didn't ask for this."

"You never do."

"What's that supposed to mean?"

"Nothing." He takes a sip of his beer and studies me. "Having fun?"

"Are you?"

"Watching Mason try to maim tourists? Always a good time."

"You're a good brother."

Something flickers across his face. "Sometimes."

"No, like…" The words are slippery. Drunk words. "You show up. Even when you don't want to. That matters."

"You're drunk."

"Still true."

We sit there, surrounded by bar noise. His knee bumps mine under the table.

He doesn't move it.

"Dean?"

"Mm?"

"I'm sorry about the forearm thing."

He laughs, low and rumbly, and dang it, that's hot. "The forearm thing. Right."

"Shut up."

"Just trying to understand what makes them criminal."

I look at him. Really look. He's relaxed tonight, beer bottle loose in his hand, sleeves rolled up because he hates me specifically.

"It's the way you…" I gesture vaguely. "When you roll them up. It's very…"

"Very?"

"Competent."

"Competent?" He's definitely laughing at me now.

"Like you could… I don't know. Build something. Or fix something. Or—"

"Or?"

Take me apart. Put me back together. Ruin me for other forearms.

"Nothing."

"Liar."

Mason crashes into our table. "Deeeean! Stop flirting and come play!"

"We're not—" Dean starts.

"Poppy thinks your arms are competent!" Mason stage-whispers. "She told everyone!"

I'm going to murder him. At his own wedding.

"Go," I tell Dean. "Before he hurts himself."

He stands and pauses. "For what it's worth?"

"What?"

"I think your everything is competent."

Then he's gone, herding Mason back to the darts.

I sit there, processing.

Did he just…?

"POPPY!" Ivy appears, grabbing my hands. "Come pee with me!"

"I don't need to—"

"Girl code. Come on." She drags me to the bathroom, which is exactly as gross as expected. I suppress a shudder.

"So," she says, fixing her lipstick. "Dean likes you."

"He tolerates me."

"He brought you water."

"That was basic human decency."

"He said your everything is competent."

"That's not even a real compliment."

"From Dean? That's basically a sonnet."

I lean against the sink. "It doesn't matter. I'm leaving Sunday."

"So?"

"So what's the point?"

She turns to me. "The point is you like him. He clearly likes you. And you have two more nights."

"To what? Have a fling with my client's brother?"

"To stop overthinking and let yourself want something."

Her words cut through me. Even drunk… could I do that? No. Not when I'm hanging on by a thread. This job is the most important thing I have in my life right now.

"I want lots of things. A functioning business. Financial stability. Carbs."

"Dean. You want Dean."

"I—"

"And that terrifies you."

I stare at her in the gross bar mirror. "When did you get wise?"

"Love does that." She grins. "Come on. Let's go watch our boys be idiots."

"He's not my boy."

"Yet."

We head back out. The guys have moved on to some drinking game I don't understand. Dean's not playing, just watching with fond exasperation.

He looks up when we approach, and our eyes meet.

Two more nights.

I'm in so much trouble.

18

REDDIT REVELATIONS

Poppy

CeCe's lying on my bed, scrolling through her phone while I panic-pack for tomorrow's wedding. She's been here for a few days, supposedly to help but mostly to drink Dean's wine and make inappropriate comments about his ass.

"Okay but seriously," she says, not looking up. "His jawline?"

"Can we not?" I'm elbow-deep in my suitcase, searching for the backup backup shoes. Because you always need backup backup shoes.

"I'm just saying. That man looks at you like—"

"Like what?"

"Like he wants to eat you for breakfast. And lunch. And a midnight snack."

I throw a shoe at her. She dodges without even looking up from her phone.

"He looks at me like I'm a problem he needs to solve."

"Yeah. With his dick."

"CECE."

"What? I have eyes. That little jaw clench thing he does when you walk by? Pure sexual frustration."

"He has TMJ."

"He has feelings."

"Same thing." I find the shoes I was looking for and toss them in the bag. "Doesn't matter anyway. Tomorrow's the wedding, Sunday I'm gone."

"Uh-huh." She's still scrolling. "That why you spent twenty minutes picking out pajamas last night?"

"It's a wedding weekend. People might see—"

"The only person who might see your pajamas is—" She stops. Sits up. "Oh. My. God."

"What?"

"Oh my GOD."

"What??"

She's staring at her phone like it personally offended her. "This absolute idiot."

"Who?"

"Your boy."

"He's not my—"

"He posted on Reddit."

Everything stops. My world narrows. "What?"

"Dean. Posted. On. Reddit." She turns the phone toward me. "About you."

I snatch it from her hands.

Am I the Asshole for wanting to evict a wedding planner from my guest house who's turning my property into a three-ring circus (even though I technically agreed to host the event)?

"No." I sink onto the bed. "No no no."

"Keep reading."
I do. Every horrible word.

She's... a lot. Energetic, constantly smiling. Basically a total type-A.

"Type-A? I'm type-A??"
"Keep going."

She's not doing anything wrong per se. She's just... everywhere. On my lawn. On my porch. In my brain.

"In his brain," CeCe says. "Interesting."
I'm going to throw up. Or cry. Or march over there and strangle him with his own perfectly pressed tie.

"Look at the comments," CeCe says.
I scroll down.

BagelDad:

As someone who has literally been pooped on by a goat at a winery wedding, I feel you. But also? You're totally gonna fall in love with her.

gayunclesrevenge:

Sir, you are not asking if you're the asshole. You're asking if it's okay to be in love with a woman who smells like vanilla and organizes for a living. Yes. It's okay.

"Oh my God."
"There's more."

"I'm going to kill him."

"With what? Your type-A organizational skills?"

I stand up. Pace. Sit down. Stand up again.

"He posted about me. On the internet. To strangers."

"To be fair, he didn't use your name." Ce-Ce's still scrolling, completely unbothered by my mounting panic.

"HE POSTED ABOUT GEORGE." My voice cracks on the goat's name. I'm pacing now, wearing a path in the guest house carpet.

"The goat deserved recognition." She says it so deadpan I almost laugh. Almost.

"CeCe!" I whirl on her, and she finally looks up from her phone.

"What?" She spreads her hands innocently, eyebrows raised. "I'm trying to find the silver lining here."

My chest feels tight. "There is no silver lining! He thinks I'm annoying!"

"He thinks you're in his brain." She taps her temple with one finger, giving me a meaningful look.

I sink back onto the bed, hands over my face. "Same thing!"

She grabs my shoulders. "Poppy. Breathe."

"I can't breathe. I'm too busy being ENER-

GETIC and CONSTANTLY SMILING."

"You are kind of constantly smiling."

"It's called customer service!"

"It's called coping mechanism but okay."

I glare at her. She grins back.

"You know what?" I grab my phone. "Two can play this game."

"What are you doing?"

"Nothing."

"Poppy Monroe, don't you dare—"

But I'm already typing.

Posted to r/weddingplanning

My client's brother is a stuck-up control freak who hates joy. How do I survive this?

I'm planning the wedding of the year at this gorgeous estate, but the owner (groom's brother) is making everything impossible. He's:

- Allergic to fun

- Measures his coffee

- Complains about EVERYTHING

- Made me move the ceremony location three times

- Has opinions about flower placement (WHO HAS OPINIONS ABOUT FLOWER PLACEMENT?)

- Looks unfairly good in a suit which is BESIDE THE POINT

He keeps showing up everywhere
I'm trying to work, making comments
about "liability" and "property damage"
like I'm some kind of chaos demon.

The worst part? He made me pasta at
midnight and now I can't stop thinking
about his hands.

WAIT THAT'S NOT RELEVANT.

Anyway. How do I get through 2 more
days without strangling him with fairy
lights?

I hit submit before I can think better of it.
"Feel better?" CeCe asks.
"No."
"Wanna go yell at him?"
My eyes flick over to hers. "Yes."
"Let's go then."
"Wait, really?"
"Girl, he called you type-A on the internet.
That's basically a declaration of war."
I love her so much.
We march across the lawn like we're storm-
ing the beaches of Normandy. I don't knock. Just
bang through the front door, because apparently we
don't do boundaries anymore.
"DEAN!"
He appears from the kitchen, dish towel over
his shoulder because of course. "Poppy? What's—"
"Reddit? REDDIT?!" My voice bounces off
his vaulted ceilings.
He freezes like I've caught him red-handed,

which—fair. The color drains from his face in a way that would be satisfying if I wasn't so furious.

"I can explain." He takes a tentative step back, and I match it with a step forward.

"Oh, you can explain why you told the entire internet I'm annoying?" I cross my arms, nails digging into my biceps.

"I didn't say annoying—" His jaw tightens, and there's that clench again. Even now, even when I want to murder him, some traitorous part of my brain notices.

"Type-A? Constantly smiling? IN YOUR BRAIN?" Each accusation comes out louder than the last.

CeCe helpfully holds up her phone. "You got 500 comments, bro."

"It was anonymous," he says weakly.

"IT WAS ABOUT GEORGE. How many wedding planners have GOATS, Dean?"

"I was… venting."

"To Reddit!"

"You vent to CeCe!"

"That's different!"

"How?"

"She's not a million strangers on the internet!"

"It was only 500!"

"OH, WELL THEN."

We're standing too close now. Both breathing hard. He's got flour on his shirt and his hair's a mess and I want to shake him and also possibly climb him like a tree.

"I didn't mean—" he starts.

"What? Didn't mean to publicly humiliate

me?"

"You're not humiliated. No one knows it's you."

"I know it's me!"

"Poppy—"

"No. You know what? Forget it." I turn to leave. "Clearly I've been 'in your brain' too long."

He catches my arm. The feel of his hand on my skin is warm and electric and *ugh!* "Wait."

"What?"

"I…" He runs his other hand through his hair. Makes it worse. "I'm sorry."

I blink. "You're what?"

"I'm sorry. I shouldn't have… it was stupid. It was several days ago, after Geroge was well, *George*. I was frustrated and—"

"And what? Decided to ask the internet if you should evict me?"

"I wasn't actually going to evict you."

"Oh good. So generous."

"Poppy."

"What?"

He steps closer. "You want to know what I really think?"

"Apparently I can read it online."

"No." His voice drops. "You can't."

"What's that supposed to—"

"I didn't write about how you looked that first day. In that blue dress with your hair down. Didn't mention how you laugh with your whole body. Or how you take care of everyone but yourself. Or how you're the first person to make me actually want to—" He stops. "I didn't write any of that."

I can't breathe. "Dean."

"I wrote the safe stuff. The annoying stuff. Because the real stuff would've been…"

"What?"

"Too much."

CeCe clears her throat. "So, uh. I'm gonna go… be anywhere else."

She disappears. Traitor.

Dean's still holding my arm. Thumb brushing over my wrist.

"I'm sorry," he says again. "I messed up."

"Yeah. You did."

"How do I fix it?"

"I don't know. Maybe don't post about me on the internet?"

"Done. What else?"

"Maybe…" I look up at him. "Maybe tell me the real stuff. Instead of telling Reddit the fake stuff."

His jaw does the thing. The clenchy thing that makes me stupid.

"The real stuff?" His deep voice has gone soft and wow I like it.

"Yeah."

"Like how I haven't been able to focus on work all week because I keep wondering what you're doing? Or how I made that pasta because the thought of you not eating made me physically angry? Or how I've checked your light every night to make sure you made it back safe?"

"Dean…"

"Or how about the fact that you're leaving in two days and I can't decide if that's the best or worst thing that could ever happen to me?"

"Why would it be the best?"

"Because maybe then I could get my damn life back."

"And the worst?"

He looks at me like I'm being deliberately obtuse. "You know why."

"I really don't."

"Poppy."

"What? I'm just a type-A wedding planner who—"

He kisses me.

Just… does it. Hands framing my face, mouth hot and desperate and tasting like mint toothpaste and lust and oh.

OH.

I kiss him back because what else am I supposed to do? My hands fist in his shirt, pulling him closer, and he makes this sound—this broken, grateful sound—that shoots straight through me.

"Still mad," I mumble against his mouth.

"I know." He kisses me again. Harder. "I'm sorry."

"You posted about me on Reddit."

"I'm an idiot." His hands slide into my hair. "Forgive me?"

"I posted about you too."

He pulls back. "What?"

"About five minutes ago. Called you a stuck-up control freak who's allergic to fun."

"Am I?"

"Little bit."

"What else?"

"Said you look unfairly good in a suit."

His mouth quirks. "Unfairly?"

"It's rude. The whole…" I gesture at him. "Thing you've got going on."

"Thing?"

"Shut up."

"Make me."

So I do.

We're kissing again, rougher this time, him walking me backward until I hit the wall. His hands are everywhere—my hair, my waist, cupping my face like I might disappear.

"Dean." I break away, breathing hard. "This is—"

"Complicated. I know."

"I was going to say probably a bad idea."

"Definitely a bad idea." He kisses my neck. I forget how words work. "Terrible idea."

"The worst."

"Should stop."

"Absolutely."

Neither of us stops.

"Poppy?"

"Mm?"

"You really think I look good in a suit?"

I laugh. Can't help it. "You're not going to let that go, are you?"

"Never." He pulls back, looks at me. Really looks at me. "I meant it. The apology. I was an ass."

"Yeah. You were."

"How do I fix it? Really?"

I think about it. About the Reddit post and the comments and how he'd said I was in his brain like that was a bad thing.

"Delete the post."

"Done." He nods once.

"And…"

"What?"

"Maybe stop acting like wanting me around is such a hardship?"

Something shifts in his expression. "Poppy. Wanting you around isn't the hardship."

"Then what is?"

"Knowing you're leaving."

Oh. Right.

We stare at each other. The kitchen's too quiet. My heart's too loud.

"I should go," I whisper.

"Probably."

"Big day tomorrow."

"Right."

But his hands are still on my waist. My fingers are still twisted in his shirt.

"Dean?"

"Yeah?"

"For what it's worth? You've been in my brain all week too."

He makes that sound again. The broken one.

"That doesn't help."

"I know."

"Poppy—" he starts.

"I'll see you later."

I extract myself. Smooth down my shirt. Try to look like I haven't just been thoroughly kissed against Dean Whitaker's kitchen wall.

"Hey," he calls as I reach the door.

I turn.

"Check Reddit later."

"Why?"

"Just… trust me."

I nod. Leave. Make it halfway across the lawn before my legs start shaking.

CeCe's waiting in the guest house, grinning like Christmas came early.

"So?"

"Shut up."

"Did you—"

"Shut up."

"But—"

"SHUT. UP."

She mimes zipping her lips. Hands me my phone.

I pull up Reddit.

His post has been edited.

UPDATE: I'm the asshole. She's incredible. I'm an idiot. That's all.

The commenters are losing their minds.

"Holy shit," CeCe whispers, leaning over my shoulder to read the screen.

"Yeah." It's all I can manage. My thumb hovers over the refresh button.

"He just—" She gestures vaguely at my phone, at me, at the universe.

"Yeah." My voice sounds hollow in my own ears.

She leans back, studying my face. "On the internet—"

"I know." I press my palms against my eyes, but I can still see his updated post burned into my retinas.

She's quiet for a beat—a rarity—then delivers the verdict: "You're totally screwed."

I collapse backward on the bed, letting gravity take me. The ceiling spins, or maybe that's just me. I think about his hands in my hair and the way he said my name like it hurt, like it cost him something.

"Yeah." The word comes out as a sigh. "I really am."

19

GEORGE RETURNS

Poppy

The bleat hits me like a personal attack.

I know that bleat.

"No." I spin around, coffee mug halfway to my mouth. Hot liquid sloshes dangerously close to the rim. "No no no no—"

George stands in the middle of the lawn, chewing what looks suspiciously like my backup veil. The one I spent forty dollars on. The one that was supposed to save the day if Ivy's grandmother's veil spontaneously combusted.

"How are you HERE?" My voice pitches up, strangled somewhere between disbelief and rage.

He tilts his head. Keeps chewing. Zero fucks given.

"You were picked up. I watched them take you. There was a truck and everything!" I'm gesturing wildly now, coffee forgotten, my free hand slicing through the morning air like I'm prosecuting a case against a goat.

CeCe pokes her head out of the guest house, sleep-mussed and squinting. "Why are you yelling at—oh shit. Is that George?"

"It can't be George. George is GONE." But even as I say it, my stomach sinks. That's definitely George's signature head tilt. That's definitely George's chaos energy.

George bleats again. Definitely George.

"Maybe it's a different goat?" CeCe offers weakly, pulling her cardigan tighter.

I stare at her. Just stare. Let the full weight of my are-you-kidding-me face do the work.

"A different goat," I say slowly, carefully, like I'm explaining physics to a toddler. "Who just happens to look exactly like George and showed up on Dean's property the day before the wedding?"

"Stranger things have—"

George headbutts the folding table. The impact reverberates across the lawn. Three centerpieces topple in slow motion. One vase shatters, crystal exploding across the grass like tiny diamonds of my failure.

"GEORGE!"

I sprint across the lawn because dignity is a luxury I can't afford anymore. George sees me coming and does that sideways hop thing that means he's about to be a complete dick.

"Don't you dare—"

He dares.

Takes off toward the ceremony arch with my veil still hanging from his mouth like some demented bridal flag. I'm chasing a goat. This is my life now.

"Need help?"

Dean's voice stops me mid-sprint. I skid to a halt, chest heaving, one sandal half-off. He's standing on the porch with his morning coffee, looking like a J.Crew ad while I'm out here living my worst life. His hair's still damp from a shower. He smells like cedar and judgment.

"Does it LOOK like I need help?" I snap, shoving my sandal back on.

He takes a slow, deliberate sip of coffee. Considers the question with infuriating thoughtfulness. "Little bit."

My eye twitches. "Your property is cursed."

"My property was fine until you showed up." But his mouth's doing that thing. That almost-smile thing that makes me want to throw something at his stupidly handsome face.

George chooses this moment to leap onto the gift table with the grace of a drunk parkour enthusiast.

"GEORGE NO—"

Too late. The table collapses. Wood splinters. Wrapped presents scatter like party confetti.

"That's coming out of your deposit," Dean says, entirely too calm for someone watching his property get destroyed.

"What deposit?" I whirl on him.

"The one I'm retroactively charging you." He raises his mug slightly, satisfied smirk playing at his lips.

I flip him off. He raises his mug in a mock toast, and I hate that it makes me want to laugh.

Twenty minutes later, George is tied to a tree with what might be excessive amounts of rope, and I'm surveying the damage. One broken vase. Three traumatized centerpieces. My dignity in pieces.

"Could be worse," CeCe says.

"How?"

"Could be raining."

I look up at the sky. "Don't you dare jinx—"

"Poppy!" Ivy's voice carries across the lawn. She's power-walking toward us in designer athleisure, Mason trailing behind. "Ready for the tasting?"

The tasting.

The menu tasting. I'd forgotten that was today.

"Um. Yes! Absolutely! Just… dealing with a small goat situation."

She stops. Notices George. "Is that—"

"Different goat," I lie. "This one's… Steve."

"Steve?"

"Steve the goat. He's… for ambiance."

Mason squints. "Looks exactly like George."

"All goats look alike," I say, which is probably racist against goats but whatever.

"Actually," Dean appears beside me, because of course he does, "statistically, goats have distinct facial features that—"

I elbow him. Hard.

"—that I'm sure vary greatly between George and… Steve."

"See?" I beam at Ivy. "Totally different goat."

She doesn't look convinced, but the caterer's van pulls up before she can interrogate me further.

"Oh good!" She claps. "Dean, you're doing the tasting with us, right?"

He freezes. "What?"

"The menu tasting. I texted you yesterday."

"I don't recall—"

"I definitely texted you." She's already heading toward the van. "Mason has a client call, so you're stepping in. Poppy will fill you in on the dietary restrictions."

And just like that, I'm being voluntold to spend the next hour eating tiny foods with Dean Whitaker.

Kill me.

"Dietary restrictions?" he mutters as Ivy bounces away.

"Sixteen of them."

"Sixteen?"

"Welcome to modern weddings." I hand him my color-coded spreadsheet. "Gluten-free, dairy-free, nut-free, joy-free—"

"That last one's not real."

"Might as well be."

Dean pauses, looks down at me and lifts one eyebrow.

"I'll just… go and compose myself and meet you back here in thirty."

He nods once, mouth twitching.

Thirty-six minutes later, I've managed to touch up my makeup and what almost constitutes a matching outfit. Cream linen pants and a basic black T-shirt. There are sandals on my feet and three bracelets on my wrist and I am ready.

Day before the wedding. I can do this. Even if George is back. Even if the sexual tension with Dean might kill me.

The caterer—a woman named Deb who looks like she could bench press me—starts setting up samples on the porch table. Tiny portions of everything. Aesthetic as hell. Probably costs more than my rent.

"Okay!" Deb claps. "We'll start with the—"

Thunder rumbles.

We all look up.

"Thought you said it wasn't gonna rain," I mutter to CeCe.

"I said it COULD be worse if it rained. That's different."

Another rumble. Closer.

"Inside?" Deb suggests.

"Inside," everyone agrees.

We relocate to Dean's dining room, which is weird because now I'm sitting next to him at his actual table, and somehow that feels even more cozy and intimate. I don't have time to be thinking about the words *intimate* and *Dean* in the same sentence.

Cool. This isn't awkward at all.

"First course," Deb announces, setting down plates with the reverence of someone presenting fine art. "Beet carpaccio with microgreens and—"

"Pass," Dean says immediately, not even looking at it.

"You haven't even tried it." I'm already irritated and we're thirty seconds in.

"Don't need to. Beets taste like dirt." He sits back, arms crossed like that settles it.

"They taste like earth," Ivy corrects, ever the peacemaker.

Dean gives her a look. "That's literally dirt."

"Just try it." I shove a fork at him, and our fingers brush. Brief. Electric. I pull back too fast.

He takes the world's smallest bite, his face going through an entire emotional journey in three seconds. Confusion. Disgust. Vindication.

"Told you. Dirt."

"You're such a child." But I'm fighting a smile.

"Says the woman who brought a goat to my property. Twice." He leans back in his chair, looking infuriatingly pleased with himself.

"Steve is a different goat!" My voice goes up an octave.

"Steve is George in witness protection." He takes a sip of water, watching me over the rim of his glass.

Deb clears her throat loudly. "Should I mark the beets as a no?"

"YES," Dean and I say in unison, then immediately glare at each other for agreeing.

The tasting continues. Dean rejects half the menu on principle. I defend foods I don't even like just to argue with him. Ivy watches us like we're dinner theater, chin propped on her hand, utterly delighted.

"The salmon—"

"Too pink." He pushes the plate away.

"That's what salmon looks like!" I'm gesturing again, fork in hand like a tiny sword.

"Suspiciously pink." He narrows his eyes at the fish like it personally offended him.

"It's SALMON COLORED."

"Which is suspicious."

I throw a microgreen at him. He catches it midair with reflexes that are frankly unnecessary, pops it in his mouth.

"Tastes like disappointment," he deadpans.

"You taste like disappointment." It's out before I can stop it.

He blinks. "That doesn't even make sense."

"Your face doesn't make sense." I sound like I'm twelve. I don't care.

Ivy giggles. Actually giggles, hand over her mouth. "You two are cute."

"We're not cute," we say together, then freeze.

"We're professionally hostile," I add quickly, cheeks warming.

"Professionally hostile but make it cute," CeCe chimes in from where she's been watching this whole disaster unfold.

Thunder crashes. The lights flicker.

"Um," Deb says. "Should we maybe—"

The wind hits like a freight train. Even from inside, we can hear it. Howling. Angry. Very much not good for tents.

"THE TENT!" I jump up so fast I knock over the tray of beets. Crimson spreads across Dean's pristine white tablecloth like a crime scene.

We all rush to the window.

The reception tent is… fighting. That's the only word for it. Fighting the wind and losing. One corner's already lifted, ropes straining, the whole structure swaying like a drunk giant.

"Oh no. Oh no oh no—"

I'm already running. Out the door, into the storm that came out of nowhere because apparently the universe hates me specifically.

The wind hits like a slap. Rain sideways. Hair immediately plastered to my face.

"POPPY!" Dean's right behind me. "You can't—"

"IT'S GONNA COLLAPSE!"

"SO??"

"SO IT'S MY TENT!"

"IT'S A RENTAL!"

"IT'S MY RESPONSIBILITY!"

I grab one of the loose ropes. The wind tries to yank it away. Dean grabs it too, his hands covering mine.

"This is insane!"

"WELCOME TO WEDDING PLANNING!"

We pull. Hard. The tent fights back.

"On three!" he yells over the wind.

"What happens on three?"

"I don't know! I'm making this up!"

I laugh. Can't help it. We're in the middle of a storm, wrestling a tent, both soaked within seconds, and he's making it up as he goes.

"ONE!"

The wind gusts harder.

"TWO!"

Lightning flashes. His face is lit up for a second—jaw clenched, rain running down his cheeks, looking weirdly beautiful for someone in crisis mode.

"THREE!"

We pull together. The rope goes taut. The tent corner drops back down.

"The stake!" I point. "It's coming loose!"

He's already moving, grabbing a rock to hammer it back in. I hold the rope steady, rain streaming into my eyes.

"Other side!" he shouts.

We run around the tent, chasing loose stakes and rogue ropes. Working together without talking, like we've done this before. Like we're a team. And drive all the stakes in deeper.

The wind starts to die. The rain softens. The tent… holds.

We stand there, breathing hard and completely drenched. Rain drips from my hair down the back of my neck, and my clothes cling to my body. I can feel my heartbeat in my throat.

"We did it," I breathe, barely audible over the dying wind.

"We did it." His voice is rough, deeper than usual.

His white shirt is see-through, his hair plastered to his head. There's mud on his cheek.

He's never looked better.

He's close enough to steal my breath, close enough to unravel every defense I've rebuilt brick by brick.

And for a second, I wish he would.

"You have…" I reach up without thinking, my thumb brushing the mud away. His skin is warm despite the rain, rough with stubble.

He goes still—completely, utterly still—like I'm a wild animal he doesn't want to spook.

We're standing too close, rain-soaked and high on adrenaline. I can see water droplets caught in his eyelashes and feel the heat radiating off him despite the storm.

I brace my palm against his soaked dress shirt to steady myself and feel his heart beating as if he's sprinted a marathon. The storm isn't the only thing crackling; it's in the half inch of air between our mouths—the taste of lightning, rain, and something terrifyingly inevitable. I should step back. Instead, my thumb traces the edge of his jaw, and the look he gives me—shocked want wrapped in lawyer-level restraint—makes me forget my own name.

"Poppy…" It's barely a word—more like a prayer, or a warning.

The sound of my name in his rain-roughened voice stirs something inside me that I don't want to examine too closely.

"We should get back," I say quickly, finally—*finally*—stepping away. Cold air rushes into the space between us.

"Right. Yes." But he doesn't move for another beat; he just stands there, looking at me as if he's trying to memorize this moment.

• • •

When we head back inside, Ivy's bouncing on her toes.

"That was AMAZING! You two were like… tent superheroes!"

"We were just—"

"Saving the day! Together! Like a team!"

Dean and I carefully don't look at each other.

"I should…" I gesture vaguely at my soaked everything. "The rehearsal dinner starts in two hours and—"

"Go!" Ivy shoos me toward the door. "We'll finish up here. You need to get ready!"

Perfect. It's just enough time to get ready, check on last minute details and to have a small, private breakdown. *Yay, me.*

Two hours later, I'm blow-dried and dressed and trying not to think about Dean in the rain. It's going poorly.

CeCe eyes me as I apply mascara for the third time, my hand shaking slightly. "You okay?"

"Fine." The word comes out too fast, too high.

"You sure? Because you've been staring at that tube for five minutes."

I blink, realizing she's right. The mascara wand is frozen halfway to my face. "Just thinking about the rehearsal."

"Uh-huh." She sprawls on the bed, watching me with those knowing eyes that see too much. "And this has nothing to do with tent wrestling in the rain with—"

"We were saving the tent." I focus very hard on my reflection, not meeting her gaze.

"Sexually?"

"How do you save a tent sexually?" But my cheeks are warm.

"I don't know, but you two managed it." She's grinning now, delighted by my suffering.

I throw my lipstick at her. She dodges easily, laughing.

The rehearsal's at some restaurant in town. One of those places that tries too hard with Edison bulbs and reclaimed wood everything. I drive with CeCe because I need the moral support and also someone to stop me from doing anything stupid.

Like thinking about Dean's hands on mine.

Or the mud on his cheek.

Or the way he said my name in the rain.

"You're doing it again," CeCe says.

"What?"

"That face."

"What face?"

"Your I'm-thinking-about-Dean's-wet-shirt face."

"I don't have a—"

"You literally just sighed."

"I'm TIRED."

We pull into the restaurant parking lot. I can see the wedding party through the windows. Everyone laughing, mingling, being normal humans who didn't just have *a moment* in a storm.

Dean's already there. Of course. Standing by the bar in a fresh shirt and dark jeans, looking like he didn't just wrestle nature itself.

He sees us pull up. Watches through the window as I get out of the car.

Our eyes meet.

And I know—I know—we're both thinking about the rain.

"Ready?" CeCe asks.

No. Not even a little bit.

"Let's do this."

We walk in together, and I can feel his eyes tracking me across the room. The rehearsal dinner officially starts in ten minutes.

But the tension between us?

That started two hours ago in a storm.

And something tells me it's only going to get worse.

20

THE REHEARSAL DINNER RESCUE

Dean

The rehearsal dinner is at a pretentious farm-to-table place that charges thirty bucks for what's essentially a salad. I'm nursing a whiskey and actively avoiding my grandmother when a woman who looks like she raided a vintage boutique and a crystal shop approaches.

"You must be Dean." Her voice has a knowing quality that immediately puts me on edge. "I'm Gloria. Poppy's aunt."

Ah, the flower witch. We haven't been officially introduced. She's wearing what I can only describe as aggressive bohemian—flowing pants, bangles that jingle with every gesture, and earrings that could double as wind chimes.

"Nice to meet you," I lie, offering my hand.

She studies me like I'm a particularly interesting specimen, her grip surprisingly firm. "So you're the one who's been giving my niece fits."

Fits?

"I haven't—" I start, but she's already smiling as if she can see right through me.

"She called me Tuesday night. Something

about a goat and a man who compartmentalizes his feelings."

My jaw tightens involuntarily. "I don't compartmentalize—" I pause. Shit. I do compartmentalize my feelings. "That's not relevant."

"Mhm." She sips what looks like champagne with flowers floating in it. Because of course. "You know, Poppy doesn't usually get this worked up about clients."

"I'm not a client. I'm an obstacle." The words come out harder than I intend.

"Is that what you think you are?" She lifts her drink, and her bangles chime softly.

Before I can answer, the door opens.

And Poppy walks in.

The world does this annoying thing where it slows down, like I'm in some awful rom-com montage. She's wearing a deep green dress that hits mid-thigh, her hair is down and wavy, and she's laughing at something CeCe is saying. The sound carries across the restaurant, bright and unguarded.

Fuck.

My brain immediately supplies a dozen inappropriate thoughts. Her legs in those heels. The way that dress would look on my bedroom floor. How her hair would feel wrapped around my—

"Dean, darling, there you are!"

My grandmother materializes like a demon summoned by impure thoughts. Perfect timing, as always. I tear my gaze away from Poppy, blinking hard to refocus.

"Grandmother." I accept her air kisses while trying not to look at Poppy. I fail. She's across the room now, but I catch her profile, the curve of her neck.

"I was just telling your mother how thin you look. Are you eating?"

"Yes." My voice sounds distant to my own ears.

"Properly? Not just those horrible protein bars?"

"I eat fine." I take a sip of whiskey, the burn grounding me.

Poppy's across the room now, checking something with the restaurant manager. She wears a professional smile, but I can see the tension in her shoulders and the way she's gripping her clipboard like a lifeline, holding herself together by sheer force of will.

"—listening to me?"

I blink, realizing my grandmother has been talking. "What?"

Her eyes narrow as she follows my line of sight. "I asked if you're seeing anyone."

"No." The answer is automatic, but something in my chest tightens as I say it.

"What about that lovely girl from the club? Patricia's daughter?"

"Married. To a woman." I drain the rest of my whiskey.

"Oh." She sniffs, her lips pursing. "Well, surely there's someone—"

"Excuse me." I abandon her mid-sentence because Poppy's got that look—the one that means something's wrong, and she's about to handle it alone. It makes my feet move before my brain catches up.

She's in the corner with the restaurant manager, her voice low but her body language screaming stress. Her shoulders are hiked up near her ears, and her knuckles are white around her clipboard.

"—understand, but we specifically requested—"

"What's the problem?" I interrupt, stepping into her space.

She glances at me, and for a second, her professional mask slips. I see exhaustion and frustration underneath. "Nothing. Just a small mix-up with the—"

"Poppy," I warn, not afraid to use my lawyer voice on her.

She looks down at her heels, biting her bottom lip, then back up at me. "They, uh, gave away our private room."

Heat floods through me, sharp and immediate. "Double-booked," the manager says helpfully, tugging at his collar.

"You double-booked the rehearsal dinner?" My voice drops to that dangerous quiet that makes junior associates sweat.

The manager shifts his weight, avoiding eye contact. "There was a miscommunication—"

"Fix it."

"Sir, I—"

"Fix. It." I use my lawyer voice—the one that makes opposing counsel sweat. I step closer, and he actually backs up. "Or I'll have my entire law firm here Monday morning going through your contracts with a microscope."

He pales, his Adam's apple bobbing. "Let me…

see what I can do."

He scurries off. Poppy stares at me, her lips parted slightly.

"You didn't have to—"

"Yes, I did." The words come out rougher than intended.

"I was handling it." Her voice wavers slightly.

"You were being polite. That's different." I cross my arms to keep from reaching for her.

She mirrors my posture, chin lifted. "I don't need you to—"

"Poppy." I step closer, close enough to catch a hint of her perfume, lowering my voice so only she can hear. "You've been handling everything all week. Let someone else be the asshole for once."

Something flickers in her eyes—surprise, maybe. Gratitude. "Why do you care?"

Because you look exhausted. Because you're trying so hard to keep it together. Because watching you stress makes my chest feel tight in a way I hate.

"It's my brother's wedding," I say instead, the lie tasting bitter.

"Right." She looks away, her jaw tightening. "Of course."

The manager returns, sweating through his shirt. "We can set up a private section for the other group. Your group can move into the private room now."

"Thank you," Poppy says quickly, already moving, already back in professional mode.

She walks away before I can say anything else. I watch her go, the sway of that green dress, and curse under my breath.

• • •

The dinner goes fine. Mason stands to make a speech, glass raised, and I realize I've never seen him like this—open, vulnerable. He's more emotional than I would have expected. I've only seen my brother cry a handful of times, and all of them were before he turned 11, but right now, he looks dangerously close.

"When I first knew I loved Ivy, it was while I watched her work in her kitchen, trying to recreate her grandmother's wonton recipe for a video. It was a total disaster. Flour everywhere. She'd been at it for six hours." He looks at her with that dopey love face, his voice cracking. "That's when I knew. Anyone who cares that much about getting it right—about honoring the people they love—that's someone worth keeping."

Ivy cries, mascara running. Everyone claps. Mason kisses his fiancée with tears in his eyes, and something twists in my gut—envy, maybe. Or grief for the part of me that used to believe in moments like this.

My parents behave themselves. Mostly.

But I keep watching Poppy.

She's everywhere and nowhere, adjusting flowers with quick, efficient movements. Checking with servers, clipboard tucked under one arm, making sure everyone has drinks, that smile never faltering. Never stopping. Never sitting.

Never eating.

"She's good at this," Gloria appears beside me

like some kind of mystic ninja, silent despite all those bangles.

"Mm." I take a sip, my eyes tracking Poppy as she laughs at something my uncle says.

"Takes care of everyone but herself, that one." Gloria's voice is gentle and knowing.

I say nothing, my jaw working.

"Bit like someone else I've been observing tonight."

I turn to meet her gaze. "Meaning?"

"You've been watching her all evening, making sure she's okay." She smiles, her crow's feet deepening. "It's sweet."

"It's practical. Can't have the wedding planner collapsing from exhaustion." But my voice lacks conviction.

"Mhmm. Keep telling yourself that, dear." She pats my arm before strolling away, leaving me with the uncomfortable truth.

But she's not wrong. I've been nursing this same whiskey for an hour, watching Poppy work the room. She has a way of making everyone feel like the most important person alive—touching arms, remembering names, laughing at terrible jokes. Her whole body lights up with each interaction, genuine warmth radiating from her.

Professional. Polished. Perfect.

Nothing like the woman who wrestled a tent in the rain two hours ago. Nothing like the woman who kissed me back in my kitchen, her hands fisted in my shirt.

"You're staring." Mason drops into the seat beside me, stealing my whiskey glass.

"I'm observing."

"With your eyes. That's called staring." He takes a swig, grinning.

"How's Ivy?"

"Nice deflection." He drains the rest of my whiskey, and I don't even care. "She's good. Happy. Thinks you and Poppy are, and I quote, 'adorable.'"

"We're not anything." The words taste wrong coming out.

"Right. That's why you've been eye-fucking her since she walked in." He sets the empty glass down with a thunk.

"I haven't—" But my protest dies when I realize he's right. I know exactly where she is right now—third table from the left, laughing with someone's aunt.

"Dude. You literally stopped mid-sentence when she bent over to fix that tablecloth."

Okay. Fair. Heat crawls up my neck.

"She leaves Sunday," I say, the words sitting heavy in my chest.

"So?" Mason leans back, studying me with that concerned-brother face.

"So what's the point?"

Mason stares at me as if I've grown a second head. "The point? The point is she makes you smile. Actually smile. Not that weird grimace thing you do at client dinners."

"It's not that simple." I run a hand through my hair, tugging slightly.

"Why?" His question is earnest, genuinely confused.

Because I knew Emily for six years—six years of conversations, shared meals, and planning a future. I knew her favorite coffee order, her childhood traumas, her favorite blue jeans, and the specific ways her best friend drove her crazy.

And it still wasn't enough.

I've known Poppy for just over a week. That's insane. Completely insane.

No matter how right it feels when she looks at me.

"Dean?" Mason watches me with that concerned-brother expression, head tilted.

"It's complicated," I mutter, staring at my empty glass.

"Everything with you is complicated." He takes another sip from somewhere. "Maybe try simple for once."

Simple. Right.

Simple is not kissing your brother's wedding planner against your kitchen wall. Simple is not spending every night checking to see if her light's on. Simple is not this ache in my chest when I think about tomorrow—about watching her leave.

"I should mingle," I say, already standing.

"You should talk to her." Mason's voice follows me.

"I should do a lot of things."

But I stay in my seat, watching Poppy charm my parents' friends. She catches me looking and winks.

Just… winks. Like we're sharing a secret. Which I guess we are. Like that kiss never happened, and also like it's all she can think about.

Damn it.

The dinner drags on—speeches about love, commitment, and forever. All the things I used to believe in before I learned better. Each speech feels like a knife between my ribs, a reminder of what I lost, what I gave up on.

By the time the evening winds down, I've had enough. Enough of watching Poppy run herself ragged. Enough of family members asking about my love life. Enough of pretending I don't notice every time she tucks her hair behind her ear, every time she laughs, every time she moves.

I find her on the restaurant's back patio, finally alone, shoes off, rubbing her feet with a grimace.

"Those look painful."

She doesn't look up, fingers digging into her arch. "Beauty is pain."

"Beauty is stupid if it cripples you." I lean against the doorframe, watching her.

"Spoken like someone who's never worn heels." But there's no heat in her tone.

"You've got me there."

She almost smiles. Almost. The corner of her mouth quirks up, then falls.

I lean against the railing, close enough to see the exhaustion around her eyes. "You haven't eaten."

"I've been busy." She continues rubbing her foot, avoiding my gaze.

"You're always busy."

"Yeah, well." She shrugs, her shoulders tight. "That's the job."

"The job is planning weddings, not martyring

yourself." The words come out sharper than I intend.

Her head snaps up, eyes flashing. "Excuse me?"

"You heard me."

"I'm not martyring—" Color rises in her cheeks.

"When's the last time you ate a full meal? Slept eight hours? Took a break that wasn't forced on you by someone else?"

She stands, though I can tell her feet are killing her. She sways slightly, catching herself on the railing. "Why do you care?"

"Why don't you?" I take a step closer.

"Because I have a wedding to pull off. Because this matters. Because if I stop for five seconds—" She cuts herself off, jaw clenching.

"What? What happens if you stop?"

"Nothing. Forget it." She grabs her shoes, clutching them to her chest like armor.

"Poppy—"

"No." Her voice cracks slightly. "You don't get to do this. Swoop in and act concerned when it's convenient."

"Convenient? You think any of this is convenient for me?" I laugh, the sound bitter. Meeting Poppy Monroe might be the least convenient thing that's ever happened to me.

"Then why are you here?" She's breathing hard now, her chest rising and falling.

Good question. Why am I here? Why do I care if she's eating? Why does watching her hurt herself make me want to shake her and hold her at the same time?

"Because someone should be," I finally say, the truth raw in my throat.

"I don't need—" She starts, but I cut her off.

"Yes, you do. You need someone to make you eat, to tell you to sit down, to care whether or not you're okay."

"And you've appointed yourself?" Her chin lifts, defiant.

"Apparently."

We stare at each other. The fairy lights strung overhead cast shadows on her face, and she looks tired, beautiful, and so freaking stubborn that I want to—

"You know what your problem is?" she says, her voice low and dangerous.

"Please, enlighten me." I cross my arms, bracing myself.

"You hide."

"I hide?" The accusation stings more than it should.

Her posture straightens, and she lifts her chin, appraising me with those sharp eyes. "Behind work. Behind this whole grumpy, emotionally unavailable persona. You hide because it's easier than actually feeling something."

"That's rich, coming from someone who can't stop moving long enough to—" My hands curl into fists.

"At least I believe in something—love, marriage, happy endings." Her voice rises, passionate now.

"Naïve."

"What?" She goes very still.

"You're naïve. You sell fairy tales to people who'll be divorced in five years." The words are cruel. I know it the moment they leave my mouth.

Her face changes. It goes hard, all the softness bleeding away. "Wow."

"Poppy—" I reach for her, but she steps back.

"No, you're right. I'm naïve. A stupid little wedding planner who believes in love." She laughs, but it's sharp and brittle. "At least I'm not so damn scared of feeling something that I've turned into a robot."

"I'm not—"

"You are. You're terrified. Of wanting something. Of someone mattering. Of being human." Her eyes are bright now, too bright.

"And you're so desperate to matter to someone that you'll kill yourself making everyone else's dreams come true." The words hang between us like grenades.

Her eyes shine with unshed tears. "Screw you."

"Poppy—"

But she's already leaving. Shoes in hand, dignity intact, walking away as if I didn't just gut her. The door swings shut behind her, and the sound echoes in the sudden silence.

Shit.

I stand there like an idiot, replaying the conversation. The way her face crumpled before she hid it. The truth in what we both said. The damage we just inflicted.

"That went well."

I turn. CeCe leans in the doorway, arms crossed, her expression unreadable.

"How much did you hear?" I run both hands through my hair, tugging hard enough to hurt.

"Enough." She studies me, silent for a long moment. "You know she's not wrong."

"Neither was I." But it sounds hollow.

"No," she agrees, pushing off the doorframe. "You're both disasters. Which is probably why you're perfect for each other."

"We're not—"

"Good grief, stop." She holds up a hand, cutting me off. "I've watched you two circle each other all week like horny vultures. Just kiss her already."

"I did." The admission slips out.

Her eyes widen, eyebrows shooting up. "When?"

"The other day." After the Reddit incident. Against my kitchen wall.

"And?" She's leaning forward now, invested.

And it was everything. It terrified me. I haven't stopped thinking about it since.

"And it's complicated," I say, the understatement of the year.

"Yeah, no shit." She pushes off the doorway. "Look, I don't know you. But I know Poppy. And she doesn't get worked up about guys. Ever. But you? You've got her twisted in knots even George couldn't manage."

"That's not—" I start, but she talks over me.

"She's leaving Sunday," CeCe continues, her voice gentler now. "So whatever this is, whatever you think you're protecting yourself from, you've got about thirty-six hours to figure it out."

She leaves me with that cheerful thought.

I stay on the patio, nursing my whiskey and my bruised ego. Poppy's words keep echoing in my mind. You're terrified. Of wanting something. Of someone mattering.

She's right. We're both hiding, just in different ways.

An hour later, the party's winding down. I've done my duty—smiled at relatives, shaken hands, pretended to care about small talk. Mason and Ivy left twenty minutes ago, glowing with pre-wedding happiness that makes my chest hurt in ways I don't want to examine.

I should go home. I should review tomorrow's timeline. I should do anything except what I'm about to do.

Instead, I go looking for Poppy.

She's not in the main dining room. Not at the bar. Not on the patio where I destroyed whatever fragile thing was building between us.

"Lost something?" Gloria appears again, materializing from nowhere. The woman has supernatural timing.

"Have you seen—"

"She left." Her expression softens slightly, knowing. "Whatever you said to her—"

"Was true." I set my jaw.

"Truth and cruelty often wear the same clothes," she says, tilting her head. "Doesn't mean you have to let them."

Cryptic flower aunt wisdom. Fantastic. As if my night couldn't get any worse.

"Where did she go?" The question escapes before I can stop it.

"Back to the house, I assume." She tilts her head, studying me like a particularly interesting bug. "Are you going after her?"

"No." But my feet are already moving toward the door.

"Liar." Her voice follows me.

"I'm going home. To sleep. Like a normal person." I grab my keys from the valet.

"Mhmm." She pats my cheek like I'm five. "She's probably checking on the tent, in case you were wondering."

"I wasn't."

"Of course not, dear."

Twenty minutes later, I'm pulling into my driveway, definitely not looking for Poppy. The headlights sweep across the property as I park.

The property is quiet. The tent is secure despite today's earlier drama. There are no lights on in the guest house—just darkness and silence.

I should go inside, leave her alone, and respect the boundary she clearly set.

Thunder rumbles in the distance.

Damn it.

Not again.

I grab a flashlight and head out because I'm apparently incapable of making good decisions when it comes to her.

The rain starts soft—a drizzle at first. But the thunder is getting closer, and I know what that means—the kind of storm that sends Nadine's neurotic dog into hysterics.

Muffin.

She'll be losing her mind right about now.

Thunder sends her into full panic mode, and Nadine mentioned she was at some wine tasting tonight.

I head for the guest house, hoping Muffin hasn't destroyed anything, my flashlight beam cutting through the drizzle.

The door is ajar.

"Poppy?"

No answer. But I can hear something—soft voices, almost crooning, off-key humming.

I push the door open.

And my heart does this weird stuttering thing.

Poppy's on the floor with Muffin, who's shaking like a leaf. The thunder vest is on, but it's not helping. Poppy has her wrapped in what looks like every blanket in the place, holding her close and murmuring nonsense. Her dress is rumpled, her makeup smudged, but she's completely focused on the terrified dog.

"Shh, baby. It's okay. Just noise. Can't hurt you." Her voice is soft, soothing.

Muffin whimpers and presses closer, burrowing into Poppy's chest.

"I know. Scary noise. But you're safe. So safe." She rocks slightly, like soothing a child.

I must make a sound because Poppy looks up. Her makeup is smudged, mascara tracking down her cheeks—from tears or rain, I can't tell. Her hair is a mess. Still in that green dress, now wrinkled and damp.

Still devastatingly beautiful.

"She was scratching at the door," she says softly, not quite meeting my eyes. "I couldn't leave her out there."

"Yeah—" I clear my throat, something lodged there. "Thanks."

Thunder crashes. Muffin yelps and tries to burrow into Poppy's chest.

"Oh, sweet girl." Poppy adjusts the blankets, her movements gentle and sure. "We need a distraction. What do you think? Story? Song?"

"She likes Motown," I hear myself say as I step inside and close the door behind me.

Poppy looks at me, eyebrows raised. "Seriously?"

"Nadine swears by it." I move closer, drawn in despite everything.

Nadine. Right.

"Okay then." Poppy starts humming—badly, off-key—but soft and sweet, and something in my chest loosens.

I should leave. Instead, I sit right there on the floor, back against the couch. Close enough to feel her warmth and catch hints of her perfume beneath the smell of wet dog.

"'Cruisin'"?" I guess, recognizing the melody despite her terrible pitch.

She laughs quietly, the sound cracking something open inside me. "I don't know the words."

"That's barely Motown."

"I don't know any Motown." She keeps humming, her fingers stroking Muffin's ears with infinite patience.

"Tragic."

"Yeah, well." She continues humming, but her voice wavers. "Add it to my list of failures."

"Poppy—"

"Don't." Her voice is barely a whisper, raw. "Not tonight."

So I don't. I just sit there while she hums to my neighbor's neurotic dog. The storm rages outside, rain lashing against the windows. Inside, it's just us, terrible humming, a wet dog, and all the things we've said to each other.

Eventually, the thunder fades. Muffin's breathing evens out, stops shaking. Her body goes heavy with sleep.

Falls asleep.

"You can go," Poppy says without looking at me, still stroking Muffin's ears. "She's okay now."

"What about you?" The question slips out before I can stop it.

"I'm fine." But her voice is hollow.

"Liar."

She finally meets my eyes, and I see it all there—exhaustion, hurt, frustration. "Takes one to know one."

Fair.

I stand, joints protesting from sitting on the floor, and brush off my jeans. "I'm sorry. About earlier."

"Which part? The robot thing or calling me naïve?" Her voice is flat, carefully neutral.

"Both. All of it. The things I said were…" I trail off, searching for the right word. There isn't one.

She looks back at Muffin, her profile sharp in the dim light. "Yeah. Me too."

"Poppy—"

"Please just go." Her voice cracks slightly, and

I hate that I did this. "I can't do this tonight."

I want to stay. I want to tell her she was right, that I am scared, that she matters. Watching her take care of everyone—including a neurotic dog that isn't even hers—makes me feel things I can't name.

Instead, I go.

But I leave my door unlocked. Just in case.

An hour later, I'm pretending to read briefs, the words swimming on the page, when I hear it—scratching at my door, insistent, desperate.

I open it, expecting Muffin.

But she's not alone.

Poppy is carrying her, wrapped in blankets like a burrito. Her hair is everywhere, no longer styled but wild around her face. Makeup gone, scrubbed clean. Barefoot, her feet probably still aching from those heels.

"She won't settle," she says, her voice small and uncertain. "Keeps crying. I think she wants—"

"Her spot." I step aside without hesitation. "Come in."

They enter like it's normal, like we do this. Poppy, with her disaster hair and someone else's dog, makes herself at home in my space as if she belongs here.

"Where's her spot?"

I gesture to the rug by the fireplace. "There. She likes the corner."

Poppy carefully settles Muffin, tucking the blankets around her. The dog immediately curls up, sighs deeply, and passes out.

"Seriously? That's all it took?" Poppy stares at

the sleeping dog, incredulous.

"She's particular."

"She's ridiculous." But she's smiling slightly, the first real smile I've seen since the patio.

"Yeah, well."

We stand there, awkward. The weight of our earlier fight hangs between us like smoke. I can still see the hurt in her eyes, the way she holds herself carefully, as if she might break.

"I should—" She starts toward the door.

"You could stay." The words are out before I can stop them, rushing out like they've been trapped. "Until she's really settled. In case the storm comes back."

She looks at me for a long moment, searching my face. "Just until she's settled."

"Right."

"On the couch."

"Of course."

"This doesn't mean—"

"I know."

She curls up on one end of the couch, pulling her knees up. I sit on the other, keeping a careful distance between us. A full cushion of space that feels like miles.

"Dean?"

"Yeah?"

"I'm not naïve. I know the statistics. I know half of these marriages won't last." Her voice is quiet, thoughtful. "But I also know that moment when they look at each other and think, 'You're it. You're my person.' And even if it ends… that moment was still real."

I don't know what to say to that. The truth of it sits heavy in my chest.

"I believe in that," she continues, staring at the dark fireplace. "I believe in fighting for that, even if it doesn't always last in the end."

"That's…" I search for words.

"Naïve?" There's a challenge in her voice.

"I was going to say brave." The admission costs me something.

She looks at me, surprised, her lips parted.

"Believing in something you know might hurt you—that's brave. Or stupid. Maybe both." I hold her gaze.

"Speaking from experience?" Her voice is soft, careful.

I think about Emily. About believing in forever until it wasn't. About closing myself off so nothing could hurt like that ever again. About the six years that weren't enough.

"Maybe."

Thunder rumbles in the distance, softer now. Muffin twitches but doesn't wake.

"We should sleep," Poppy says, but neither of us moves. "Big day tomorrow."

"Right."

But neither of us moves. The space between us feels charged, electric.

"Dean?"

"Mm?"

"This is complicated."

"Everything with you is complicated." But I'm almost smiling.

She almost smiles back. "Is that bad?"

"I'm starting to think complicated might be worth it."

"Yeah?" Hope flickers across her face.

"Ask me in thirty-six hours."

"What happens in thirty-six hours?" She's watching me carefully now.

You leave. And I either let you go or do something stupid.

"The wedding's over," I say instead, the coward's answer.

"Right. The wedding." Something dims in her expression.

Silence settles. Comfortable this time. The storm's passing. Muffin snores softly.

"Stay," I say, the word coming out rough. "Tonight. Here. The guest house is cold and—"

"Okay."

"Okay?" I wasn't expecting that.

"Just sleeping."

"Just sleeping."

"On the couch."

"Sure."

"Dean?"

"Yeah?"

"Thank you. For earlier. With the restaurant. For coming to check on us. For… this." She gestures vaguely at the space, at us, at whatever this is.

Something in my chest shifts. Loosens. Like a knot coming undone, like breathing after holding your breath too long.

"Get some sleep, Poppy."

"You too."

I grab blankets from the hall closet and pillows

that actually match, making the couch as comfortable as possible by tucking everything around her. She curls up, dress and all, looking small, exhausted, and perfect.

I head upstairs to shower, letting the hot water beat against my shoulders. After changing into sweats and a T-shirt, I try not to think about her downstairs on my couch.

I fail spectacularly.

When I come back down to check, she's asleep, curled on her side with one hand tucked under her cheek like a child. Muffin has migrated from her spot and is pressed against Poppy's stomach, protective.

They look… right. Like they belong here. Like this is how it should be.

That feeling in my chest intensifies. Or maybe it gets better. It's hard to tell.

I grab a book from the shelf and settle into the chair across from them, just for a minute, to make sure they're okay.

• • •

I wake up four hours later, the book resting on my chest and my neck cramped. Early morning light filters through the windows, gray and soft.

Poppy's still asleep, but she's shifted. The blanket is half off, and her dress has ridden up slightly, exposing more of those legs.

Muffin is awake, watching me with judgmental eyes from her spot against Poppy's stomach.

"Don't start," I mutter, my voice rough with sleep.

She huffs and settles back down, but keeps one eye on me.

I stand slowly, my joints protesting, and fix Poppy's blanket, being careful not to wake her. My hand brushes her shoulder, and she sighs, turning into the touch, seeking warmth.

That thing in my chest?

Yeah. I'm fucked.

Completely, thoroughly fucked.

And tomorrow's the wedding.

The day after that, she leaves.

I look down at her sleeping on my couch, at Muffin guarding her like a tiny, neurotic sentinel, and I know with absolute certainty that I'm going to do something stupid.

The only question is whether it'll be letting her go or asking her to stay.

21

WEDDING DAY CHAOS

Poppy

I wake up on Dean's couch at 5:42 a.m., Muffin snoring against my stomach, and reality hits me like a sledgehammer.

Shit.

I slept here. In my dress. After ugly-humming Motown to a neurotic dog while Dean watched with that look that made my chest crack open.

I can't process that now. It's wedding day.

I carefully extract myself from the blanket—when did that get here?—and tiptoe toward the door. My dress is wrinkled beyond salvation, my hair feels like a bird's nest, and there's definitely dog drool on my shoulder. Perfect.

Muffin cracks one eye open, judges me with that special contempt only dogs can muster, and goes right back to sleep.

Smart dog.

The guest house is freezing when I stumble in, the morning air biting through my thin dress. CeCe is still passed out, one leg hanging off the bed, yesterday's mascara giving her raccoon eyes. She's snoring softly, dead to the world.

I shower, change, and armor myself in my responsible wedding planner outfit—a burgundy silk dress that projects "I definitely didn't just do the walk of shame from your brother's couch." The fabric is smooth and professional, a shield against the chaos threatening to swallow me whole.

By the time my phone buzzes at 6:47, I'm already three coffees deep and cross-referencing my lists. My hands are steady now, controlled. I can do this. I've done this a hundred times.

TEXT:

> Can't make it today. Food poisoning. Sorry.

I stare at the screen, blink, and read it again.
No.
No, no, no.
"Fuck." The word comes out small. Broken. The phone trembles in my grip. "Fuck, fuck, FUCK."

CeCe pokes her head out of the bathroom, toothbrush in her mouth, foam at the corners. "What's wrong?"

"The guitarist." My voice sounds weird. Far away, like it's coming from underwater. "For the ceremony. He just… canceled."

"Oh shit." The toothbrush stops mid-brush.

"The ceremony's in a matter of hours." I'm doing that thing where my voice gets higher with each word, tighter, like a string about to snap. "Where am I supposed to find a classical guitarist in rural New York in a matter of HOURS?"

"Okay, breathe." CeCe steps out of the bathroom, concern creasing her forehead.

"I can't breathe. This is Ivy's wedding. The wedding that's supposed to save my career. The wedding that—" I stop. I can't say the rest out loud. My throat closes around the words.

The wedding I've been using to prove I'm not a complete failure.

"We'll figure it out," CeCe says, but even she sounds worried. Her eyes are too wide, her usual confidence cracking.

I'm already scrolling through my phone, fingers flying, calling every musician in a fifty-mile radius. Each ring feels like an eternity.

"Hello, hi, I need a guitarist for—"

"Booked." Click.

"Is there any way—"

"Lady, it's Saturday." The dismissal in the voice stings.

Call after call. Same answer. Booked. Busy. One guy actually laughs at me, the sound harsh through the speaker.

My hands are shaking now. That scary kind of shaking where you can't make it stop. The phone keeps slipping in my sweaty palm.

"Poppy—" CeCe's voice is gentle, worried.

"I've got it." I don't have it. The lie tastes bitter. "Just… give me a minute."

I stumble outside because the guest house is too small, the walls pressing in. I need air, need space, need the sky above me. I need a freaking miracle.

And I almost run straight into Dean.

He's carrying coffee, steam rising from two cups. His hair is still damp from a shower, curling slightly at the ends. He looks unfairly good for someone whose couch I just snuck away from—dress shirt and jeans, barefoot, looking relaxed and put-together while I'm falling apart.

"Whoa." He steadies me with his free hand, warm and solid against my arm. "You okay?"

"Fine." I step back, breaking contact. Heat blooms where he touched me. I can't look at him. Not after last night. Not after being so close to him while I hummed off-key to a dog. Not after whatever that moment was.

"You left early." His voice is careful, neutral.

My stomach flips. "I had to—wedding stuff."

"Right." Something flickers in his eyes—disappointment, maybe. Or understanding. "Wedding stuff."

We stand there for a beat too long, the morning air cold between us.

"Dean, I really don't have time—" I start, already turning away.

"What happened?"

The question stops me. Something in his tone—genuine concern, not just polite inquiry.

"Nothing. Just… a vendor thing." I wave a hand dismissively, but it's still shaking.

"What vendor thing?" He steps closer, and I catch a whiff of his soap—cedar and something else.

"The guitarist canceled." The words tumble out, too fast, tripping over each other. "For the ceremony. Ivy specifically wanted acoustic guitar, and he's sick, and I can't find anyone else, and—"

"Give me an hour." He's already setting down

the coffee cups on the porch railing.

"What?" I blink at him, not understanding.

"One hour." He's backing away, keys appearing in his hand like magic. "Trust me."

"Dean—" But he's already moving, purpose in every step.

But he's gone, jogging toward his car like a man on a mission, leaving me standing there with my mouth open and my crisis temporarily forgotten.

"So," CeCe says from the doorway, wrapped in a blanket now. "What was that all about?"

I watch Dean's car disappear down the driveway, taillights winking in the early morning gray. "Shut up."

"Okay, babe. You're the boss." But she's grinning, that knowing smile that makes me want to throw something at her.

I flip her off and go back to panic-calling musicians, even though something in my chest has loosened just slightly.

• • •

An hour later, I'm helping Ivy with pre-wedding prep—her suite is chaos, makeup everywhere, hair tools plugged in, bridesmaid dresses hanging like pastel ghosts—when she starts screaming.

"IT'S NOT SYMMETRICAL!"

I nearly drop the veil I'm steaming. My heart slams into my throat as I run into the bathroom, disaster scenarios flooding my brain. Fire. Blood. Torn dress.

She's staring at her face in the mirror like it

betrayed her, leaning so close her breath fogs the glass.

"My eyebrows," she whispers, voice thick with horror. "Look at them."

I look. They're… eyebrows. Perfect eyebrows, actually. Better than mine have ever been.

"The left one is half a millimeter higher!" Her finger jabs at the mirror, leaving a smudge.

"Ivy. Breathe." I step closer, gentle.

"I can't breathe! I have 13 million followers, and they're going to notice and—" Her chest is heaving now, eyes too bright.

"Hey." I grab her shoulders, firm but careful not to wrinkle the robe. "Look at me."

She does. Mascara already smudging at the corners, threatening to run. Her bottom lip trembles.

"Nobody's going to notice your eyebrows."

"But—" Her voice cracks.

"Know what they're gonna notice? How happy you look. How Mason can't stop staring at you. How freaking gorgeous this entire estate is. How beautiful you are, inside and out." I squeeze her shoulders gently, trying to ground her.

"But the photos—" She's still staring at her reflection, critical.

"Forget the photos."

Her eyes widen, snapping to mine in the mirror.

"I mean—we'll get beautiful photos. But that's not why you're doing this, right?" I turn her to face me properly, away from the mirror and its cruel magnification.

She's quiet. For so long, I start to really regret yelling 'forget the photos.' What kind of wedding planner am I? Her breathing is shallow, rapid. Then she whispers, "I'm scared."

"Of what?" I soften my voice, my grip.

"What if people think—" She stops, swallowing hard. Her hands are twisting in her robe.

"You of all people know better than to care about what people think. There are always going to be a few haters." I wait until she meets my eyes. "But you and Mason?"

She smiles involuntarily when I say his name. It transforms her face, chasing away the anxiety.

"You and Mason are going to have a beautiful wedding and an even more beautiful life together."

She inhales slowly, nodding. Her shoulders drop from where they've been hunched near her ears. "Thanks, Poppy."

"Anytime." I grin, relieved.

Something in her face shifts. The influencer mask cracks, and I see the real Ivy underneath—vulnerable, uncertain, human.

"Where'd you sleep last night?" she asks suddenly, tilting her head.

My hands freeze on her shoulders. Heat floods my cheeks. "What?"

"Dean mentioned you helped with Muffin during the storm." Her tone is carefully casual, but her eyes are sharp in the mirror now.

"Oh. That was… nothing." I busy myself adjusting her robe, smoothing nonexistent wrinkles.

"Uh-huh." She's watching me in the mirror now, a small smile playing at her lips. "Is that why you're being weird?"

"I'm not being weird." But my voice pitches up

slightly, defensive.

"You're totally being weird." She turns to face me fully, studying my expression.

Before I can argue, Mason appears in the doorway looking green. Actually green, like he might be sick all over Ivy's pristine white bathmat.

"Babe? We need a minute." His voice is tight, strained.

Ivy's face falls, all the calm I just built evaporating. "What's wrong?"

"Nothing. Just… wedding jitters. Guy stuff." But his hands are shaking where they grip the doorframe.

"Guy stuff?" I question, because that's the worst lie I've ever heard.

"Just need to talk. Privately." He looks at me pointedly.

I give them space but hover near the door because I'm nosy and also because Mason looks like he might puke or bolt, and I need to know which emergency I'm dealing with.

"—Mom's being impossible," I hear him say, voice muffled. "And Dad brought Kevin."

"Your cousin Kevin?" Ivy's voice rises slightly.

"My perfect surgeon cousin Kevin who Mom wishes was her son instead." The bitterness in his tone is sharp, cutting.

"Mason—"

"What if she's right? What if I'm not—" His voice cracks, and my heart squeezes.

"Stop." Ivy's voice is firm now, steel underneath the gentleness. "Look at me."

There's shuffling. Soft voices I can't make out.

The quiet murmur of comfort, reassurance.

Then Ivy laughs, bright and clear. "Your mom can suck it. I'm marrying you, not her perfect son fantasy."

"Yeah?" He sounds young, uncertain.

"Yeah. I love you, Mace. Forever."

"I love you too," he says softly. Then there are kissing sounds, and just as I'm starting to feel like a creeper, Ivy laughs again, lighter this time.

"Now go. Poppy needs to fix my allegedly wonky eyebrows."

I step away quickly, pretending I wasn't listening. Crisis averted. Thank God.

"Poppy!" CeCe calls from downstairs, her voice echoing up. "Hair and makeup's here!"

Right. Back to work.

My phone buzzes. Flower delivery is here. Caterer's on schedule. DJ confirmed. Everything is falling into place like dominoes, one after another. Everything except my ability to function around Dean Whitaker. Oh, and my missing guitarist. The thought hits me like cold water, and my stomach drops. Now I feel like the one who might puke.

I can't think about last night. About sleeping on his couch. About him tucking a blanket around me while I slept, the gentleness of it. About waking up to find him in the chair across from me, a book on his chest, like he'd been watching over us.

I can't do any of this right now. Six hours until the wedding.

Six hours to pull off a miracle.

Six hours until I prove I can do this.

Or six hours until everything falls apart.

22

WEDDING DAY COUNTDOWN

Dean

I break at least six traffic laws getting to my storage unit.

Haven't been here in months. Years, maybe. The lock sticks, protesting when I yank it open. The guitar case is exactly where I left it, buried under boxes of Emily's shit I never returned and law school textbooks I'll never open again. Dust motes dance in the fluorescent light as I pull things aside, creating a small avalanche of my past.

The Martin D-28 is still perfect. Still smells like rosewood and regret.

I tune it in the car, muscle memory taking over. My fingers remember even if my brain would rather forget. Each string hums to life under my touch, the sound achingly familiar. Like coming home to a place you swore you'd never return to.

Back at the estate, I find Mason in the kitchen, stress-eating cereal. He's hunched over the counter, tie already loosened, shoveling Cheerios into his mouth like they hold the answers to life.

"I need your help," I say.

"If this is about the bachelor party, I already

apologized for the—" He looks up, spoon halfway to his mouth, then stops. His eyes drop to the guitar case. "Is that—"

"Can you still play bass?" I cut him off before he can finish that thought.

He blinks. "Uh. Yeah? Why?" The spoon clatters back into the bowl.

"Because Poppy's guitarist canceled, and she's about to have a breakdown."

"So?" But his posture's already changing, straightening.

"So we're fixing it." I set the case down on the counter with a thunk.

"We?" His eyebrows climb toward his hairline.

I hold up the guitar case, popping the latches. His eyes go wide when he sees the Martin.

"Dude. You haven't played since—" His voice drops, careful now.

"I know." I fix him with a hard stare, daring him to say more.

"Are you sure you want to—"

"Mason," I cut him off, jaw tight. "It's your wedding. Poppy's worked her ass off. We're doing this."

He studies me for a long moment, cereal forgotten. Then grins like a love-drunk idiot, that dopey expression I've been seeing all week. "Hell yeah, we are."

We spend the next hour in the basement, running through processional music, the songs Ivy requested, trying to remember how to harmonize. My fingers hurt, the tips burning where calluses used to be. It's a good hurt, though. Like waking up something that's been sleeping too long. Like remembering you're still alive under all the armor.

"You know," he says during a break, adjusting his bass strap, "you could just tell her you like her."

I keep my eyes on the fretboard, fingers finding the next chord. "Tell who what?"

"Poppy. That you're stupid about her." He's grinning again; I can hear it in his voice.

"I'm not—" I start, but the protest dies.

"You're literally learning guitar again for her." He plucks a string, the note hanging in the air between us.

"It's for the wedding." But the words sound hollow even to me.

"Right." He starts playing a bassline, something jazzy and knowing. "That's why you've been moping around since she started avoiding you."

My fingers slip on a chord. "She's not avoiding me."

"Bro. She literally hid behind a tent yesterday afternoon when you walked by." He's laughing now, the sound bouncing off the basement walls.

Yeah. She did. I'd pretended not to notice, but I saw the flash of burgundy, the way she ducked behind the white canvas.

"I posted about her on Reddit," I admit, the confession scraping out.

Mason stops playing. The sudden silence is deafening. "You what?"

"I asked Reddit if I was an asshole for wanting her gone." It was days ago, in my defense. Before I knew what she'd become to me.

"Are you freaking serious?" His voice climbs

an octave.

I frown and fiddle with the tuning pegs, not meeting his eyes. "She found out."

"No shit she's avoiding you!" He sets the bass down with more force than necessary.

"I apologized."

"How?" He crosses his arms, waiting.

"We, uh, kissed." The memory floods back—her hands in my shirt, the desperate sound she made, how right it felt.

Mason drops his pick. It hits the concrete floor with a tiny plastic tap. "What?"

"In my kitchen. After she yelled at me." I can still taste her—vanilla and fury and something sweet.

"And?" He's leaning forward now, invested.

The memory of her on my couch hits like a sucker punch. Curled up in that green dress, looking wrecked and perfect and so vulnerable it made my chest crack open. She'd hummed off-key Motown to my neighbor's neurotic dog like it was the most natural thing in the world. Like she belonged there. Like she belonged with me. And when I found them both asleep—Poppy with her hand tucked under her cheek, Muffin pressed against her stomach—something fundamental shifted. The kind of shift that makes you realize you've been living your life wrong. That maybe all those walls you built weren't protecting you from pain, just preventing you from this. From her. From the terrifying possibility that someone could matter this much.

"And now I'm pretty sure she's avoiding me."

My voice comes out rougher than intended.

"Because you kissed?" Mason picks up his bass again, fingers finding the strings.

I shrug, the motion feeling heavy. "Because she's leaving tomorrow, and we both know this is complicated and—"

"And you're an idiot." He says it gently, but it still lands like a punch.

"Thanks. Super helpful." I adjust my grip on the guitar neck, focusing on the wood grain.

He picks up the bass again. "Play the processional again. And maybe think about why you're doing this."

"For the wedding—"

"Dean." Just my name, but it carries weight.

I shut up and play.

• • •

The day's already trying to kill me, and it's only noon.

I'm in the kitchen, third coffee burning my tongue, pretending to read emails when my phone buzzes with a call from an unknown number. The screen glows accusingly on the marble counter.

"Dean Whitaker," I answer, expecting it to be a work call. Another fire to put out.

"Mr. Whitaker? This is Tom from Harvest Table Catering. We've had an accident."

My stomach drops, coffee turning to acid. "Define accident."

"Our van hit a deer. We're okay, but the vehicle's totaled and—" His voice is shaking, young and scared.

"Where are you?" I'm already moving toward my keys.

"Route 9, about forty minutes out. The food's mostly intact, but we can't—"

"Text me your exact location. Don't move." I hang up before he can protest.

I stare at the ceiling. Count to five. Breathe through the surge of adrenaline.

Then I grab my keys.

Mason's in the hallway, adjusting his tie for the fifteenth time. His hands are shaking slightly. "Where you going?"

"Errand." I don't slow down.

"Now? The ceremony's in—" He checks his watch, panic edging into his voice.

"I know when the ceremony is." The words come out sharper than intended.

He narrows his eyes, that brotherly radar activating. "What's wrong?"

"Nothing. Practice the processional again. Your transition's still rough." I'm already pulling on my jacket.

"Dean—"

But I'm already out the door, gravel crunching under my shoes as I jog to the car.

• • •

The drive takes thirty-seven minutes. I know because I watch every minute tick by on the dashboard clock. I find the catering van on the shoulder, front end crumpled like a crushed soda can, the driver looking shell-shocked and pale.

"Mr. Whitaker?"

"Tom?" I climb out of my car, assessing the damage.

"Yeah. I'm so sorry, we've never—" He's young, maybe twenty-five, looking like he might cry or throw up.

"Is the food salvageable?" I cut through his panic with efficiency.

He blinks at me, surprised by the question. "Most of it. The appetizers took a hit, but the main courses are in the back—"

"Good. Help me load my car." I'm already popping my trunk.

"Sir?" He stares at me like I've suggested we fly.

"We're transferring everything. Now." I start pulling out the first container, still warm.

It takes two trips to get it all safely loaded. My BMW smells like salmon and anxiety, the leather seats probably ruined. Tom rides with me on the last run, clutching a tray of something that might be bruschetta like it's a newborn.

"I should call your brother—" he starts, voice uncertain.

"No." The word is final.

"But—" He shifts in his seat, uncomfortable.

"You call no one. Got it?" I bark, eyes on the road as I push the speed limit.

He nods, terrified, shrinking against the passenger door.

Smart kid.

Back at the estate, we unload everything into the kitchen. It takes twenty minutes of careful maneuvering, my back protesting as we carry the last of the heavy trays.

"Set up here," I tell Tom, pointing to the prep station. "Use whatever you need. Can your team make it?"

"They're getting a rental. Should be here by—" He's already pulling out his phone, fingers flying.

"Good. Make it work." I turn to leave, loosening my tie. The salmon smell is clinging to my clothes.

"Wait. Should I tell the wedding planner—"

"No." The word comes out harder than intended. "She's got enough to deal with. This stays between us."

"But—" His eyes are wide, confused.

"Tom. The bride wants salmon. She's getting salmon. End of story." I level him with a look that's closed more than one business deal.

He stares at me, processing. "You're doing this for the bride?"

No. I'm doing it for the woman who stayed up all night making sure every detail was perfect. Who forgot to eat because she was too busy taking care of everyone else. Who looked at me last night like I might actually be worth something.

"Sure," I lie, the word tasting bitter. "For the bride."

• • •

My phone rings as I'm heading back to the house. Gideon's name flashes on the screen.

I let it go to voicemail.

He calls again immediately. Persistent bastard.

This time, I answer. "What?"

"Where the hell are you? Feldstein wants—" His voice is tight, professional panic mode.

"I'm busy." I keep walking, phone pressed to my ear.

"Busy? Your next brief is due—"

"Monday. It's due Monday." I can picture him in his office, pacing, tie loosened.

"He wants to review it today." Each word is clipped, stressed.

"Well, he's going to review it Monday."

Silence. Gideon doesn't do silence, which probably means he's about to go nuclear.

"Are you seriously blowing off Feldstein? Now? When you're this close to partnership?" His voice climbs, incredulous.

I watch through the window as Poppy races across the lawn, clipboard in hand, hair already escaping from whatever style she'd attempted. She's talking to three people at once, somehow making each one feel heard. Gesturing with the clipboard, smiling, solving problems with that endless energy.

"Dean?" Gideon's voice pulls me back.

"I'll call him back." My gaze stays on Poppy, tracking her movement across the property.

"You'll call him—are you insane? This is your career we're talking about!" He's nearly shouting now.

"I'm aware." My voice is calm. Too calm, probably.

"Then why—"

I hang up.

Turn off my phone. The screen goes dark, and something in my chest loosens.

Fuck Feldstein. Fuck the brief. Fuck partnership.

Today, nothing matters except making sure this wedding goes perfectly.

For her.

• • •

I head inside to shower and change. The house is chaos—bridesmaids shrieking about something, someone's lost a shoe, Mason's guitar playing drifts from the basement, off-tempo and anxious.

I make it to my room without being spotted. I strip off the salmon-scented clothes, tossing them in a pile for the dry cleaner to deal with. I take a quick, brutal shower, scrubbing away the smell of fish and highway.

The tux hangs in my closet like an accusation. When's the last time I wore this? Some firm event? A client's daughter's wedding where I spent the whole time reviewing contracts on my phone?

This feels different.

Everything about this week feels different.

I'm adjusting my bow tie, fingers fumbling with the silk, when Mason appears in my doorway.

"Dude." He's already in his tux, looking nervous and happy and terrified all at once.

"What?" I focus on the mirror, the tie finally cooperating.

"Mom's looking for you." He leans against the doorframe, grinning despite the warning.

"Tell her I died." I move to my cufflinks, silver and simple.

"Funny. She wants to discuss your 'life choices'." He makes air quotes and smirks.

"My life choices are fine." But I can feel his eyes on me, assessing.

"Sure they are." He shifts his weight, crossing his arms. "Is that why you just hung up on your boss?"

"You were listening?" I glance at him in the mirror.

"These walls are thin." He grins wider. "Also, you were yelling."

Oops.

"I wasn't yelling." I check my reflection, smoothing down my jacket.

"You were aggressively speaking." His tone is teasing, but his eyes are serious.

I finish with the tie. Check my cufflinks. Avoid his eyes in the mirror.

"So," he says, drawing out the word. "Poppy."

"What about her?" I busy myself with my pocket square.

"You're really gonna let her leave tomorrow?" The question lands heavy.

"She has a life in California. A business. I have—" I gesture vaguely at nothing.

"A job that makes you miserable and an empty house?" He raises an eyebrow.

Ouch. That was a low blow, even for him.

"Mason." I give him a stern look, turning to face him.

"What? Someone's gotta say it." He shrugs, unapologetic.

"No. They don't." I cross the room and check my reflection in the full-length mirror. The tux fits perfectly. I look like someone who has his life together.

The mirror's a liar.

"She's good for you." His voice softens.

"She's—" Complicated. Terrifying. Everything. I straighten my tie even though it's perfect. "She's leaving."

"So ask her to stay." He says it like it's simple. Like words can fix this.

I almost laugh, the sound bitter. "It's not that simple."

"Why?" Genuine confusion colors his voice.

Because I don't know how. Because the last time I asked someone to stay, she left anyway. Because Poppy deserves better than an emotionally stunted lawyer who just learned how to feel again.

"It just isn't." I turn away from the mirror, from my own reflection.

Mason shakes his head, disappointed. "You're an idiot."

"So everyone keeps telling me." I grab my jacket, shrugging it on.

"At least you're a well-dressed idiot." He claps my shoulder, the gesture grounding. "Come on. Time to go play guitar for the woman you're pretending not to love."

"I'm not—"

"Save it for Reddit, bro." He's already walking away, laughing.

He leaves. I stare at myself in the mirror, trying to see what Poppy sees. What makes her look at me like I'm worth saving.

My phone—still off—sits on the dresser. Eighteen missed calls, probably. Emails piling up. My entire career potentially circling the drain.

I leave it off.

Grab my guitar and head downstairs.

Time to play wedding music and pretend my entire life isn't reorganizing itself around a woman who's leaving in twenty-four hours.

• • •

The estate looks like Poppy's Pinterest board exploded. In the best way. Flowers everywhere—peonies and roses and things I can't name. Fairy lights even though it's still daylight, strung between trees like captured stars. White chairs lined up in tidy, perfect rows. The freaking porta-potties that are somehow classy, disguised with lattice and climbing vines.

And Poppy. Standing by the arch, adjusting something that doesn't need adjusting. Nervous energy radiating off her in waves I can feel from here.

She's in a burgundy dress that should be illegal. Hair twisted up with what looks like—is that a pencil?

Of course it is.

She sees me. Freezes. Her clipboard drops a few inches, forgotten.

I cross to her, guitar in hand, my shoes crunching on the grass.

"Hey." Brilliant opening. Truly.

"Hey." She won't meet my eyes, focusing instead on something over my shoulder. "You look…"

"Like a penguin?" I offer, trying for humor.

That gets a smile. Small, but real. Her shoulders drop slightly. "A very handsome penguin."

"The caterers are all set," I say quietly, close enough now to catch her perfume.

She nods, still not quite looking at me, then stops. Her head tilts, confusion crossing her face. "Wait. How do you know that?"

Shit.

My gaze drops to her mouth without permission. Focus, idiot.

"I just—checked. Everything's fine." The lie sits uncomfortably on my tongue.

She narrows her eyes, that sharp intelligence zeroing in. But before she can interrogate me, the photographer appears, breathless and harried.

"Need the groomsmen! Ten minutes!" She's already backing away, camera bouncing against her chest.

"That's my cue." I start to leave, taking a step backward.

"Dean?" Her voice stops me.

I turn back, waiting.

"Thank you. For… everything." The words are quiet, sincere, and they hit me square in the chest.

There are words I should say. Important words. Life-changing words about how she's turned my entire world sideways in the span of a week.

Instead, I just nod. "Just doing my part."

"Right. Your part." Something flickers in her expression—disappointment, maybe.

We stare at each other. The space between us feels electric, charged with everything unsaid. I can feel the pull of her like gravity.

"Dean!" Mason's voice carries across the lawn, breaking the moment. "Stop making heart eyes and get over here!"

Poppy's cheeks turn pink, color flooding her face. She looks down at her clipboard. "You should go."

"Yeah." But my feet don't move.

Neither of us moves.

"After," she says suddenly, meeting my eyes. "After the ceremony. Can we—"

"Yes." The word comes out before she finishes.

"You don't even know what I was going to say." But she's smiling now, that real smile that makes my chest tight.

"Doesn't matter. Yes." I mean it. Whatever she wants to talk about, whatever she needs, yes.

She bites her lip. That thing that makes me stupid, that thing that makes me want to close the distance between us and—

"Okay." Her voice is soft, hopeful.

"Okay."

"Dean! Seriously, bro!" Mason again, more insistent.

I back away, still watching her. Committing this moment to memory—the late afternoon sun catching in her hair, the burgundy dress, the way she's looking at me.

One more smile. Then she's back to her clipboard, and I'm jogging toward my brother and this wedding that changed everything.

Twenty minutes until showtime.

And I've never been more terrified in my life.

Not of playing guitar in front of people, but of what I'm going to say to her afterward.

When there are no more distractions, no more wedding to hide behind.

Just me and her and the truth I've been running from all week.

23

IT'S GO TIME

Poppy

The ceremony starts in thirty minutes, and I'm trying not to have a complete mental breakdown.

Everything else is perfect. The flowers are stunning—peonies and roses exactly like Ivy wanted, arrangements I spent hours perfecting. The well-dressed guests are seated, chattering quietly, sunlight filtering through the trees. Ivy is glowing in her saved dress. Mason is looking nervous but happy in his tux.

Just… no music.

"We can use Spotify," CeCe suggests, already pulling out her phone. "I'll hide a speaker—"

"No." The word comes out sharper than intended.

"It's better than silence." She's scrolling through playlists, trying to help.

"It's not—" I press my palms against my eyes. Hard. Stars burst behind my eyelids. "Ivy specifically wanted acoustic guitar. She had this whole vision of walking down the aisle to actual music, not some crummy speaker playing—"

That's when I hear it.

Guitar.

An acoustic guitar.

Coming from the ceremony space.

I rush outside and stop dead. My feet literally stop working. Cement shoes in the grass.

Dean's sitting on a stool near the arch, guitar in his lap, playing something soft and beautiful. His long fingers pluck the strings to produce something that can only be described as enchanting. He's bent over the instrument, completely focused, and the late afternoon light catches in his hair. Mason's beside him with a bass, grinning like he knows a secret.

Three hundred guests are seated, listening to Dean freaking Whitaker play guitar. Like it's normal. Like my entire world isn't tilting off its axis.

"What…" I can't finish. Can't breathe. Can't process. My clipboard dangles forgotten at my side.

He looks up. Our eyes meet across the rows of white chairs. And there's something in his expression that makes my knees forget how joints work—vulnerability, determination, something raw and open. But I make my way closer, weaving between chairs, amazed at how good they sound. The notes hang in the air like something sacred.

"Musician's here," he says when I reach him. Casual. Like he didn't just save my whole ass.

"You play." It's not a question. More like an accusation of withheld information.

"Used to." His fingers keep moving over the strings, finding chords with muscle memory. The sound is… God. It's beautiful. "Bit rusty."

Rusty, my ass. He sounds like he was born with that guitar in his hands. The way his fingers move—confident, sure, creating something achingly lovely. And he looks hot. Infuriatingly, devastatingly hot.

"Dean—" My voice cracks.

"We've got the processional, the recessional, and that song Ivy wanted for the unity ceremony." He's talking to the guitar now, not looking at me. His jaw's tight, shoulders tense. "Mason helped with the arrangements."

"Helped?" Mason snorts, shaking his head. "Bro, I basically—"

"Mason." Dean's voice carries that older brother warning, sharp and final. "Not now."

"How did you—" I stop. Start over. Try to make words happen through the lump in my throat. "When did you—"

"This morning." Still not looking at me, eyes fixed on the fretboard. "After you needed help."

After I needed help.

Like it's that simple. Like learning guitar music in a couple of hours is just something people do. Like resurrecting buried parts of yourself for someone else's crisis is normal behavior.

"Poppy." Now he looks at me. Really looks at me. And there's so much in his eyes I can't catalog it all—fear and hope and something that looks dangerously close to the thing I've been trying not to name. "Let us do this. Please."

Us. The Whitaker brothers, who spent most of the week bickering about grass and liability insurance but are now sitting here with instruments because I needed them.

Because I needed help and Dean… Dean chose this. Chose me. Chose to make sure this wedding—my wedding—went perfectly.

I'm going to cry. Right here. In front of three hundred guests and God and everyone. My eyes are already burning, vision blurring. Ugh, my makeup!

"I can't—" My throat closes up. "This is—"

"If you cry, your mascara will run." His mouth quirks, that almost-smile that makes me stupid. "And then Ivy will cry. And then everyone will cry. It'll be a whole thing."

A laugh bubbles out—watery and ridiculous, half-sob, half-giggle. "You're an ass."

"Yeah." He starts playing again. Something soft and warm that sounds like a lullaby, like coming home. "Now go do your thing. We've got the music."

I should go. Should check on Ivy. Should do literally anything except stand here staring at Dean Whitaker like he just handed me the moon. This softer, sweeter version of Dean that I never knew existed. But I can't move. My feet are rooted to the grass.

"That song," I whisper, barely audible over the music. "What is it?"

He glances at Mason, who suddenly finds his bass very interesting, studying the strings like they hold the secrets of the universe.

"Just something I wrote," Dean says quietly, his voice rough around the edges. "A long time ago."

He wrote it?

He writes music?

This man, who drives me insane and works drafting prenups, writes music that sounds like heartbreak and hope had a baby. I'm sorry, but what?

"It's beautiful." The words feel inadequate, too small for what I'm feeling.

"It's yours."

The words land between us like a grenade. The air leaves my lungs.

"What?"

"For the ceremony." He clears his throat, uncomfortable. "If you want it. For the... you know. Prelude music. While people are sitting."

"You're giving me your song?" My voice pitches up, incredulous.

"It's just notes, Poppy. No big deal." But the muscle in his jaw jumps, betraying him.

Except it is. It's the biggest deal. It's Dean Whitaker cracking himself open and handing me pieces I didn't even know existed.

"POPPY!" Ivy's voice carries from the house, shrill with pre-wedding panic. "WHERE ARE YOU? I NEED YOU!"

Reality crashes back. I'm working. This is a job. I have responsibilities.

"Shit. I have to—" I gesture vaguely toward the chaos, the house, my actual purpose here.

"Go." His voice is gentle, understanding. "Before she sends a search party."

I turn to leave. Make it three steps, grass crunching under my heels. Turn back.

"Dean?"

"Mm?" He looks up again, waiting.

"Thank you."

He looks at me. Does that thing where his eyes say everything his mouth won't. The intensity of it hits me in the chest, steals my breath. I feel it everywhere.

"Go," he says softly. "We'll be here."

I go.

But I can hear his music following me. A song he wrote years ago that he's playing now, for me, and I know—I know—I'm completely screwed.

Because how do you not fall in love with a man who resurrects his buried dreams just to save yours?

• • •

Twenty-eight minutes until showtime. Ivy's pacing in the bridal suite like a caged leopard in Vera Wang, the dress swishing with each agitated turn.

"Where were you?" She spins, veil whipping around, nearly taking out a lamp. "I'm freaking out. What if Mason changes his mind? What if I trip? What if—"

"Breathe." I grab her shoulders, grounding her. "Dean and Mason are playing music for your ceremony."

She blinks, the words not computing. "What?"

"Guitar and bass. They learned all your songs this morning." I squeeze her shoulders gently.

"Dean's playing guitar?" Her voice goes up an octave.

"Apparently." I'm still processing it myself.

Her face does something complicated—surprise melting into understanding, then into something soft and knowing. "Oh. Oh, Poppy."

"What?" I don't like that tone. That's the tone of someone who sees too much.

She's still looking at me. Still concerned, eyes too perceptive. "He hasn't played since Emily."

The name hits me cold. A bucket of ice water down my spine. "Who's Emily?"

Ivy sits carefully on the upholstered bench, gathering her skirt with practiced movements. Careful with the dress. "His ex-fiancée, Emily."

Ex-fiancée. There's an ex-fiancée?

I sit too, sinking into the nearest chair like my legs have given up. Because, frankly, that does not compute. Dean was engaged? Dean, who acts like feelings are a communicable disease?

"They were together six years," she continues, staring at her hands. "Met in law school. Dean was different then. Played music all the time. Open mics, little gigs. He was gonna—" She stops, swallows hard. Clears her throat. "Anyway. They got engaged. Had a loft downtown. Two weeks before the wedding, she left."

"She left?" My voice sounds hollow.

Ivy stands, walks toward the mirror, adjusting her veil with shaking fingers. "Just... left. Said she'd fallen out of love. That he was too much. Too intense. Too... Dean."

My chest hurts. Actually physically hurts, like something's squeezing my ribs. "That's—" Of course he's too Dean. But, like... maybe in a good way?

"She took half his savings, maxed out their joint cards, and moved to Seattle with some tech guy she'd been seeing." Ivy's voice is flat, reciting facts.

"She cheated?" The word tastes bitter.

"For months, apparently." Ivy's fixing her lipstick, but her eyes are on me in the mirror, watching my reaction. "Dean packed up the guitar that day along with anything else that reminded him of her. Haven't seen it since."

Until today.

Until I needed help.

The weight of that settles over me like a blanket, heavy and suffocating.

"Why are you telling me this?" I whisper, almost afraid of the answer.

She turns, meeting my eyes directly. "Because that man out there? The one who just excavated six years of buried grief to play at my wedding? He didn't do it for me."

"Ivy—" I start to protest, but she cuts me off.

"He did it for you." She straightens, smooths her dress with decisive movements. "And if you let him get away because you're scared? I will haunt your ass from beyond the grave."

"You're not dying." But my voice shakes.

"Metaphorically haunt. With strongly worded texts." She's smiling now, but her eyes are serious.

My brain feels scrambled, thoughts tumbling over each other. "I'm leaving tomorrow."

"So?" She tilts her head, waiting.

"So what's the point of—"

"The point?" She grabs my hands. Hard. Her grip is almost painful. "The point is he chose you over his own pain. Do you get that? He literally picked emotional torture because you needed him."

Something weird pinches in my chest, sharp and insistent. "That's not—"

"Two minutes!" CeCe bursts in, breathless. "Holy shit, you look gorgeous. Also, Dean's playing guitar? What the hell? He's good. Also also, we need to go. Like, now."

Ivy takes a last look in the mirror. Breathes deep, centering herself. Smiles—and it transforms her face. She's a stunning bride. Olive skin glowing, perfect makeup, shiny black hair cascading over her shoulders. Her dress is a freaking dream—all lace and silk and fairy tale magic.

"Let's do this."

We file out. Me first, checking my clipboard one last time. Then the bridesmaids in their blush pink, giggling nervously. Then CeCe, winking at me. Ivy and her dad wait at the top of the aisle, and I can see him squeezing her hand.

And Dean starts playing.

Not the processional yet. That other song. His song. The one he wrote years ago that sounds like every feeling he's ever buried trying to claw its way out.

It's gorgeous.

And perfect.

And so achingly beautiful, I have to press my hand to my chest to keep my heart from breaking out of my rib cage.

I stop breathing.

"You good?" CeCe whispers, close to my ear.

No. I'm not good. I'm standing at the edge of something massive and terrifying, and I don't have a parachute. I'm watching the man who posted about me on Reddit play music he buried with his broken engagement, and I'm supposed to get on a plane tomorrow like none of this happened.

"Fine," I lie, the word barely making it past my lips.

I close my eyes and take a breath, trying to think through all the things I need to do next. Check on the reception space, make sure the DJ is ready, coordinate with the caterers, ensure the cake is properly displayed.

But I can't focus because all I can hear is his music. The melody wraps around me like arms, like a promise, like a question I don't know how to answer.

And I'm starting to think it might follow me all the way to Italy.

Hell, who am I kidding?

It's going to follow me everywhere.

24

THE WEDDING SHIFT

Dean

My fingers remember.

That's the weird part. Six years of nothing, and they still know where to go. Still find the chords like they've been waiting.

The guests are seated. Waiting. Mason's nervous-tapping his foot against his stool.

"You good?" I ask.

"Getting married, bro." His voice has that edge of disbelief.

"I noticed." I transition to a different chord progression, something softer.

"To Ivy." He's got a dreamy, faraway look on his face as he says this.

"That's generally how weddings work." I almost smile despite the tension coiling in my shoulders.

"Shut up." But he's smiling. "Thanks for this."

"Thank Poppy. She's the one who—" I start, but he cuts me off.

"I meant playing again." He looks at me now, really looks at me. His expression is serious, understanding. "I know it's been hard since—"

"Don't." The word comes out sharp. My fingers press harder into the strings.

"I'm just saying. This is big." His voice is gentle, careful.

I frown, focusing on the fretboard. "It's one song."

"It's more than that." He knows. Of course he knows.

Maybe. Probably. But I can't think about that now. Can't think about why I drove to a storage unit I've been avoiding for years. Can't think about the look on Poppy's face when she saw me playing.

Can't think about how she's leaving tomorrow. Definitely not that.

"Here we go," Mason says.

The wedding party starts walking. I play the music Poppy picked—something soft and romantic that makes my chest tight.

Each bridesmaid passes. Then CeCe, coming up from the side, who winks at me like she knows something.

Then the music changes. The song Ivy specifically requested.

And there she is.

Not Ivy.

Poppy.

Standing at the back, clipboard forgotten, watching me play. Tears swimming in her eyes.

Damn.

I almost miss a chord. Mason covers, keeps the bassline steady.

Ivy appears, radiant and perfect, but I can't stop looking at Poppy. The way she's pressing her hand to her chest. The way she's looking at me like…

Like maybe I'm not the only one who's screwed here.

Mason sets down his bass and takes his spot at the front.

The ceremony passes in a blur. Vows, rings, the unity thing where I play the song that makes everyone cry. Mason kisses his bride. Everyone cheers.

And Poppy's gone.

Disappeared somewhere between "I do" and "I now pronounce you."

"That was beautiful," someone says.

"Thanks," I manage.

Pack up the guitar. Shake hands. Accept compliments I don't deserve.

But all I can think about is the look on her face.

And how I have less than twenty-four hours to figure out what the hell to do about it.

25

PERFECT CHAOS

Poppy

The sun's doing that golden hour thing where everything looks like it's been dipped in honey and Instagram filters. I'm standing at the edge of the reception tent, clipboard abandoned somewhere between the cake cutting and my second glass of champagne, watching my perfectly planned wedding become something else entirely.

Something better.

Mason's got Ivy on the dance floor, spinning her like they're in their own music video. Her dress flares out. He dips her. She laughs so hard she snorts. Three of her influencer friends are filming, but she doesn't even notice.

That's love, I think. When you forget about the cameras. When you forget about everything except the man in front of you.

"Miss?" A server appears with another champagne flute. "From the gentleman at table twelve."

I don't need to look. Table twelve is where Dean's been holding court with his grandmother, who's had four martinis and is now telling anyone who'll listen about Dean's "awkward phase."

But I look anyway.

He's loosened his tie. Ditched his jacket and rolled up his sleeves, because apparently he's trying to kill me. His hair is slightly tousled now. And he's watching me with this expression that makes my stomach do stupid things. Idiotic things.

I raise the glass in a mock toast. He smirks.

God help me.

"Poppy!" Gloria materializes in a cloud of patchouli and silk. "The flowers are still perfect!"

Facts. "That's because you're a genius."

"True." She links her arm through mine. "But also because you knew exactly what you wanted. Even when you didn't."

"That doesn't make sense."

"Sure it does." She nods toward Dean. "Like him."

"We're not talking about—"

"You've been not talking about him all night." She steals my champagne. "While he's been not looking at you from across every room."

My stomach bottoms out. "He's looking at me right now."

"Mhmm. Like you're dessert and he's been on a diet."

"Gloria."

"What? I have eyes. That man wants to eat you alive."

I choke on air. "Can we not—"

My phone buzzes.

It's Miranda.

Shit.

I'm standing at the edge of the tent, watching everything sparkle—candles flickering, music drifting, the bride glowing like a fairy tale—and Miranda freaking Coleman who fired me is calling.

I let it go to voicemail.

She calls again.

I roll my eyes and answer. "Let me guess—you saw the social media posts?"

A tight laugh. "I always knew you had it in you, Poppy. Truly. The vision, the execution—it's impressive."

"That's funny," I say. "Because last I checked, you fired me for letting a Pomeranian eat a cake. But now you want to talk because there are a million people gushing online about this wedding?"

She powers through it. "You've made quite the splash. If you're open to it, I'd love to talk about bringing you back. Under the Coleman Events umbrella, of course. Think of the exposure—"

"Oh, Miranda." I sigh like I'm bored. "You taught me so much. Like how to smile while being undermined. And how not to seat the mistress at the family table."

She's quiet.

I smile, slow and sharp. "But I think I'm good. I'm building something of my own now. It's called freedom. You should try it sometime."

Then I hang up, rename her contact to: Miranda – Do Not Resurrect, and toss my phone back in my bag just in time to hear Gloria chuckling.

"Oh look, the goat's being photogenic."

I glance over to where she's pointing. And she's right. George—who has spent the entire week being a terrorist—has chosen this exact moment to become a Disney character. He's grazing on the hill behind the tent, silhouetted against the sunset like he's posing for a wedding blog.

"Are you kidding me?" I mutter.

"Even chaos behaves when it matters," Gloria says. "Speaking of which…"

Dean's walking over. Of course he is. Because my body language probably screams 'please come make this more complicated.'

"Ladies." He stops just close enough that I can smell his cologne. It's crisp and perfect and way too distracting. "Gloria, beautiful work on the flowers."

"I know." She doesn't do false modesty. "Though Poppy deserves the credit. She has exquisite taste."

They both look at me. I suddenly need to be anywhere else.

"I should check on—"

"Everything's perfect." Dean's voice is soft. Different. I love it way more than is possibly healthy. "Stop working."

"I'm not working. I'm… observing." But the lie sounds weak even to me.

"You're hiding." He says it gently, but it still lands like an accusation.

Heat crawls up my neck. "I'm not—"

"Poppy." He steps closer. "Take the compliment. You did it. Look around."

So I do.

Really look.

The tent glows with the fairy lights I fought to hang at midnight. The centerpieces Gloria and I designed catch the light just right. The dance floor is packed. People are laughing. Ivy's mom is teaching Dean's mom some TikTok dance, which should be horrifying but is actually hilarious.

It's… perfect.

"Oh," I breathe.

"Yeah." Dean's voice is right by my ear. When did he get that close? "Oh."

Gloria clears her throat. "I'm gonna go dance with that silver fox at the bar. You two… continue whatever this is."

She floats away, leaving us standing too close while the world happens around us.

"You played guitar," I say, because apparently I can't let it go.

"You noticed." His tone is careful, guarded.

"Dean." I turn to face him fully, forcing him to look at me.

He meets my eyes for a beat, then looks away. "What?"

"You know what." My voice drops, softer now.

He sighs. Runs a hand through his hair, messing it up further. "It wasn't a big deal."

"Ivy told me about Emily."

He goes still. That scary kind of still that means he's processing seventeen emotions at once.

"Ivy talks too much." The words come out tight, clipped.

"She said you haven't played since—" I start, but he cuts me off.

"Poppy." He turns to face me fully, jaw set. "Do we have to do this now?"

"When else? I leave tomorrow." The reminder

sits heavy between us.

Something flickers across his face—pain, maybe, or resignation. "Right. Italy."

"Dean—" I reach for him without thinking, but he's already moving.

"Dance with me."

I blink at the sudden shift. "What?"

"Dance. With me." He holds out a hand, his expression unreadable. "Unless you're too busy observing."

I should say no. Should maintain professional distance. Should remember this is complicated and I'm leaving and he's still dealing with what sounds like massive emotional trauma.

Instead, I take his hand, like it's the most normal thing in the world.

He leads me to the dance floor right as the band slides into something slow. Because of course they do. The universe has zero chill.

"Fair warning," I say as he pulls me close. "I'm terrible at this."

"Shocking." He smirks at me. "You're so coordinated with everything else."

"Was that… did you just make a joke?" I stare at him, genuinely surprised.

His mouth quirks. "I make jokes."

"No, you make observations. Jokes are different." I'm smiling despite myself.

He spins me. Smooth. Practiced. "Maybe you bring out my sense of humor."

"Or your open bar."

"That too."

We're quiet for a minute. Just swaying while

Mason and Ivy have their moment in the middle of the floor, lost in each other.

"She's happy," I say.

"Yeah."

"Really happy. Like, disgustingly happy."

"That's what love looks like, apparently."

"You say that like you don't believe in it."

His hand tightens on my waist. "I used to."

"And now?"

He looks down at me. Really looks at me. And for a second, I see everything. The hurt. The hope. The terrifying possibility that maybe he's starting to believe again.

"Now I think maybe I was just doing it wrong."

My heart forgets how to beat. "Dean—"

"EVERYONE LOOK AT GEORGE!"

We break apart as the crowd turns toward the hill where George has decided to…

"Is he posing?" Dean asks.

He is. The asshole goat is literally posing against the sunset like he's auditioning for a Hallmark movie.

"I hate him," I say.

"No you don't." Dean's watching me, not the goat.

I glare at George, who's now turned to show his better side. "I really do."

"You're taking pictures right now."

I lower my phone. "Shut up."

Dean laughs. Real, actual laughter. The sound hits me right in the chest. It's magnificent. Deep and unfiltered and perfect.

"What?"

"Nothing." But he's still smiling. "Just… you. This week. Everything."

"That's not nothing."

"No," he agrees. "It's not."

The band starts another song. People drift back to dancing. But we just stand there, him looking at me like I'm a puzzle he's finally solving, me trying not to do something stupid like ask him to come to Italy.

"Poppy! Dean!" Mason appears, flushed and grinning. "Family photo!"

And just like that, the moment breaks.

But as we follow Mason to where the photographer's setting up, Dean's hand finds the small of my back. Guiding. Gentle. Possessive in a way that makes me shiver.

"Cold?" he murmurs.

"No."

"Liar." He smirks.

"Takes one to know one."

His thumb traces a small circle through the fabric of my dress. "We're really doing this? Now? Trading barbs during family photos?"

"You started it."

"Pretty sure you started it when you showed up with a goat."

"That was an accident!"

"So you keep saying."

"PLACES!" The photographer's waving us around like we're chess pieces. "Bride and groom center! Family around them! Wedding planner— oh, you're not family? Well, stay anyway. You look gorgeous in that light."

I try to step away but Ivy yanks my arm. "She's practically family. She stays."

So I end up in the Whitaker family photo, tucked between Dean and Mason while the photographer snaps away and the sun paints everything gold.

"Smile like you mean it," Dean says under his breath.

"I am smiling." I keep my face frozen in place, aware of the camera.

He leans in slightly, his shoulder brushing mine. "No, you're panicking."

"Same thing." But my smile softens, becomes real.

"Poppy." His voice drops. Serious. "You belong here."

The camera clicks before I can respond. Before I can tell him that belonging somewhere for a week doesn't mean you get to stay. Before I can ask why he's making this harder than it needs to be.

"Beautiful!" The photographer's already moving on. "Now just the brothers!"

I escape to the bar, order something stronger than champagne. CeCe slides up beside me.

"So."

"Don't start." I know that tone. That's her I-have-opinions tone.

"I'm just saying, I've never seen you in a family photo before. Three years and you've never once been in a family photo."

The words hit harder than they should. I grip my glass tighter. "Ivy insisted."

"Uh-huh." CeCe's watching me too closely.

"And Dean's hand on your back? Did Ivy insist on that too?"

I down my drink. "I need you to not."

"Not what?"

"Not make this into something."

"Babe." She turns me to face her. "It's already something. The question is what you're gonna do about it."

Before I can answer, the band announces the last dance. Couples flood the floor. The lights dim to just fairy lights and stars.

And Dean's there. Again. Always.

"One more?" he asks.

I should say no.

I take his hand instead.

This time when he pulls me close, I let myself feel it. The warmth of him. The way we fit. The absolute certainty that I'm fucked.

Cool.

"Poppy?"

"Mm?"

He's quiet for a moment, and I can feel the tension in his body, like he's working up to something. "This week…"

"Don't." I press my face into his shoulder, breathing him in. "Please. Just… let me have this."

His arms tighten around me. "Okay."

We sway while Mason and Ivy kiss under the stars and George provides ambient scenery, and everything is exactly as perfect as I planned.

Except for the part where I'm falling for someone I can't have.

But that's tomorrow's problem.

Tonight? Tonight I'm dancing with Dean Whitaker while the fairy lights blur into stars and his heartbeat keeps time with mine.

And for now, that's enough.

It has to be.

26

THE EDGE OF EVERYTHING

Dean

The song's ending and I can't let go.

Won't let go.

Poppy's pressed against me, face buried in my shoulder, and I'm trying to memorize everything. The vanilla scent of her hair. The way her hand fits in mine. The small sigh she makes when I pull her closer.

"Dean." Her voice is muffled against my jacket.

"Not yet."

The band's packing up. Guests are filtering out. Mason's carrying Ivy's shoes while she laughs at something our cousin said.

Normal wedding shit.

Except nothing about this week has been normal.

"People are leaving," she says.

"So?"

"So I should—"

"You should come with me."

She pulls back. Looks up at me with those eyes that have been destroying my sanity since she showed up with a goat and an attitude. "Where?"

Anywhere. My bed. Italy. The fucking moon.

"Just… somewhere quiet." My voice sounds shockingly in control.

I can see her wrestling with it. The smart part of her brain versus whatever this thing is between us.

"Dean—"

"Five minutes." My hand finds her face. Thumb tracing her jaw. "Give me five minutes."

She leans into my touch. "That's all?"

"That's all I'm asking for."

Lie. I want hours. Days. A lifetime to figure out how she crawled under my skin so quickly.

"Okay," she whispers.

I take her hand. Lead her away from the tent, the lights, the noise. Around the side of the house where it's just moonlight and the sound of her heels on gravel.

"Where are we—"

I spin her against the wall. Stone at her back, me crowding her space, and lower my face to hers.

"Hi," she breathes.

"Hi."

"This is very—"

I kiss her.

Not soft. Not careful. This is a kiss that's been building for days. Weeks. Months. *Years*. My hand is in her hair, tilting her head back, swallowing the sound she makes when I press closer.

She tastes like champagne and bad decisions.

Perfect.

There's been no one in so long that I should be out of practice. I'm not. Because this is Poppy and it's perfect.

Her hands fist in my shirt, pulling me down, and hell. The little noise she makes when I bite her bottom lip. The way her body arches into mine.

"Fuck," I mutter against her mouth.

"Yeah."

I kiss her again. Harder. Tongue sliding against hers, and she gives as good as she gets. Nips at my lip. Nails dragging down my chest through the shirt.

My hips pin hers to the wall and she gasps. Can she feel how hard I am through the suit pants? She has to. Nothing I can do about that.

"Dean—" she gasps.

"I know." I trail kisses down her throat. Find that spot behind her ear that makes her shiver. "I know."

"We can't—"

"We're not." Another kiss. "Just this."

Her leg hooks around mine. Dress riding up. My hand finds her hip, squeezes.

"This is insane," she pants.

"Yep."

"We barely know each other."

This isn't part of the plan. But maybe—just maybe—I'm tired of plans.

Maybe I want reckless. Messy. Her.

"Maybe." I pull back. Look at her. Hair wrecked, lips swollen, eyes wild.

She laughs. Low and breathless.

I press closer. Let her feel exactly what she does to me. "You really have to go tomorrow?"

A warm breath punches out of her and something flickers across her face. "That's the plan."

Right. The plan. Italy. Her real life that doesn't include me.

"When's your flight?"

"Two."

I check my watch. Fourteen hours.

Not enough.

She kisses me. Soft this time. Sweet. Which is somehow worse.

"We're adults," she says against my mouth.

"So?"

"So we both know what this is."

"Do we?"

She pulls back. "Chemistry. Bad timing."

"That's all?" My heart thuds in my chest.

"What else could it be?"

Ask her to stay. The thought hits like lightning. Insane. Impossible. Who asks someone to change their entire life after little more than a week?

"Right." I step back. Give her space. Give myself space before I say something stupid. "You're right."

She fixes her dress. Smooths her hair. Puts herself back together while I fall apart.

"Poppy."

She stops, hand still in her hair.

"Yeah?"

"Come on." I tug her hand, leading toward the house.

"Where are we—" She's following but confused, looking back at the reception still going strong.

"When's the last time you ate?"

She blinks at me like I just asked her to solve

calculus. "I… what?"

"Food, Poppy. Actual food. Not champagne and whatever crumbs you stole from the catering trays."

"I ate." But her voice lacks conviction.

"When?" I push through the back door, pulling her with me into the quiet of the kitchen. The music fades to a distant thrum.

"Earlier." She's not meeting my eyes now.

"Try again."

She's quiet. Too quiet. Which means I'm right. I can see her trying to calculate when she last sat down, came up empty.

"Thought so." I pull her through the back door into my kitchen. "Sit."

"Dean, I'm fine—" She's still standing, stubborn.

"Sit." I point at the chair, using my closing argument voice.

She sits. Probably because her feet are killing her in those heels. I can see her trying not to wince every time she shifts, the micro-grimace she thinks she's hiding.

"Shoes off," I order, already raiding the fridge.

"Bossy." But there's no heat in it.

"You like it." I glance back in time to see her cheeks flush.

"I absolutely do not." The protest is immediate, automatic.

But she's kicking off the heels, sighing when her feet hit the cool floor. The sound goes straight through me—relief mixed with exhaustion mixed with something that makes my chest tight.

Focus. Food. Not the way she's stretching her legs under my kitchen table, rolling her ankles.

"Grilled cheese?" I ask, pulling out butter, bread, cheese.

"Seriously?" She's watching me with this expression I can't quite read.

"What's wrong with grilled cheese?" I set the pan on the stove, butter sizzling as it hits the heat.

"Nothing. Just… you're making me a sandwich? Now?" Her voice is softer, uncertain. Like she can't quite believe this is happening.

"You need to eat. I need to do something with my hands that isn't—" I stop. Turn back to the stove.

"Isn't what?"

Touching you. Undressing you. Finding out what other sounds you make.

"Cooking," I finish.

She laughs. Soft. Knowing. "Right. Cooking."

I focus on the simple task. Butter. Bread. Cheese. The familiar rhythm of something I can control while everything else spins out.

"I can't believe you got the caterers here," she says quietly.

My hands still. "How did you—"

"Tom told me. During cleanup. About their totaled van. You saved the entire reception."

"He wasn't supposed to—"

"Tell me that you drove forty minutes to rescue salmon? That you took control? That you specifically told him not to worry me?"

I flip the sandwich. "It wasn't a big deal."

"Dean."

I turn. She's sitting at my table, bare feet tucked under her, still in that burgundy dress that's been murdering me all night. Hair starting to fall from whatever complicated thing she did to it. Looking at me like I'm something more than a workaholic robot.

"Thank you," she says.

"You already thanked me. For the guitar."

"This is different."

"Why?"

"Because you didn't have to. Because I never would've known. Because you just… fixed it."

I plate the sandwich. Slide it across to her. "Eat."

She takes a bite. Her eyes close. "Oh my gosh."

"It's just grilled cheese."

"It's perfect." Another bite. "How is it perfect?"

"Garlic butter. Touch of rosemary."

"You put rosemary in grilled cheese?"

"You got a problem with that?"

"No. It's just very… you."

"What's that supposed to mean?"

She grins around another bite. "Overachieving. Even with sandwiches."

I lean against the counter, watching her demolish the food. It's strangely satisfying. "When's the last time someone took care of you?"

She pauses mid-chew. "I take care of myself."

I give her a stern look.

She looks at me. Really looks. "That's part of the reason for my vacation to Italy."

The words hang between us. Too honest for whatever we're pretending this is.

"Couch?" I ask once she finishes the sandwich.

"Couch."

We migrate to the living room. She curls into one corner; I take the other. Careful distance. Like that'll help.

"Tell me about Emily," she says.

"Why?"

"Because I'm leaving tomorrow and we're being honest tonight."

Fair.

"We met when I was still in law school." The words come easier than expected. "She was… everything. Smart. Driven. Understood the hours, the pressure. We made sense on paper."

"But not in reality?"

"I thought we did. Six years. Had an apartment together. Planned a future." I stare at the ceiling. "Two weeks before the wedding, I came home early. Found her in our bed with someone else."

"Shit."

"Yeah." I laugh, but it's sharp. "Best part? She'd been seeing him for months. Using my money to fund their dates. Maxed out our cards buying him things."

"Dean…"

"She said I was too much. Too intense. Too focused on work." I look at Poppy. "Too Dean."

"That's bullshit."

"Is it?"

"Yes." She shifts closer.

My chest does something complicated. "Poppy—"

"I know. Wrong time. Wrong place. Wrong everything." She laughs, but it's watery. "Story of my life."

"Tell me."

"What?"

"Your story. The real one. Why you're really running to Italy."

She pulls her knees up. Makes herself smaller. "I got fired," she says suddenly.

"What?"

"The day I arrived. My boss called. Fired me over the phone on my drive here." She's not looking at me now. "This wedding was supposed to be my comeback. My proof that I could do this on my own."

"And you did."

"Did I? Or did I just get lucky with a guitar-playing lawyer and his chaos-loving brother?"

She moves closer. Close enough I can smell her shampoo. See the faint freckles across her nose. Count the ways this is going to hurt tomorrow.

"Hey." I catch her chin. Make her look at me. "You pulled off a perfect wedding with no team, no backup, and a possessed goat working against you."

She laughs and the sound hits me square in the chest. "George isn't possessed."

"Debatable." I trace my thumb along her jaw. "You're incredible. You know that, right?"

"I'm a mess."

"You're my mess."

The words hang there. Too much. Too real.

"For tonight," I add.

"Right. Tonight."

She kisses me. Softly. Slowly. Like we have time we don't actually have.

I pull her closer, onto my lap. Her hands tangle in my hair, my arms wrap around her waist, and fuck being careful.

"Dean," she breathes against my mouth, my name a prayer and a question.

"I know." The words rumble between us, acknowledging everything we're not saying.

"We should stop." But even as she says it, her fingers tighten in my hair, holding me to her.

"Probably." I don't sound convinced. I'm not convinced.

But she's kissing my neck now, and my brain shorts out. Her teeth graze my pulse point, and—

"Poppy," I groan, the sound wrecked and desperate.

She pulls back just enough to look at me, lips swollen, breathing hard. "Too much?"

"Not enough." My hands slide up her back, pressing her closer. "Never enough."

She pulls back further, looking at me with eyes gone dark, pupils wide. Her chest heaves, her dress askew. "We can't."

"I know." But my hands remain on her waist, thumbs stroking slow circles that contradict my words.

"I'm leaving." Her voice cracks on the word, and something in my chest breaks with it.

"I know." The reminder sits between us like a third person, unwelcome and undeniable.

We stare at each other. The weight of everything we're not saying crushing the air from the room.

Then she yawns.

She's exhausted. Been running on fumes for days, and here I am keeping her up because I can't let go.

"You need sleep," I say.

"I need to pack."

"Pack tomorrow."

"My flight—"

"Is at two. You can pack in the morning."

She should argue. Should go back to the guest house. Should put distance between us while she can.

Instead, she curls into my side. Rests her head on my shoulder. "Five minutes."

"Sure."

"I mean it. Just five minutes then I'll go."

"Okay."

Her breathing evens out in three.

I sit there, her weight against me, staring at the clock. 12:47 a.m.

Thirteen hours.

She shifts in her sleep. Burrows closer. Her hand finds mine, fingers threading together like they belong there.

I should wake her. Send her to bed. Protect us both from whatever this is becoming.

Instead, I hold her tighter.

Because in thirteen hours she'll be gone.

And I'll go back to being the guy who doesn't feel things.

Except now I know that guy was bullshit.

Now I know what it's like to have Poppy Monroe asleep in my arms.

And tomorrow, I have to let her go.

I close my eyes. Not to sleep. Just to memorize this.

The weight of her.

The sound of her breathing.

The way she fits against me like she was always supposed to be here.

Thirteen hours.

27

THE MORNING AFTER

Poppy

I wake up in the guest house at 6:47 a.m., and my whole body aches like I've been hit by a truck named Bad Decisions.

The couch. Right. I slept on Dean's couch until after midnight, then stumbled back here like some kind of romance novel martyr. Because staying would've meant… what? Admitting I wanted more than post-wedding exhaustion cuddles?

My phone buzzes with a flight reminder.

Check-in now available.

Cool. Thanks, phone. Super helpful.

George bleats from the porch, because apparently he's my roommate now.

"Morning, asshole," I mutter, dragging myself vertical.

He bleats again. Louder. Like he's personally offended by my life choices.

"Yeah, well, join the club."

I stumble to the door, and there he is—my demon goat therapist, already judging me with those creepy rectangle pupils.

"What?" I ask. "You want life advice? From

me? The woman who just spent a week falling for someone completely unavailable?"

He headbutts the doorframe.

"Right. That's what I thought."

I leave the door open, because why fight it, and start shoving clothes into my suitcase. The safe green dress from the rehearsal dinner. The silk burgundy dress from last night. The heels that witnessed me wrestling a tent in a storm. The backup planner I didn't need because turns out I'm really good at memorizing disaster scenarios.

George wanders in, settles on the rug like he owns the place.

"You know what's messed up?" I tell him, folding a shirt badly. "I actually pictured it. The whole thing."

He tilts his head.

"Not like, wedding bells and babies." I chuck a shoe in the general direction of my bag. "Just… Tuesday nights, arguing about takeout. Him accepting that sometimes I'm going to prioritize my work over food, sleep, basic human interaction. Me accepting the same about him. Fighting over the thermostat. Stupid, normal couple shit."

George snorts.

"I know, right? We hardly know each other. That's not—people don't—"

I stop. Sit on the bed. Stare at my half-packed disaster.

"But it was kind of intense," I admit. "Living on his property. The wedding pressure. Everything accelerated, you know? Like relationship boot camp."

George chews thoughtfully on what looks like my phone charger cord.

"Hey! No!" I yank it away. "I need that for Italy."

Italy. Right. My big escape plan. A week of pasta and wine and definitely not thinking about Dean Whitaker's eyes. Or his laugh. Or the way he looked last night dressed in a tux and dancing with one of his little cousins.

"Nope." I stand up. "Not going there."

I attack the packing with renewed determination. George watches, occasionally offering commentary in the form of aggressive bleating.

"What did I expect?" I ask him. "For him to chase me to the airport? Beg me to stay? That's not—that's rom-com bullshit. This is real life."

Although last night felt pretty freaking rom-com, with the dancing and the guitar and the way he—

"Stop it," I tell my brain. "Besides," I continue, cramming products into my toiletry bag, "we both have careers. Important careers. His is here, mine is…" I pause. "Nonexistent. But it'll exist again. In California. Where I live."

George looks skeptical.

"Don't give me that look. It's called being a grown-up. You make rational decisions based on logic, not on how someone's voice sounds when they say your name."

Poppy.

Damn. Even in my memory, it wrecks me.

My phone buzzes. It's CeCe.

Ugh.

Fair.

I finish packing—badly—and hop in the shower. The water's perfect, which feels like a personal attack. Even the guest house is trying to make me sad about leaving.

"Get it together," I mutter, shampooing aggressively.

By the time CeCe arrives, I'm dressed and pretending to be a functional human. She takes one look at me and shakes her head.

"Oh, honey."

I glance up from zipping my suitcase, defensive already. "What?"

She sets down the pastries and coffee, studying my face with that knowing look. "You're wearing your feelings on your face."

"No I'm not." But my hand goes to my cheek automatically, like I can wipe them away.

"You're literally pouting."

She hands me a chocolate croissant and coffee that smells like heaven and bad decisions.

"Talk to me," she says, settling on the bed and patting the space beside her.

"Nothing to talk about." I take a massive bite of croissant, chewing deliberately. "Wedding's over. I'm going to Italy. End of story."

"Uh-huh." She sips her coffee, waiting. "And Dean?"

The name alone makes my stomach drop. "What about him?"

"Poppy." It's not a question. It's an accusation wrapped in concern.

I swallow the most delicious bite of croissant, buying time. "What? We had a moment. Now the moment's over. That's how things work." I wish they didn't, but they do.

"A moment," she repeats, eyebrows climbing. "Is that what we're calling it?"

I focus on my croissant like it holds the secrets of the universe. "Yes."

"Not 'the first time you've clicked with a guy in three years'?"

"Dramatic."

"Not 'the only guy who's ever made you forget about your to-do list'?"

"That's not—"

"Not 'the reason you've been lit up like a lighthouse all week'?"

"I have not been lit up."

George bleats in what sounds suspiciously like disagreement.

"Even the goat knows you're lying," CeCe says.

I slump next to her, the fight draining out of me. "It doesn't matter. He didn't ask me to stay."

"Did you ask him to?" She sets down her coffee, turning to face me fully.

"That's not—no. Why would I?" I pick at the croissant, pulling it apart into tiny pieces.

"Because you're in love with him?"

The word hangs there like a challenge.

My hands go still. The croissant crumbles forgotten in my lap. My heart is doing something arrhythmic and painful in my chest.

"I'm not—we barely—it's not possible, CeCe."

"So?" Her expression is serious, unflinching.

"So people don't fall in love in a week!" I wipe flakes of croissant crumbles from my cheek with more force than necessary.

"Says who?"

"Says… I don't know. Science. Logic. Common sense."

"Right. Because you're such a fan of common sense." She gestures around the chaos. "That why you're running away to Italy?"

"I'm not running. It's been planned for months."

"Convenient." She nods, but there's no judgment in it. Just sad understanding.

I stand up, needing to move, and pace to the window. The main house sits there, all perfect and haunting in the morning light.

"What was I supposed to do?" I ask quietly, my

breath fogging the glass. "Wait around hoping he'd suddenly develop feelings? Beg him to try long-distance?"

"Maybe tell him how you feel? Go from there?"

"I don't—" I stop. Can't even lie about it any-more. My reflection stares back at me, hollow-eyed and tired. "It doesn't matter how I feel. He's got his life, I've got mine. That's how it works."

"That's how it works when you're scared," CeCe says gently.

My shoulders hitch up, defensive. "I'm not scared. I'm practical."

"Honey." She stands, coming to join me at the window. "You organized a wedding with no team. You wrestled a tent in a storm. You tamed George." She gestures at the goat, who's now eating my lap-top cord. "You're the least scared person I know. Except when it comes to this."

"This is different."

"Why?"

Because this matters. Because he matters. Be-cause I can handle losing clients and jobs and dig-nity, but I'm not sure I can handle losing something I never really had.

I turn away from the window, from the view of his house. "I have a brunch to get to," I say instead.

CeCe sighs, long and disappointed. "Right. The farewell tour."

"Ivy specifically requested—"

"I know. I'll drive you." She's already grabbing her keys, resigned.

"You don't have to—"

"Yes, I do. Because you're about to go pretend

everything's fine when we both know you're dying inside."

"Dramatic."

"Accurate."

She's not wrong. But what's the alternative? Sob into my croissant about feelings I shouldn't have for a guy I barely know?

No. I'm going to that brunch. I'm going to smile and hug people and pretend my chest doesn't feel like it's caving in. Then I'm getting on a plane to Italy, where I'll eat my feelings in pasta like a normal person.

"Besides," I tell CeCe as we head out, grabbing my purse and avoiding looking at the main house again, "I haven't taken a real vacation in three years. Every weekend's been a wedding. I deserve this."

"You deserve a lot of things," she mutters, holding the door open.

"What?"

"Nothing. Get in the car."

I turn back to George, who's watching from the porch with what I swear is disappointment.

"Don't look at me like that," I tell him. "This is the right thing to do."

He bleats.

"Your opinion is noted and ignored."

But as we drive away, I can't shake the feeling that I'm leaving more than just a guest house behind.

I'm leaving the first place that's felt like home in years.

And the first person who's made me want to

stay.

28

THE GOODBYE TOUR

The country club smells like old money and regret. Perfect.

I'm doing this thing where I hover near the mimosa station like it's home base in a really bad game of tag. Dean's across the room talking to his mother, and I'm pretending the orange juice needs my complete attention.

"You're being weird," CeCe mutters beside me.

"I'm being strategic."

"You're hiding behind fruit juice."

"Strategically hiding."

She grabs a mimosa. Downs half of it. "Just go talk to him."

"Pass."

"Poppy—"

"Look, there's Ivy!"

I abandon CeCe and her judgy eyes, and make a beeline for the bride. Safe territory.

Ivy's glowing in that post-wedding way, all soft edges and stupid happiness. Mason's got his arm around her, and they're doing that thing where they can't stop touching. Little brushes. Fingers intertwined. Casual PDA that makes my chest hurt.

"Poppy!" Ivy extracts herself to hug me. "Tell me you're not leaving yet."

"Flight's at two."

"Italy!" She bounces a little. "I'm so jealous. Please eat everything."

"That's the plan."

Mason joins the hug, because apparently we're those people now. "Seriously, Poppy. Can't thank you enough."

"Just doing my job."

"Bullshit," he says. "You went above and beyond. The guitar thing alone—"

My stomach twists. "That was all Dean."

They exchange one of those married people looks. Great. They know. Everyone knows. The whole world knows I spent last night on Dean Whitaker's couch like some pathetic—

"Poppy?"

His voice hits me like a physical thing. Low. Careful. Too close.

I turn. Try for casual. "Hey."

He looks tired. Good tired, but still. Hair's doing that thing where it's trying to be messy but can't quite commit. He's in jeans and a button-down that's probably worth more than my car payment.

"Hi," he says.

Hi. That's it. That's all we get?

Ivy clears her throat. "We're gonna go… check on the buffet."

"The buffet's fine—" Mason starts.

She drags him away. Subtle as a brick.

And then it's just us. Standing too close. Not

close enough.

"So," I say.

"So."

Quality conversation. Really nailing this good-bye thing.

"You left early," he says quietly.

"I had to pack."

"Right. Pack."

He's doing a thing with his jaw. Some tense thing that means he's thinking too hard.

"Dean—"

"Have a good flight."

Wait. What?

"That's… that's it?"

Something flickers across his face. "What else is there?"

Stay. Ask me to stay. Tell me last night meant something. Tell me this week meant something. Tell me I'm not the only one who's drowning here.

"Nothing," I say instead. "Just. You know. Thanks for letting me use your guest house."

"It's what we agreed to."

Right. Our business arrangement. How silly of me to think—

"Take care of George," I blurt out.

His mouth twitches. Almost a smile. "George isn't my responsibility."

"Someone should probably tell George that."

"I'll add it to my list."

We stare at each other. His eyes are filled with something… but I can't tell what. The room's too loud. Too bright. Too full of people who aren't having the world's most awkward goodbye.

"I should—" I gesture vaguely toward the exit, the words catching in my throat like broken glass.

"Yeah." His voice is flat, resigned. Like we're discussing the weather instead of whatever this thing between us was.

But then he reaches out, his fingers barely grazing my wrist. The touch is so light I might have imagined it, except for the way my skin burns where he's made contact.

"Poppy."

I freeze. My name on his lips shouldn't sound like a prayer and a goodbye all at once, but it does.

"Be careful," he says.

The words hit me like cold water. Be careful? That's what we're going with? Not 'I'll miss you' or 'this has been incredible' or 'please don't go.' Be freaking careful? Odd choice, but okay.

"Always am," I lie, forcing the words past the lump in my throat.

He lets go. Steps back. The distance between us might as well be an ocean. And that's it. That's our goodbye. No fanfare, no dramatic declarations. Just two people pretending this doesn't hurt as much as it does.

I turn and walk away before I do something stupid. Like cry. Or scream. Or ask him what the hell last night was if this is how it ends. My feet carry me toward the door on autopilot while my heart stays behind, scattered in pieces on the floor.

CeCe intercepts me at the door, her timing impeccable as always. "You okay?"

"Peachy." The sarcasm drips from my voice like poison.

"That bad?"

"He told me to *be careful*." The words come out as an accusation, as if CeCe is somehow responsible for his emotional cowardice.

"Oh honey." Her voice is soft with understanding.

"Like I'm his elderly aunt going on a cruise. Or his niece who's staying in a shady hostel." The comparison would be funny if it didn't hurt so much.

"Maybe he just—"

"Don't." I grab her arm, probably harder than necessary. "Just. Can we go? Please?"

She nods, understanding written all over her face. We head for the exit together, and I don't look back. Can't look back. Because if I do, if I see him standing there watching me leave, I might not have the strength to keep walking.

Because if I do, if I see him standing there with that stupid jaw thing and those stupid sad eyes, I might—

"Poppy!"

Gloria appears like a sequined guardian angel, blocking our escape. Of course she does. My aunt has impeccable timing when it comes to emotional interventions.

"Aunt Gloria. Hi." My voice comes out smaller than intended.

She studies my face with those all-seeing eyes of hers. "Oh, sweetheart."

"I'm fine." The lie tastes bitter on my tongue.

"Liar." She cups my cheek with one perfectly manicured hand. "But that's okay. Sometimes we need to lie until it becomes true."

"I don't—"

"Italy's going to be good for you," she says firmly, cutting off my weak protest. "A little distance. And perspective, pasta, and prosecco."

I nod, feeling numb. The attempt at humor comes automatically. "The three P's of healing."

"Exactly." She pulls me into a hug that smells like patchouli and possibilities. The familiar scent threatens to undo all my carefully constructed walls. "But Poppy?"

"Yeah?"

"When you're ready? Don't let fear make your choices."

"I'm not—"

"Yes, you are. You both are." She pulls back, gives me that look that sees too much, knows too much, understands things I haven't even admitted to myself. "Pride's a cold bedfellow, darling."

"Gloria—"

"Go. Catch your flight. Eat gelato. Find your joy." She kisses my forehead like she used to when I was small and the world was simpler. "But remember—running toward something and running away from something feel the same until you stop."

Cryptic aunt wisdom. My favorite. Just what I need when my heart is already in pieces.

CeCe tugs my arm. "Come on. Traffic's gonna be a bitch."

I let her lead me away. Through the overdone lobby. Past the valet stand. Into the car where I can finally, finally breathe.

"That was—"

"Don't," I cut her off. "Just. Drive."

She drives.

I stare out the window, watching New York blur past, and try not to think about Dean standing in that stupid country club with his stupid perfect face and his stupid "be careful."

It wasn't long.

Barely more than a week.

But in that time—chaos, goats, reluctant smiles that felt like victories.

In that time, I watched him slowly crack open, only to slam shut the second things got real. In that time, it felt like a lifetime, and now it's just… over.

"Hey," CeCe says softly. "For what it's worth? I think he wanted to say more."

"Yeah, well." I swipe at my cheek. Ugh, allergies. "Wanting and doing are different things."

"Maybe—"

"Can we just… not? Please? I need to not think about it until I'm at least three wines deep in Italy."

"Okay."

"Okay."

More tears stream silently down my cheeks.

The airport looms ahead. My great escape. My big adventure. My definitely-not-running-away vacation.

"You sure you're good?" CeCe asks as she pulls up to departures.

"I'm great. Living the dream. About to eat my bodyweight in carbs."

"Poppy."

"I'll be fine," I say. Softer this time. "I just. I need to go."

She hugs me over the center console. "Text me when you land."

"Will do."

"And Poppy? Maybe he just needs time to—"

"CeCe. *Please*. For the love…"

"Right. Shutting up."

I grab my bags. Head for the automatic doors.

International departures.

Don't look back.

Don't think about him.

Don't wonder if he's wondering where I am.

Just go.

Because Gloria's wrong. Sometimes running away is exactly what you need.

Even if it feels like leaving half your heart behind.

29

SAME SHIT, DIFFERENT DAY

Dean

The conference room smells like disappointment and overpriced coffee. Same as always. Except now I hate it.

"—quarterly projections show a fifteen percent increase in billable hours," Gideon drones on.

I'm supposed to care. That's my job. Caring about billable hours and win rates and whatever soul-sucking metric we're measuring this week.

Instead, I'm watching a pigeon outside systematically destroy someone's lunch.

Good for you, pigeon. Burn it all down.

"Dean?"

Shit.

"What?"

Gideon's giving me that look. The one that says pay attention, asshole. "Your thoughts on the Morrison settlement?"

My thoughts? My thoughts are that it's been three days since Poppy left and Muffin won't stop scratching at the guest house door like she's waiting for someone who's never coming back.

"Aggressive but fair," I say. Safe answer. Always works.

"That's what you said about the Henderson case."

"And?"

"The Henderson case was a custody dispute. This is one involves blackmail."

Crap.

"Right. I meant aggressive but… fraudulent."

The room goes quiet. That special quiet that happens when you've just said something spectacularly stupid.

"Meeting adjourned," Feldstein says. His voice could freeze hell. "Dean. Stay."

Everyone files out. Gideon shoots me a what the hell look. I shoot him back a mind your business look.

"Want to tell me where your head's at?" Feldstein asks once we're alone.

"Right here."

"Bull." He leans back. Studies me like I'm a problem to solve. "You've been off lately. Distracted. Sloppy."

"I've been—"

"You missed the Patterson deadline."

"By an hour."

"You called opposing counsel by the wrong name. Twice."

"They all look the same."

"Dean." His voice goes soft. Dangerous. "I went to bat for you. Told the partners you were ready. That you could handle the pressure."

"I can."

"Can you?" He stands. Walks to the window.

Gazes out. "Because from where I'm sitting, it looks like something's got you twisted up."

Someone, my brain supplies helpfully. Someone has me twisted up. Not something. Big difference.

"I'm fine."

"No. You're not." He turns. "Take the week. Get your shit together. Come back ready to work or don't come back at all."

"You're suspending me?"

"I'm saving you from yourself." He heads for the door, pauses. "Whatever happened upstate? Fix it or forget it. But decide."

The door closes with a click that sounds final.

I sit there for ten minutes. Staring at nothing. Damn.

This is really not good.

• • •

Muffin's on my porch when I get home. Again. Because of course she is.

"Why are you here? Thought you stayed with Nadine while I was at work?" I ask.

She waddles over, snorts, then heads straight for the guest house.

"No." I follow her. "We've talked about this."

Scratch scratch scratch.

"She's not there."

Scratch scratch scratch.

"Muffin. Come on."

She looks at me with those stupid sad eyes. Like I'm the jerk for pointing out reality.

"I know," I mutter. "I miss her too."

The words slip out before I can stop them. Muffin tilts her head like finally, some honesty.

"But missing people doesn't bring them back." I scoop her up. "Trust me. I'm an expert."

I carry her back to my house. She goes limp, full passive resistance mode.

"You're being dramatic."

She farts.

"That's just petty."

Inside, I set her on her designated spot. She immediately gets up and waddles back to the door.

"We're not doing this again."

Scratch scratch scratch.

"Fine. Stay there. See if I care."

I make coffee. Check emails. Pretend to review a brief. Muffin keeps scratching.

"You know what your problem is?" I tell her. "You don't know when to quit."

She pauses. Looks at me. Goes back to scratching.

"She left, okay? Went to Italy. Probably drinking wine and… eating pasta and… being happy without us."

Muffin whines.

I microwave leftover risotto and eat it straight from the Tupperware, standing by the kitchen counter while Muffin sighs into her bowl. The dining table sits across the room—set with exactly zero place settings, surrounded by chairs I haven't used since the night I made risotto for Poppy. I built this life for efficiency. For order. And yet lately, all I can see is the empty space where something could be. Should be.

I rinse the container, wipe down the spotless counter, and open my laptop again.

There's nothing lonelier than silence pretending to be peace.

My phone buzzes. Work email. I delete it without reading.

"You want to know something messed up?" I sit on the floor next to Muffin. "I keep catching the scent of her. Like, everywhere. How can someone's perfume linger like that?"

Muffin settles next to me, finally giving up on the door.

"Found a bobby pin in my couch yesterday. Just… sitting there. Like it belongs."

She rests her head on my knee. I pat it softly.

"And George won't shut up. Just stands on the lawn screaming at nothing. Nadine says he's 'processing'." I huff out an exhale. "Remind me I need to order him more goat feed from Amazon, by the way."

A soft wheeze. Muffin's version of agreement.

"Be careful," I mutter to myself, sitting on my living room floor with Muffin sprawled across my lap. "That's what I said. After everything that happened between us, I told her to be careful."

The words taste like regret every time I replay them. Which is approximately every five minutes.

I keep seeing that look in her eyes when I said it. Like I'd kicked something small and defenseless. Or destroyed some small part of her. I hate it. Hate myself even more.

I wanted to say more. God, I wanted to say everything. The words were right there, caught in my throat like shards of glass. But maybe that's the problem—she makes me feel things I can't name. Things I definitely can't want.

I sigh, running my hand through Muffin's fur. "Could've said anything else. 'Thank you.' 'I'll miss you.' 'Please don't go.' But no. I went with 'be careful' like I'm her damn travel agent."

"Well, isn't this cozy."

I look up. Nadine's standing in my doorway because apparently nobody knocks anymore.

"It's called depression," I say flatly.

"It's called Tuesday afternoon." She lets herself in, naturally. "Is Muffin bothering you?"

"Always."

"Want me to take her?"

"No." The word comes out sharper than intended.

She raises an eyebrow. "No?"

"She's… fine. We have a system."

"Uh-huh." She settles on my couch uninvited, making herself at home like she owns the place. "How's work?"

I lean back against the wall, arms crossed. "Fantastic."

"That why you're home at two o'clock on a Tuesday?" Her tone is too knowing, too sharp.

"Early day." I avoid her eyes, focusing on Muffin instead.

"And yesterday? Also an early day?"

I glare at her. "Are you stalking me?"

"I have a Ring camera. And too much time." She studies me with those sharp eyes that miss nothing. "You look terrible, by the way."

"Thanks."

"Why haven't you shaved? And when's the last time you ate actual food?"

"I eat."

"Scotch isn't food."

"It's made from grain."

"Dean." Her tone carries that warning I've heard a thousand times.

"What do you want, Nadine?"

She's quiet for a moment. That's never good. The silence stretches between us like a taut wire.

"How long are you planning to mope around like this?" she finally asks.

My chest does something stupid and painful. "I'm not moping."

"You're sitting on the floor with my dog discussing bobby pins." She gestures at our pathetic tableau.

"That was a private conversation." I scratch behind Muffin's ears, defensive.

"Dean." Her voice softens, which is somehow worse than her judgment. "She really got to you, didn't she?"

I don't answer because what's the point? We both know the truth. The silence hangs heavy, suffocating.

"She's in Italy," I blurt out, the words escaping before I can stop them.

"How do you know?"

"Because that's where she said she was going." My jaw tightens.

"But you haven't actually confirmed—"

"Nadine." It's a warning.

"I'm just saying. People change plans." She shrugs, too casual.

"Not Poppy. She's a planner. She follows through. It's her whole thing." Even saying her name hurts. Some stupid foreign ache in my chest that won't go away.

"Hmm." She stands, and I can practically see the wheels turning in her head. "Well. If you're sure."

"I'm sure."

"Although Italy's a big place. She could be anywhere. Rome. Venice. That cute little beach town with the lemons…"

"Portofino." The word slips out automatically.

"Oh?" Her smile is pure evil. "She mentioned that specifically?"

I've walked right into her trap, and we both know it.

She heads for the door with purpose. "You know, the guest cottage is just sitting there empty. Might be therapeutic to check on it. Make sure everything's… in order."

My shoulders tense. "I'm not going in there."

"If you say so." She pauses at the door, playing her final card. "Though people leave things behind sometimes. Might want to make sure it's ready for the next guest."

"There won't be a next guest." The words come out hard, final.

"Ever?" She turns back, eyebrow raised.

I don't answer because the thought of anyone else in that space, in her space, makes me want to punch something.

"Right." She shakes her head like I'm a lost cause. "Three years, Dean. Never seen you like this."

Same, I think but don't say it.

"Maybe she'll come back." Nadine shrugs, trying to act casual.

Something twists in my gut—hope and dread tangled together. "She's not coming back. She has a life in California. A business." Each word is another nail in the coffin of whatever we almost were.

"Right." She pauses at the door, delivering her killing blow. "You know what's funny?"

"Nothing about this is funny."

"I've lived next door to you for three years. Never seen you smile. Not once." She looks at me with something like pity. "A week with that girl and you smiled every day."

"That's not—"

"Even at that damn goat."

I give her a stern look because nothing about George was funny. That goat is a disaster.

She opens the door. "The goat made her laugh. And when she laughed…"

"What?"

"You smiled." She shrugs like she hasn't just eviscerated me. "Just an observation."

She leaves.

I sit there with Muffin, both of us staring at the door like idiots waiting for something that's never coming back.

"She's not wrong," I tell the dog. "I did smile more."

Muffin grunts in what I choose to interpret as

sympathy.

"So what? Smiling's overrated."

She gives me a look that clearly says I'm full of it.

Three days. Feels like a lifetime. Feels like yesterday. Feels like I'm drowning in the space she left behind.

"Be careful," I mutter again. "What a complete moron."

Muffin leans against my leg, warm and solid and understanding.

At least someone gets it.

I make myself get up off the floor, trying not to notice how empty everything feels.

Same house. Same job. Same life.

Except I hate it now.

All of it.

Without her here to make it make sense.

30

PARADISE IS OVERRATED

Poppy

The villa is stupid beautiful.

Like, offensively beautiful. The sort of beautiful that makes you want to punch something because how dare a place be this perfect when you feel this… not.

White stone walls. Warm terracotta tiles under my bare feet. Bougainvillea dripping purple over every railing like nature's showing off. The infinity pool bleeds into the Mediterranean, all impossible blues that hurt to look at— they're so pretty.

I'm on my third limoncello.

At 2 p.m.

Because that's what you do in Portofino, right? You drink local liqueur and stare at the water and pretend you're living your best life.

"This is amazing," I tell no one.

The words echo off marble countertops.

I take another sip. It's too sweet. Everything here is too sweet. Too bright. Too much.

My phone buzzes. CeCe, probably. Checking in again.

A glance at my phone confirms it.

Yep.

CECE:

How's paradise?

I send back a photo of the view. Let her think what she wants.

The truth? I'm not okay.

Not even a little.

Paradise is boring as hell when you're alone. But it's more than that.

I wander through the villa—because what else am I doing? The kitchen has one of those fancy espresso machines that I have no idea how to operate.

I flop on the bed. Thousand-thread-count sheets. A view that belongs on postcards.

And all I can think about is a grumpy lawyer's guest cottage that smelled like lemon cleaner and came with a complimentary farting dog. The cutest little farting dog…

"Stop it," I tell myself.

But my brain's already there. Wondering if Muffin misses our morning scratches. If George has destroyed anything new. If Dean—

No.

I sit up and grab my planner from the nightstand because, of course, I brought my planner to Italy. I flip through pages of absolutely nothing because—surprise—I have no plans.

For the first time in years, I have nowhere to be. No timeline to manage. No crisis to solve.

It's supposed to feel like freedom.

Instead, it feels like drowning.

I pour another limoncello. Walk out to the terrace. The town spreads below like a watercolor painting—pastel buildings tumbling down to the harbor, boats bobbing like toys, tourists wandering cobblestone streets.

Beautiful.

Empty.

Wrong.

My phone rings. Unknown Italian number.

"Pronto?" I answer, proud of my limited Italian vocabulary.

Rapid Italian fills my ear. Something about delivery? Tomorrow?

"Uh… no parlo italiano?" I try.

More Italian. Faster now. Frustrated.

"I don't—sorry, I—"

They hang up.

Great. Even Italy thinks I'm a mess.

I lean against the railing. The sun's perfect here. That golden Mediterranean light everyone writes poems about. Sings songs about. It makes my skin glow, turns my hair to honey, probably does wonders for my vitamin D.

I hate it.

"This is what you wanted," I remind myself. "A break. Peace. No one needing you."

Except, it turns out, maybe I like being needed. Like being in the middle of chaos.

Maybe I'm one of those pathetic people who only knows who they are when they're fixing someone else's problems.

Maybe—

"Signora!"

I turn. There's a woman at my gate. Older, wearing an apron, holding what looks like a covered dish.

"Si?"

She launches into Italian, gesturing wildly. I catch maybe three words. *Benvenuta.* Welcome. *Mangiare.* Eat. *Sola?* Alone?

That last one hits weird.

"Si," I admit. "Sola."

Her face crumples with sympathy. She practically forces the dish into my hands, patting my cheek and making soft, pitying noises like I'm an abandoned puppy.

Then she's gone, shuffling back down the path, probably to tell the whole neighborhood about the sad American girl alone in the big villa.

I lift the cover. Lasagna. Real, homemade, someone's-nonna-recipe lasagna.

And suddenly I'm crying.

Not pretty tears either. The ugly kind that make your face splotchy and your nose run. Because a stranger just showed me more warmth than this whole perfect villa, and I'm standing here in paradise feeling sorry for myself, slightly drunk, and somewhere in New York there's a man who brought me a sandwich when I was covered in goat water.

I eat the lasagna standing over the sink like a savage.

It's perfect. Of course it is.

Everything here is perfect.

And I've never felt more alone.

I pour another limoncello and go back to the

terrace.

The sun's starting to set. The whole sky's on fire, turning the water to molten gold. Couples walk the beach below, holding hands. A yacht glides past, laughter drifting up on the breeze.

"Be careful," I mutter, mocking his last words to me.

What kind of goodbye is that? After a week of... whatever that was?

Be careful.

Like I'm just another stranger. Just another wedding planner passing through.

"Asshole," I tell the sunset.

It doesn't argue.

I should be journaling. That was the plan— come to Italy, journal about my feelings, have some big epiphany about my next chapter.

Instead, I'm drunk on limoncello, crying over lasagna, and talking to myself in a villa that costs more per night than most people make in a week.

Living the dream.

I check the time. 8 p.m. here. 2 p.m. in New York.

He's probably at work. Being important. Intimidating junior associates. Definitely not thinking about—

I throw my phone across the terrace before I can finish that thought.

Then immediately run to check if I cracked the screen because I'm not that much of a disaster.

It's fine. Unlike me.

"One week," I tell myself. "Give it one week. You'll feel better."

But even as I say it, I know it's a lie.

Because this view, this villa, this whole Instagram-perfect moment?

It's just really expensive emptiness.

And the only thing I want—the only stupid, impossible thing—is to be back in a guest cottage, fighting with a goat, watching a grumpy lawyer try not to smile.

I finish the limoncello.

Tomorrow I'll do better. Tomorrow I'll enjoy paradise.

Tonight?

Tonight I admit what I've been avoiding since I left New York.

I miss him.

And that's the most pathetic truth of all.

31

THE TRUTH TASTES LIKE BOURBON

Dean

Sullivan's looks exactly like it did in law school. The same sticky floors, the same bartender who pours heavily, and the same lies I tell myself about why I keep coming back.

"You look like shit," Nate says, sliding into the booth across from me.

"Thanks. Really needed that," I reply, tipping my chin at him.

He grins, the same stupid grin that got us through Torts. Except now there are crow's feet, a wedding ring, and probably some spit-up on his shirt.

"Amelia sends her love." He pulls out his phone. "And approximately four thousand photos of Rosie's first attempt at sweet potatoes."

"Thrilling."

But he's already swiping through the photos. Baby in a high chair, orange goop everywhere, Amelia laughing in the background with her hair in a messy bun, looking exhausted yet radiant—everything I pretended I'd never want.

When Emily left, I told myself that was it—

focus on work, make partner, and don't get hurt again. Lock it down.

"She's basically a tiny dictator," Nate says, pure worship in his voice, his eyes still glued to his phone. "Yesterday she screamed for forty minutes because I gave her the wrong spoon. The. Wrong. Spoon."

I take a long pull of bourbon. "Sounds awful."

"It's the best."

He means it. The bastard actually means it. I can read it all over his face.

More photos flash by—a baby in a bathtub, a baby asleep on his chest, and a baby giving the camera a gummy smile.

"This one's my favorite." He shows me a video of Amelia dancing in their kitchen, baby on her hip, both of them covered in what looks like applesauce. She's singing off-key while the baby shrieks with laughter.

Something cracks in my chest.

"She's cute," I manage to say.

"She's perfect. Even when she's demonic. Which is often." He pockets his phone and finally looks at me directly. "How's the firm?"

I take another sip, the bourbon warming my throat. "Great."

"And the house?" He's watching me too closely now, reading between the lines.

"Still standing." I shift in my seat, uncomfortable under his scrutiny.

"That wedding planner Mason mentioned?" He leans forward slightly, and I know this is what he's been working up to.

Dammit, Mason.

I signal for another bourbon and rub my temple. "In Italy."

"Ah." He leans back, nodding as if that explains everything. "Is that why you look like someone killed your dog?"

"I don't have a dog."

"Right. Just borrowing the neighbor's emotional support animal."

"It's not—" I stop and take a breath. Why is everyone against me? Tonight was supposed to be about moving on—grabbing drinks and dinner with an old law school buddy. Not whatever this hell is. "How's work?" I manage, gritting my teeth.

Nice deflection, asshole.

"Good. Boring. Exactly how I like it." He steals a fry from the basket between us. "Nine to five. Home for dinner. Bedtime stories. The whole suburban nightmare you always mocked."

"I didn't mock it."

"You literally called it 'death by minivan.'"

"That was—"

"Last year. At my birthday." He grins. "Right before you gave that whole speech about freedom and choices and not being tied down."

The bourbon burns. Good.

"Things change," I mutter.

"Do they?" He studies me, that lawyer look we perfected in mock trial, checking for weaknesses. "Because from where I'm sitting, you're still doing the exact same thing. Big cases. Empty house. Pretending you're too evolved for basic human connection."

"Screw off."

"She must've been something."

I don't answer.

"Mason said she handled his entire wedding solo. Said she charmed everyone. Even you."

"She was… competent." The word feels wrong. Of course she was competent. But she was so much more.

Nate laughs. Actually laughs. "Competent. Damn, Dean. You're thirty-five, not dead."

"Thirty-six."

"Whatever. Point is, when are you going to stop this?"

My fingers tighten around the glass. "This?"

"The whole tortured genius routine. It's getting old." He says it gently, but it still lands like a punch.

I want to argue. Want to tell him he doesn't understand. That some of us are built differently. That not everyone needs the house and the baby and the—love of his life.

His phone buzzes, and his face softens.

"Amelia?" I guess.

"Rosie's bedtime." He shows me the screen, it's a FaceTime request. "You mind?"

Yes.

A lot, actually.

"Go ahead."

He answers. The screen fills with a baby—droopy eyes, clutching a stuffed elephant, with Amelia's voice in the background saying, "Show Daddy your new trick."

The baby blows a raspberry.

Nate acts like she just solved world hunger. "That's my girl! Can you do it again?"

She does. With more spit.

"Genius," he declares. Then to me, "Want to say hi?"

"I'm good."

But the phone's already turned. The baby stares at me through the screen, huge eyes and a suspicious expression, as if she knows I'm full of shit.

"That's Uncle Dean," Nate tells her. "He's pretending he doesn't want one of you."

"I'm not—"

The baby raspberries at me.

"See? Even she knows."

I flip him off below the camera line.

Five minutes later, after a bedtime song, promises to be home soon, and more kisses than seem necessary, he hangs up.

"Sorry," he says, the dopey grin on his face suggesting he's not really sorry at all.

"It's fine."

"You know what your problem is?"

I curl my fingers around my glass. "Please, enlighten me."

"You think wanting something normal makes you weak."

I finish my bourbon. "I don't think that."

"No? Then why are you sitting here looking like death while some wedding planner in Italy is probably wondering why you let her go?"

"I didn't let her—she was always going. It was temporary."

"Everything's temporary if you decide it is."

"That's not—"

"I used to be you," he interrupts. "Remember? Same speeches, same bullshit about freedom and not needing anyone. Then Amelia happened."

"And now you're covered in applesauce."

"And I've never been happier." He's serious. Completely serious. I shift in my seat, my jaw tightening, because the certainty in his eyes makes something in my chest ache. "It's terrifying, yeah. Having someone who could destroy you just by leaving. But Dean… the alternative is this."

He gestures at me, at my empty glass, at my expensive suit and crooked tie, and at the perfect life that has a hole where something should be.

"I should go." My voice comes out rougher than I intended.

"You should go to Italy."

"What?" I blink, my pulse kicking hard, as if he's just ripped open a thought I've been fighting to bury.

"Whatever happened with that wedding planner, fix it."

My chest tightens, defensive walls slamming up. "There's nothing to fix."

"Right." He stands and throws cash on the table. "That's why you've checked your phone six times since I got here."

I haven't. Have I? I glance at my phone anyway, guilt prickling hot under my collar.

"Go home," he says. "Think about what you actually want. Then maybe, for once in your life, be brave enough to take it."

He leaves, and I order another bourbon.

I stare at my phone.

She hasn't texted. Why would she? I told her to be careful, like she was a stranger, like our time together meant nothing.

I'm not sitting here drowning in baby photos and pretending I still believe my own bullshit.

The thought of her meeting someone new and moving on isn't pleasant. It sits in my stomach like a rock.

I pay and drive home. The estate is dark except for the security lights.

No George. No chaos. No woman in a sundress making everything difficult.

Just quiet.

I head inside, pour a scotch, and sit on the couch.

I get up, pour more scotch, and stare out the window at the guest cottage.

"Damn it."

Ten minutes later, I'm standing at the cottage door with the spare key.

This is stupid. She's gone. There's nothing—

I open the door.

The scent hits me immediately—vanilla, her perfume, that damn cucumber face mask she wore one morning. There's a physical ache in my chest where my heart used to be.

I should leave.

Instead, I walk in. Everything is exactly as she left it. The bed is made with military corners. One coffee mug sits in the drying rack. Her planning binder is gone, but a sticky note is stuck to the counter—*Thank you for everything. Take care of*

George. And Muffin. And yourself. - P

"Take care of yourself," I mutter. "Real original."

I'm pathetic. Standing in an empty cottage, smelling the hint of her leftover perfume.

I turn to go, and that's when I see it.

There, on the floor by the couch, catching the light.

An earring.

Small. Gold. One that probably has a match somewhere in Italy.

I pick it up and study it like it holds answers.

It doesn't.

But now I'm thinking about her losing it, taking them off after that first long day, too tired to notice one rolling away. I'm imagining her in Italy, reaching for her earrings, finding only one.

"This is insane," I tell the empty room.

I pocket the earring anyway.

Back at my house, I pour more scotch and open my laptop.

I type: *Is it crazy to fly to Italy to return an earring?*

Delete.

I type: *Found something that belongs to someone in Italy. Worth returning?*

Delete.

I pour more scotch.

I navigate over to Reddit.

I create a new post.

Need Advice pls

Would I be crazy if I flew to Italy to return jewelry to a woman who was only temporarily in my life but left me questioning everything?

I stare at it.

I post it to r/relationships.

The responses come in fast.

thisdude:
BRO. YES. FLY TO ITALY. NOW.

cottagecore_cynic:
If you don't go, you'll regret it forever. Speaking from experience.

ladyinred:
This is rom-com stuff, and I'm here for it. UPDATE US.

Bageldad:
Life's short. Flights are long. But regret lasts forever. Book the ticket.

cottagecore_cynic:
Dude, asking Reddit means you already know the answer.

hyperforty:
What's the worst that could happen? She says thanks, and you see Italy? GO.

Bageldad:

I flew to Japan for a girl once. Married
for 12 years now. YOLO.

cottagecore_cynic:
The earring is just an excuse, and you
know it. Stop being a coward.

That last one stings.

But they're right. All of them. Even the person who just commented with a bunch of peach emojis and the words GET IT in all caps.

I open a new tab and search for flights to Italy.

There's one leaving tomorrow afternoon.

My cursor hovers over 'Book Now.'

This is insane. I have the week off work. But still, I have a life that makes sense without her in it.

Had. I had a life that made sense.

I think about Nate, his baby, his applesauce-covered happiness.

I think about Poppy laughing at George, swaying in my arms under fairy lights, looking at me like maybe I wasn't a lost cause.

I type in my credit card info and click 'Book Now.'

The confirmation email comes through immediately.

Flight to Milan. Connection to Genoa. Car to Portofino.

I screenshot it and send it to Nate.

His response is immediate.

I stare at the earring. Such a small thing. It barely weighs anything.

But maybe that's the point.

Maybe the big things start small.

Maybe they begin with admitting that your perfect life is perfectly empty.

And maybe they start with a flight to Italy, an earring, and the kind of hope I swore I'd never let myself feel.

"Be careful," I mutter to myself.

Then I book a rental car for good measure.

Because careful is overrated.

And I'm done pretending I don't want what everyone else seems to have figured out.

Connection. Chaos. Someone to come home to.

Even if she tells me to get lost in Italian.

At least I'll know I tried.

The earring rests on my coffee table, catching the light.

Less than twenty-four hours until my flight.

Twenty-four hours to figure out what I'm going to say when I see her.

No pressure.

32

MINE

Dean

She's on the terrace when I find her.

Because of course she is. Backlit by the sunset like some Renaissance painting, hair loose and catching gold, wearing this white linen thing that makes my chest tight.

Four days. It's only been four days, and she's more beautiful than memory served.

I clear my throat.

She turns.

And the look on her face—shock morphing to something else, something raw—nearly drops me.

"Dean?" Her voice breaks on my name. Just cracks right down the middle.

"Hi."

Smooth. Real smooth. Fly four thousand miles to say 'hi.'

She blinks. Once. Twice. Her hand grips the terrace railing like she needs the anchor. Like I might disappear if she lets go.

"What are you—how did you—"

I hold up the earring. My hand's not quite steady. "You left this."

The words hang between us. Stupid. Inadequate. The Mediterranean breeze picks up, sending her hair across her face. She doesn't move to fix it.

Her face changes. Something shutters behind her eyes, and when she looks at me again, it's pure steel.

"You're joking."

"I thought you might want—"

Her expression changes. "Don't."

She's across the terrace in three steps, sandaled feet slapping against stone. Her sundress whips around her legs. Fury radiates off her in waves, but there's something else too. Something raw underneath the anger.

"Don't you dare. You flew to Italy to return an earring?"

"Poppy—"

"No." She's right in my space now.

Close enough that I can see the sun freckles across her nose. Smell the lemons from her shampoo mixed with wine and salt air. Her chest rises and falls too fast.

"You don't get to do this. You don't get to show up here and pretend—"

"I'm not pretending—"

"Bullshit." Her voice cracks. Her hands ball into fists at her sides. "You're not here for the earring. Don't lie to me."

The words hit like a slap. Physical. Deserved.

She's right. Of course she's right. My throat closes up.

"I—"

"What, Dean? What possible reason—"

She stops. Laughs, but it's sharp and not at all amused. Tears gather in her eyes but don't fall. Not yet. I always knew how strong she was, but this cements it for me.

"You told me to be careful. Remember? Your big goodbye. 'Be careful.' Like I was some… some stranger you were sending into traffic."

"That's not—"

"Then you let me leave." Her voice drops to almost nothing. "Let me walk away thinking I imagined everything. The way you looked at me. The way we—"

She breaks off. Inhales a shaky breath. Wraps her arms around herself like she's cold despite the summer heat.

"And now you're here? With an earring? Like that makes sense?"

I shift, knowing how badly I've messed this up. "Nothing about this makes sense."

"Next you're going to tell me you came because Muffin misses me."

My mouth twitches. "She does, but that's beside the—"

"Then why—"

"Because I'm an idiot."

That stops her. Her mouth opens. Closes. A tear finally escapes, tracking down her cheek.

"What?"

"I'm an idiot."

The words pour out now. I can't stop them. My hands shake as I shove them in my pockets.

"A coward. A disaster who's spent years convinced I was too smart to need what everyone else wants. Too evolved. And too… broken, maybe."

She's still. Watching. Another tear falls. She doesn't wipe it away.

"I sat in that house after you left, and it was exactly what I wanted, right?"

I laugh, but it sounds wrong. Hollow.

"Peace. Quiet. No chaos. No goats. No woman reorganizing my life and making me feel things I specifically decided *not* to feel."

"Dean—"

"And it was hell." The words scrape out. "Complete hell. Because it turns out I don't want quiet. I want you arguing with me about tent placement. I want you covered in goat… muck. I want you on my couch eating sandwiches and making everything complicated."

"You said—"

"I know what I said. I lied." I step closer. She doesn't back away. "To you. To myself. To everyone. Because it was easier than admitting the truth."

"Which is?" Her gaze is on mine.

"That you wrecked me." My voice drops. "In one week, Poppy. You were in my life for just over a week, and you wrecked everything I thought I knew about myself."

Her breath catches.

"My friend has a baby," I continue because apparently, I'm doing this. "Showed me eight thousand photos. Of his daughter. His wife. Their life. This whole messy, chaotic, beautiful disaster of a life. And all I could think was how I used to mock him for wanting that. For choosing that. For being brave enough to admit he needed someone."

"Dean—"

"I can't." The admission burns coming out. It's the brutal, awful, messy truth, and I can't hold it in any longer. The idea of Poppy as my wife—mine forever, pregnant with my baby—should scare the ever-loving hell out of me. But it doesn't. In fact, warmth spreads through me at the thought of it. I take a breath and continue, "I can't go back. To the quiet. To the empty house. To pretending this"—I gesture between us—"isn't everything."

She makes a sound. Small. Wounded.

"So yeah. I flew to Italy. With your earring. Because I needed an excuse. Because even now, even after everything, I'm still the guy who needs a prop to say what should be simple."

"What should be simple?" Her voice is small, uncertain.

I meet her eyes. Endless blue pools of worry. No more running.

"You—" I pull a breath into my lungs, trying to compose myself. "I want this… a shot with you. If, uh, that's something you want too."

She wipes her face. Glares. "Right now, I mostly want to push you off this terrace."

"Poppy—" I smirk.

"I'm not done." She jabs a finger at my chest. "You don't get to just show up and declare feelings and fix everything. You hurt me."

"I know."

"You let me leave." The pain behind her eyes is evident, and I *hate* that I'm the one who put it there.

"I know."

"You—"

I kiss her.

I probably shouldn't. She's still mid-rant. But something inside me snaps. Built-up want, plus days of regret. My declaration still hanging between us.

She makes a noise against my mouth. Fury or need or both. Then her hands are in my hair, and she's kissing me back like it's war. Like she's still mad but also desperate. Like maybe she's been as wrecked as me.

"This doesn't fix it," she gasps when we break apart.

"I know."

"I'm still angry." Her eyes flash on mine.

"Good."

"Good?"

I frame her face with my hands. "Be angry. Be furious. Push me off the terrace if you want. But do it tomorrow. Just—" My voice breaks. "Just don't make me leave right now."

She studies me. Long enough that I think maybe—

"You're really bad at this."

"The worst," I agree.

"The earring thing was stupid."

"Incredibly." I chuckle.

"And you're going to have to work for this."

"Whatever you want."

"Whatever I want?" Something shifts in her eyes. "Dangerous offer."

"I'm done being safe."

She kisses me again. Different this time. Slower. Deeper. Like she's trying to tell me something words can't reach.

When she pulls back, we're both breathing hard.

"For the record," she says, her voice soft but steady, "I kept trying to hate you. That whole week. Tried to convince myself you were just some grumpy control freak who happened to look good in a suit."

She thinks I look good in a suit. The thought catches me off guard, warmth spreading through my chest.

"And?" I manage, trying to sound casual when I'm anything but.

Her eyes search mine, vulnerable and honest in a way that makes my heart stutter. "And then I'd remember how you looked at George." A small smile tugs at her lips. "The way your whole face changed when that ridiculous goat followed you around. Like you were trying so hard not to care, but you did."

I want to protest, but she's not done.

"How you brought me dinner that night when I was drowning in spreadsheets. You didn't have to. I brought nothing but chaos, but you fed me. Who does that for someone they claim to barely tolerate?"

"Poppy—"

"How you quietly fixed things. How you quietly fixed things… the tent, the salmon, the guitar… How you smiled when you thought I wasn't watching." Her thumb traces my jaw, leaving a trail of fire. "You thought I didn't notice, but I noticed everything."

My throat feels tight. "I didn't—"

Her eyes are bright with unshed tears. "A real smile. Not your polite lawyer smile or your 'handling difficult clients' smile. But actual joy. Like maybe I wasn't driving you completely insane."

"You were," I admit. "Just not in the way I expected."

She laughs, soft and sweet. "I'd remember how you made me feel like maybe I wasn't too much. Like maybe all my chaos was exactly right if it made you look at me like that."

"Like what?"

"Like I was something wonderful." Her voice drops to a whisper. "Like I was worth changing for."

"Poppy—" My voice breaks on her name.

"I'm still mad." She says it firmly, but her hands haven't left my face.

"Okay." I'll take mad. I'll take anything as long as she's here.

"Really mad."

"I deserve it."

"But also…" She presses closer, her body fitting against mine like it was made to be there. "I missed you so much I couldn't breathe. Coming here alone was awful; it was like losing something I never really had."

Something in me breaks. The last wall. The final defense. Three years of carefully constructed armor just crumbles under the weight of her confession.

"Tonight, you're mine." The words come out raw. Possessive. Everything I've been holding back.

She shivers against me. "Yours." The single word is a promise, a surrender, a claim of her own.

"And tomorrow, we figure everything else out."

"Everything," she agrees.

"But tonight—"

She shuts me up with another kiss. This one's different again. Hungry. Certain. Like we're done talking. Done pretending. Done being apart. It's my new favorite kiss, erasing the memory of every careful, hesitant touch we've shared before.

My hands find her waist, spanning the warmth of her through the thin fabric.

"Dean." My name on her lips undoes me completely.

"Yeah?" My voice is rough, unrecognizable.

"The earring thing really was incredibly stupid."

I laugh against her throat, feeling her pulse jump under my lips. "You mentioned that."

"Monumentally stupid."

"Noted."

"But also…" She pulls back, frames my face with her hands. Meets my eyes with that direct gaze that's always seen too much. "Thank you. For being brave. Finally."

"Only took a complete emotional collapse and a Reddit thread."

Her eyes widen with delight. "Reddit?" She's practically vibrating with glee. "Don't tell me you asked Reddit again?"

"Mistakes were made."

"Oh my God. What was your username? GrumpyLawyer69?"

"I'm not telling you that."

"ControlFreakCottageOwner?"

"Poppy."

"Oh, I'm going to need details." Her hands slide under my shirt, finding skin, and my brain short-circuits. "Every. Single. Detail."

"Later," I manage.

"Later?" She's doing something with her fingernails that should be illegal.

"Much later." She's walking backward, pulling me with her, and I follow helplessly.

"Because right now I need you to show me exactly how sorry you are."

"So sorry," I agree immediately.

"How much you missed me."

"Every second."

"How you're never letting me walk away again."

"Never," I agree, following her inside. The word feels like a vow.

"Good." She stops in the doorway, framed by the fading light, looking like every dream I've tried not to have. "But Dean?"

"Yeah?"

"If you ever tell me to 'be careful' again instead of how you actually feel, I'm getting a restraining order."

"Fair."

"And moving George into your living room."

"Absolutely not." The words are automatic.

She raises an eyebrow, and I see my future flash before my eyes. A future that definitely involves a goat in my living room.

"Fine. For a supervised visit," I concede, since I'm pretty sure I'd agree to just about anything right now. World peace. Skydiving.

"Deal." She pulls me inside, her smile turning wicked. "Now stop negotiating and kiss me like you mean it."

So I do.

And for the first time in my extremely careful life, I mean every reckless second of it.

33

NO MORE PRETENDING

Poppy

He looks exhausted.

Good.

He should be exhausted. Should've lost sleep. Should've suffered like I've suffered in this stupid perfect villa with its stupid perfect views and its stupid perfect emptiness.

But also—

He's here. Actually here. In Portofino looking wrecked and uncertain and holding my earring like it's precious.

"Mine," he says again, and I'm gone.

Done pretending I haven't been dying without him. Done acting like four days wasn't enough to rewire my entire existence.

His hands are everywhere. My waist. My hair. The curve of my hip where linen meets skin.

"Missed you," he breathes against my neck. "So much."

"Show me."

And he does.

He backs me against the wall and kisses me like he's trying to make up for lost time. For stupid goodbyes. For every moment we've been apart.

"The bedroom's—"

"Don't care."

"Dean—"

"Here." His voice is rough. Desperate. "Need you here. Now. Can't—"

I get it. The urgency. The fear that if we move, if we think, if we do anything but this, one of us might remember why this is crazy.

So I don't move. Don't think.

Just pull him closer. Let him press me into the wall. Let myself feel how much he wants this. Wants me.

"You're shaking," I realize.

"You scare me, baby," he admits against my throat, his lips making me dizzy. "Absolutely terrify me."

"Why?"

"Because I don't know how to do this. Any of this. Because you could wake up tomorrow and realize—"

I shut him up the only way that works. With my mouth. My hands. My whole body telling him what words can't.

That I'm here. That this is real. That we'll figure out the rest later.

"Bedroom," I gasp when we come up for air. "Now."

He doesn't argue. Just lifts me—actually lifts me—and carries me through the villa like he owns it. Like he owns me. And right now, he does.

But I think might own him right back.

His hands are steady now as he sets me on the

bed. Sure. Like something's settled in him.

"Let me see you," he says, voice low.

I reach for the hem of my dress.

"No." He catches my hands. "Let me."

And damn, the way he looks at me. Like I'm something precious. Something worth savoring.

He slides the straps down slowly. Presses his mouth to each shoulder as he bares it.

"Thought about this," he murmurs against my skin. "Every night. How you'd taste. How you'd sound."

"Dean—"

"Shh." His fingers trail down my spine, finding the zipper. "My turn to talk. You've been running this show since day one."

The dress pools at my feet. His eyes go dark.

"Fuck, Poppy."

"That's the idea."

He laughs. Low. Rough. Then his mouth is on mine again and coherent thought becomes optional.

His shirt has too many buttons. I tell him so.

"Patience," he says.

"Forget patience."

But he catches my hands again. Pins them gently above my head with one of his.

"What did I say about who's running things?"

Oh. Oh.

"You think you're in charge now?" I arch against him. "Just because you showed up with some grand gesture—"

"Nothing grand about it." He traces my jaw with his free hand. "Just a man who finally figured out what he wants."

"Which is?"

"You." Simple. Certain. "However I can have you."

My breath catches.

"That's not fair," I manage. "You can't just say things like—"

"Watch me." He releases my hands and runs his knuckles along my cheek. "You're brilliant. Infuriating. Beautiful. You reorganize everything you touch, including me, and I—" He stops. Swallows. "I'm completely gone for anyone who isn't you."

"Dean—"

"Still talking." But he's smiling now. That rare, real thing that transforms his whole face. "Let's see what other things we can do with that mouth of yours."

He kisses me then. Different from before. Slower. Deeper. Like we have time now. Like maybe the urgency's settling into something else. Something that might last longer than tonight.

"You're still wearing too many clothes," I point out when we break apart.

"Bossy."

"You love it."

He pauses. Studies me. "Yeah. I really do."

His shirt finally comes off. Then everything else, with a lot less finesse than I'm sure he planned. But I don't care about finesse. I care about his hands on my skin. His weight above me. The way he says my name like a prayer.

"Tell me what you want," he says.

"You. Just you. All of you."

He moves then, and we both gasp. A shocked,

helpless sound—like we've opened a door we've been leaning against for months. For a moment we're still. Adjusting. Remembering. Relearning. Foreheads pressed close. Noses brushing. My fingers clutch at his shoulders, feeling the tremor there that matches mine.

"Okay?" he asks, breathless.

"Perfect." I pull him down for another kiss. It's messy and grateful and a little desperate. "You're perfect."

"Poppy—"

"Shut up and move."

He does. Slow at first. Careful. Like I might break. His hand finds mine above my head; our fingers lace, anchor-tight.

"I'm not fragile," I tell him.

"No." He picks up the pace. "You're not." His mouth finds my pulse point. "Perfect for me," he breathes into my neck.

Something in my chest loosens. It's nothing like before. Nothing like the fumbling, rushed, what's-the-fuss-about experiences I've had in the past. Not that there were many. A handful of forgettable encounters that left me wondering if maybe I was broken. If everyone was lying about how good this could be.

This is… everything. This is deliberate. Intentional. This is choosing each other.

"Look at me," he says when my eyes drift closed.

I do. Find him watching me with something like wonder.

"So good," he murmurs. "So perfect. So mine."

"Yours," I agree.

His rhythm falters. "Say it again."

"Yours, Dean. Yours."

"Damn." He drops his forehead to mine. "You can't just—"

"Yes, I can." I wrap my legs around him. Pull him deeper. "My grumpy, emotionally constipated, perfect—"

He kisses me quiet. Moves harder. Faster. Until words become impossible and there's just sensation. Connection. The two of us figuring out how we fit.

Spoiler: We fit perfectly.

34

PIZZA IN BED

Dean

She's draped across my chest like a blanket. A very satisfied, slightly sweaty blanket that keeps drawing patterns on my skin.

"So," she says.

"So."

"That happened."

I trace lazy circles on her back, still catching my breath. "Three times."

She laughs. I feel it everywhere. "Show-off."

"You started it."

She smiles. "Did not."

"Did too." I catch her hand. Kiss her palm. "Had to prove I wasn't all talk."

"Mm. Good follow-through."

"Thanks. I aim to please."

"Such a giver."

We're quiet for a minute. It's a quiet that should probably feel awkward but doesn't. Outside, I can hear the ocean. Boats in the harbor. Real life happening while we hide in this bubble.

"I'm hungry," she announces.

"Worked up an appetite?"

"Mm." She stretches like a cat. "Think we can find any good Italian takeout?"

"In Italy?" I deadpan. "Might be tough."

She laughs into my chest. "Shut up. You know what I mean."

"There's probably menus somewhere." I trace lazy circles on her hip. Can't stop touching her. "Or we could be really American about it and order pizza."

"God yes. Extra cheese. Maybe some of that fancy prosciutto."

"Classy."

She props herself up on an elbow, sheet slipping down to reveal one perfect shoulder. The moonlight through the window catches the sheen of sweat on her collarbone. My mouth goes dry.

"You're different," she says, studying me with those eyes that see too much.

"Different how?"

She traces her finger along my jaw, featherlight. I fight the urge to turn into her touch like some desperate thing.

"Relaxed. Like you finally stopped clenching."

"I don't clench."

"Dean." She laughs, low and knowing. "You're basically a human fist."

The truth of it stings. But then—

"Was," I correct.

Something shifts in her face. Soft. Real. Like maybe she gets it. Gets me. Like maybe I'm not too much for her.

"Was," she agrees.

We find menus in a kitchen drawer, both of us

padding around mostly naked like this is normal. Like I fly to Italy all the time to chase wedding planners who turn my life inside out. The tile is cold under my feet. She shivers when she leans against the counter, and I wrap myself around her from behind, skin to skin.

"Your Italian is shit," she informs me, squinting at the app.

"Yours is better?"

"I know important phrases. Like 'more wine' and 'where's the bathroom'."

"Practical."

She tilts her head back against my shoulder. "Did we just order six pizzas?"

I look at the confirmation. "Or six toppings. Hard to tell."

"Either way, we're committed now."

While we wait, she raids the villa owner's wine collection, pulling out bottles like she owns the place. There's something intoxicating about watching her move through space—confident, unself-conscious. She's wearing my shirt now, and every time she reaches up, I catch a glimpse of the bruise I left on her hip.

Mine.

"This feels illegal," she says, examining a Barolo.

"You said the host told you to make yourself at home."

"Pretty sure they didn't mean bang in every room and steal the Barolo."

The image flashes—her against every surface, crying out my name. My voice comes out rough.

"We haven't banged in every room."

"Yet." She grins over her shoulder. Pure trouble. "The night's still young."

"You're gonna kill me."

"What a way to go though." She laughs.

Fifteen minutes later, the doorbell saves me from doing something stupid like bending her over the kitchen island. Though from the look in her eyes, she's thinking the same thing.

Six pizzas. Because of course.

We sprawl across the bed like teenagers, boxes everywhere, no plates, no dignity. Just her legs tangled with mine and tomato sauce that's definitely gonna stain these sheets.

"Oh, good grief." The sound she makes around her first bite goes straight to my groin. "This is pornographic."

"The pizza?"

"Everything. This whole night." She gestures with her slice, and a piece of cheese lands on my chest. She leans over to lick it off, and I forget how to breathe. "You show up. We fight. We destroy the bedding. Now there's cheese. It's perfect."

I chuckle. "Your standards are concerningly low."

She bites my chest. I jerk hard enough to upset a pizza box.

"My standards are exactly where they should be." She settles back against the pillows, stealing a piece of my prosciutto. "Right here. In bed. With you. And roughly seventeen pounds of carbs."

The casual way she says it—like this is obvious, like we're obvious—does something to my chest. We eat in comfortable silence for a minute, just the sound of chewing and the distant harbor bells.

"Tell me something," she says eventually, wiping her hands on a napkin.

My guard comes up automatically, walls starting to rebuild themselves. "What?"

"Something real. Something you haven't told anyone." Her voice is soft, coaxing.

I watch her lick sauce off her thumb. My brain short-circuits for a second before I can answer.

"I hate my house."

Her hand stills. "What?"

"Always have." The admission feels weird in my mouth. True but foreign. "It's too big. Too quiet. Bought it because it seemed like what I should want."

I shrug, but she's watching me now with that look. The one that strips me bare.

"Turns out, 'should' is bullshit."

"Huh." She goes back to her thumb, and I have to look away. "What do you actually want?"

"In a house?"

"In general."

Dangerous question. Especially when she's sitting there in my shirt with sex hair and pizza grease on her fingers, looking like everything I never knew I needed.

"Noise," I say finally. The words come slow, careful. "Chaos. Someone to fight with over dinner. A dog that steals the covers. A goat that commits crimes."

"That's oddly specific." She's trying not to

smile.

"Wonder why."

She's on me before I see it coming. Pizza boxes fly. She pins me in place, straddling my hips, and I could flip us in a heartbeat but why would I want to?

"You're a closet romantic," she accuses.

"Am not." But I can feel my defenses crumbling under her gaze.

She shifts her weight, settling more firmly against me. "Are too." She pokes me in the chest. Then she grinds down just enough to make me groan. "Dean Whitaker wants a family."

"I want—"

The word sticks. You. Too much. Too soon. Too real. I don't say it. Not yet. Not tonight.

"What?" Her face softens.

"This," I manage. "Whatever this is."

She studies me for a long moment. I can feel her pulse where she's pressed against me. Then she smiles, small and private.

"Me too."

"Yeah?"

"Yeah." She curls against my side like she belongs there. Because she does. She really does. "Even though you're emotionally stunted and can't admit you are a total softy."

She's laughing into my shoulder, her whole body shaking with it. I'm laughing too, and the bed's a disaster zone of pizza and wine and us, and somehow this is the happiest I've been in… ever?

"We should clean up," she says without moving.

"Should we though?"

"The grease is gonna—"

I shrug. "Tomorrow's problem."

She props up to look at me. "You're really embracing this new spontaneous thing."

"When in Rome."

"We're not in Rome."

I blank, jetlag already setting in. "True. When in… what's this place called?"

"Portofino, you absolute disaster."

"Right. When in Portofino."

She kisses me, and she tastes like wine and marinara and possibility. Her tongue slides against mine, lazy and thorough, like we have all the time in the world.

I hop up to clear away the pizza boxes and then rejoin her on the bed. We settle in together. Her back to my chest. My arm around her waist. Perfect fit.

"Dean?"

The contentment in the room shifts slightly, becomes something heavier. "Yeah?"

"What happens tomorrow?"

I pull her closer, buying time, feeling the warmth of her against me. "We'll figure it out."

She's quiet for a beat, and I can feel her processing, deciding whether to let it go. "That's not really an answer."

"I know." The truth is, I'm not sure.

She turns in my arms. Studies my face in the dim light. "I'm scared too, you know."

"I know."

"But I'm glad you're here."

"Yeah?"

"Yeah." She kisses me. Soft. Sweet.

And tomorrow? Tomorrow can wait.

Tonight, we have this. Pizza and laughter and skin against skin. No promises except the ones our bodies make. No plans except to wake up together and see what happens next.

It's terrifying.

It's perfect.

It's enough.

For now.

35

WHEN IN PORTOFINO

Poppy

I wake up to Dean cursing in Italian.

Not good Italian. Terrible, American, possibly just made-up Italian.

"What are you doing?" My voice comes out scratchy. Everything is sore in the best way possible.

He's standing at the window in his boxers, glaring at something outside. Morning light hits the planes of his back, highlighting scratches I definitely left there.

"There's a goat."

I bolt upright, the sheet pooling around my waist. "What?"

"A freaking goat. On the terrace. Eating the..." He squints. "I think those were roses."

"You're hallucinating." But I'm already scrambling out of bed.

"Come look."

I wrap the sheet around myself and pad over. Sure enough, there's a white goat on the terrace, methodically destroying what was probably a very expensive flower arrangement.

"Oh my gosh."

"It's like George followed us." He sounds personally offended, running a hand through his already messy hair. "Is this my life now? Stalker goats?"

The goat looks up, makes direct eye contact with Dean, and knocks over a potted lemon tree.

"I think he's establishing dominance," I say, biting back a laugh.

"I'm going out there." He's already moving toward the door.

"Dean, no—"

But he's already sliding open the door, marching out in his boxers like some kind of deranged warrior. The goat bleats. Dean points at it with the authority of someone used to winning arguments.

"No. Bad goat. Drop the... whatever that is."

The goat eats faster, chewing with vindictive pleasure.

"I'm serious. I flew four thousand miles to get away from this."

I'm laughing so hard I can't breathe, clutching the doorframe for support. "Please stop arguing with the goat."

"He started it!" Dean's voice rises, incredulous.

The goat hops onto a table. Dean's face goes through about seventeen emotions, ending somewhere between rage and resignation.

"That's it. We're leaving. Getting dressed. Going into town. Somewhere goat-free."

"But he's so cute—" I'm still giggling, watching this whole disaster unfold.

"Poppy." Just my name, but it carries a warning.

"Fine." I watch the goat demolish another plant with apparent glee. "But I'm taking a picture first."

"Of course you are." He shakes his head, but his mouth is twitching.

Twenty minutes later, we're walking down narrow stone steps toward the harbor. I'm wearing a sundress I'm really glad I packed—it's white, hits mid-thigh, and Dean's been staring at my legs since we left the villa.

"You're going to make us crash," I inform him as he walks into his third lamppost.

"Worth it." He doesn't even look apologetic.

"Smooth talker."

"You want smooth?" He spins me against an ancient stone wall, caging me in with his arms. "How's this for smooth—you look positively edible, and I'm considering dragging you back to bed."

My breath catches, my heart stuttering. "That's not smooth. That's caveman."

"You like caveman." His voice drops to that register that makes my knees weak.

I do. I really do.

"Weren't we escaping livestock?" I manage, though my voice comes out breathy.

He grins, slow and satisfied, stepping back. "Right. Goat-free zones only."

We wander without a plan. That's the thing about Dean, I'm learning—when he lets go of control, he really lets go. No itinerary. No schedule. Just his hand in mine and wherever our feet take us.

The town is stupidly charming: pastel buildings

stacked like cake layers, boats bobbing in water so blue it looks fake. Tourists are everywhere, but it doesn't matter because Dean keeps pulling me into tiny alleyways to kiss me senseless.

"You're insatiable," I gasp after he's basically attacked me behind a gelato shop.

"Your fault." He nips at my throat, his teeth grazing sensitive skin. "That dress is criminal."

"Want me to change?" I tease, though my pulse is racing.

"Hell no. I want you to wear it forever. Or nothing. Preferably nothing."

An elderly Italian woman passes us, saying something that sounds judgmental. Dean grins and responds in his terrible Italian. She laughs, pats his cheek, and continues walking.

"What did you say?" I ask, straightening my dress, my cheeks warm.

"No idea. Either 'sorry for the public display' or 'your fish is on fire.' My pronunciation needs work."

We find a tiny café overlooking the water. The owner knows zero English, and Dean knows zero real Italian. Somehow, we end up with espresso, pastries, and what might be fish but could also be chicken.

"This is nice," I say, looking out at the boats.

"The possible fish?" He pokes at it with his fork, suspicious.

I laugh. "This." I gesture between us. "Being normal. Like we're just..."

"Just what?" He sets down his fork, giving me his full attention.

"People. On vacation. Together."

He studies me over his espresso, his eyes searching my face. "Is that what we are?"

"I don't know." I steal a bite of his maybe-fish, needing something to do with my hands. "What do you think we are?"

"Disasters," he replies immediately. "Absolute disasters who can't keep their hands off each other."

"Romantic." I'm smiling despite the sarcasm.

"You want romantic?" He leans across the tiny table, close enough for me to smell his cologne mixed with espresso. "Fine. I think we're whatever makes you tackle me in pizza grease. Whatever makes me fly to Italy with jewelry. Whatever this is that makes me want to buy every goat in this country just to see you smile like that."

I can't help but smile. "Every goat?"

"Don't test me." He's completely serious, which makes it funnier.

"Dean Whitaker, goat collector."

"Has a nice ring to it."

The waiter brings more espresso, judging Dean's Italian pronunciation. They appear to have an argument about conjugation. I watch, charmed by how bad he is at this, how he gestures with his hands as if that will somehow correct his terrible grammar.

"You're really terrible at Italian," I inform him when the waiter leaves, shaking his head.

"Good thing I have other skills." He's using that voice that makes me think of last night. And this morning.

"Like?" I aim for casual but miss by several time zones.

His foot finds mine under the table, his dress shoe sliding against my sandal in a slow, deliberate movement. "Wouldn't you like to know?"

"I already know. Three times, remember?"

"Four. You're forgetting the shower."

Heat crawls up my neck. "The shower doesn't count. That was just—"

"Just what?" His voice drops to that dangerous register that should come with a warning label. "Just you pressed against the tile while I—"

"Check, please!" I practically shout, flagging down our long-suffering waiter.

Dean laughs, the sound rich and genuine. He throws euros on the table with the confidence of someone who has no idea how much anything costs here. "Come on. Let's go buy you something inappropriate."

"More inappropriate than this dress?" I stand, smoothing down the sundress that's already riding up my thighs.

"Is that a challenge?" The look he gives me suggests he's already planning exactly how to make good on it.

We wander through the narrow streets, passing shops that sell everything from handmade pasta to questionable "designer" handbags. Dean immediately gravitates toward a stall displaying the tiniest bikinis I've ever seen outside of a dental hygiene convention.

"Absolutely not." I cross my arms and shake my head.

"This one's nice." He holds up what might generously be called a string with aspirations.

"That's not a bathing suit. That's dental floss with delusions of grandeur."

"Fashion-forward dental floss." He drapes it over me, considering it with the focus of a man making important fashion decisions. "We have a pool at the villa..."

"We have a goat at the villa." I push the string away.

"Good point. Wouldn't want to scandalize him." He pauses, hanging the bikini back up. "Although after the shower incident, I think that ship has sailed."

"George II has seen things," I agree solemnly.

"George II needs therapy."

Instead, I try on enormous sunglasses that make me look like a bug from a 1960s sci-fi movie. Dean takes approximately forty pictures, each more ridiculous than the last, laughing the entire time.

"Delete those." I'm trying to look stern but failing.

"Never. This is blackmail material." He's still snapping photos, circling me like a demented photographer.

"For what?"

"Future negotiations." He pulls me close, his hands settling on my waist as if they belong there. "When you're being stubborn about something."

"I'm never stubborn." I tilt my chin up, defiant.

He just looks at me.

"Okay, rarely stubborn." I'm wavering under his gaze.

The look continues.

"Shut up." I swat his chest.

We buy the sunglasses, a leather journal that I can't resist because of the smell, and a bottle of limoncello because Dean insists we need more. We sit by the harbor, eating gelato—pistachio for him, stracciatella for me. We people-watch, making up elaborate backstories for tourists, pointing out dogs and rating them on a scale from one to Muffin. We argue about whether that building is coral or salmon-colored.

"It's clearly coral," I insist, pointing with my gelato spoon.

"That's salmon. Look at the way the light hits it." He's squinting at the building like a serious art critic.

"That's not how color works."

"I have excellent color vision. I once won a case based on my ability to distinguish between burgundy and maroon."

I lower my gelato. "That's not a thing that happened."

"It could have happened." He's fighting a smile.

"Dean."

"Fine. But that building is still salmon."

"You're salmon." It's childish, but I don't care.

"That doesn't even make sense." But he's laughing.

"Your face doesn't make sense."

An elderly Italian woman pauses to stare at us. We're clearly disturbing the peace with our silly argument. Dean says something to her in his terrible Italian, probably trying to ask her opinion about the building. She pats his cheek like he's a particularly slow child and continues walking.

"This is fun," I say, surprised by how much I mean it.

He turns to me, gelato forgotten. "What?"

"You. Being fun. It's disconcerting. Like finding out your tax attorney secretly does stand-up."

"I'm incredibly fun. A delight. A joy to be around. Ask anyone." He's using his lawyer voice, making his case.

"You tried to evict me via a Reddit post." I point my spoon at him accusingly.

"That was before." His voice softens, becoming serious.

"Before what?"

He kisses me instead of answering. Right there on the street, with gelato-sticky fingers and tourist crowds around us. He tastes like pistachio and possibility, all the words he still can't quite say.

"Before that," he says against my lips.

We're heading back when we pass a jewelry store. One of those places with a window display that whispers "expensive" in twelve languages. Dean stops so abruptly I almost run into him. He's staring at the window display with an expression I can't read—intense, focused, almost hungry.

"See something you like?" I tease, but my voice comes out breathier than intended.

"Yeah."

The way he says it—soft, certain, like he's not talking about jewelry at all—makes my stomach do a complicated flip. His hand tightens on mine, and for a moment I think he's going to say something else. Something important.

But then he shakes his head, as if clearing it, and pulls me along. "Come on. I want to show you something."

He leads me through winding streets that get progressively steeper. And steeper. And dear God, even steeper. By the time we reach a small church on a hill, I'm wheezing like an asthmatic.

"You did that on purpose," I gasp, clutching the stone wall for support. My thighs are burning.

"The view's worth it," he says, not even slightly out of breath. The bastard.

And then I turn around, and okay, he's right. The entire coast spreads out below us—impossibly blue water dotted with boats like scattered confetti, buildings tumbling down the hillside in shades of amber and rose, the sun starting its descent and painting everything gold.

"Oh," I breathe, all annoyance forgotten.

"Yeah." He's not looking at the view. He's looking at me. "Oh."

We stand there as the light changes, as the church bells ring the hour, as the world goes soft and golden around us. His arms come around me from behind, and I lean back into his warmth, feeling his heartbeat against my back.

"I could stay here," I say quietly.

"In Italy?" His voice rumbles through his chest.

"In this moment." I turn in his arms, looking up at him. "With you."

Something shifts in his expression—hope and fear tangled together. "Poppy—"

"I know. We have to go back. Deal with real

life. Figure out what this is when we're not in vacation mode." I touch his face, feeling the slight stubble under my palm. "But right now, can we just—"

"Yes," he says, before I can finish. "Whatever you were going to say. Yes."

He kisses me as the sun sets over Portofino, and for once, I don't think about plans or business or what comes next. I just think about this—his hands in my hair, his solid warmth against me, the way he makes me feel like maybe chaotic disasters can have happy endings too.

"Ready to head back?" he asks eventually, when the light has faded to purple and the first stars begin to appear.

"Can we take a taxi? My feet have filed a formal complaint." I wiggle my toes in my sandals, feeling the blisters forming.

"I'll carry you." He's already bending as if he's going to scoop me up.

"Down a million stone steps? I've seen your coordination." I push against his chest, laughing.

"Not fair. I was distracted."

"Everything's distracting to you when I'm in a sundress."

"Guilty." He takes my hand, lacing our fingers together. "Come on. Let's go home."

Home. The word lands soft and warm in my chest.

"Yeah," I say. "Let's go home."

And maybe that's the whole thing—the answer to what we are and what we're doing. We're just two people who can't imagine being anywhere else.

"Ready to face the goat?"

"Together." The word comes out more serious than I intend.

"Together," I agree.

He helps me up but doesn't let go of my hand.

We find a taxi, and by the time we reach the villa, the sun has disappeared. The goat's gone, but it has left devastation in its wake.

"Poor roses," I mourn, surveying the carnage.

"They died for a good cause." He's already pulling me toward the door.

"Which is?"

"Getting us out of bed." He drops the bags and pulls me against him. "Although now that we're back…"

"You're predictable." But I'm already melting into him.

"You're beautiful." His hands slide up my back.

He laughs, kisses me, and walks me backward toward the door.

"Inside," he says against my mouth. "Now."

"Bossy."

"You love it."

I do. God help me, I really do.

Tomorrow we'll have to talk. About what this is, where we go, and what happens when real life crashes back in.

But tonight?

Tonight, I'm his.

Dean wraps himself around me like he's afraid I'll disappear. One arm is under my pillow, the other is tight across my waist. Even almost unconscious, the man doesn't do anything halfway.

"Your brain's too loud," he mumbles into my hair.

"Sorry." I try to still my racing thoughts.

"Don't apologize. Just talk to me." His thumb traces circles on my hip.

I turn in his arms and study his face in the dark. "Tell me about Emily."

His whole body goes rigid, every muscle tensing. "What?"

"That's not really a 2 a.m. conversation." His voice has gone careful and guarded.

"When is it a conversation?" I keep my tone gentle, not pushing.

"Never."

"Dean—" I start, but he cuts me off.

"Poppy. Please. I'm here with you, and she's the last person I want to be thinking about. She doesn't deserve any more of my headspace." There's pain in his voice, old and deep.

The "please" gets me. Dean doesn't say please. I don't know what to say, so I just hold him tighter, pressing my face into his chest.

"Tell me something else," I say eventually.

"Like?" He's relaxing slightly, the tension bleeding out.

"What were you like as a kid?"

He groans and rubs the back of his neck like he wants to dodge it. "Pass."

"Tell me, or I'm putting my cold feet on you." I wiggle my toes threateningly.

"Terrorist." But he's smiling—a small, reluctant smile that I love. "Fine. I was exactly what you'd expect. Quiet. Serious. Read constantly."

"What'd you read?" I prop myself up on an elbow, intrigued now.

"John Grisham. All of them. Multiple times."

"Nerd." I poke his chest affectionately.

"I conducted mock trials."

I sit up completely. "What?"

"I had a whole courtroom setup, with stuffed animals as the jury. This teddy bear—Mr. Bear, real original—was always the defendant." He's now talking to the ceiling, avoiding my gaze.

"Why?" I'm trying not to laugh.

"He had shifty eyes."

I'm laughing so hard the bed shakes. "You prosecuted a teddy bear?"

"Multiple times. He was clearly guilty." His defensiveness makes it even funnier.

"Of what?"

"Various crimes. Mostly theft. Sometimes fraud." He says it with such seriousness.

"Oh my God, you were adorable." I collapse back onto his chest, still giggling.

"I was weird." I can hear the old self-consciousness in his voice.

"Adorably weird." I settle back against him, kissing his shoulder.

I laugh into his shoulder. I can picture it: a serious, dark-haired little boy lining up his stuffed animals just so, presiding over them…

He reminds me a lot of the Dean I first met when I arrived at the estate—full of control, order, and iron-clad boundaries.

Then I think about the Dean who's currently naked in bed after flying to Italy on a whim, and I smile.

He pulls me closer, his arms tightening around me. "What about you? Ever been in love?"

Ugh. Fair's fair, I guess.

"I thought I was, in college. Jake." The name still tastes bitter.

"Jake." He spits it out as if it personally offended him. "Tell me Jake died tragically."

"He teaches kindergarten in Portland." I can't help but laugh at Dean's tone.

"Even worse." He sounds genuinely appalled.

I laugh despite myself. "He was nice—"

"Nice." He says it like it's a curse word.

"Stop saying it like that." I poke him again.

"Like what?" He's playing innocent, but I can hear the smile in his voice.

"Like 'nice' is code for having the personality of wheat toast."

"Isn't it?" He shifts beneath me to get more comfortable.

Okay, maybe. "We dated for two years. He liked that I had everything planned out and called me his little CEO."

"I already hate him." Dean's voice has gone flat, dangerously so.

"Dean." I try to sound warning, but it comes out fond.

"What kind of condescending—"

"He slept with my roommate." I say it quickly, ripping off the band-aid.

Dean goes rigid, actually rigid. "What?" His voice is low, concerned.

"I came back from winter break early. They

were in my bed. My actual bed, Dean."

"I just need a name. His full name. I know people." He's sitting up now, genuinely angry.

"You're not having someone murdered." I pull him back down.

"Just light maiming."

"Dean." But I'm laughing; I can't help it.

"Fine. Heavy maiming." He settles but keeps me close.

I kiss him to silence him. When I pull back, he's still frowning.

"In your bed though?" He sounds personally offended on my behalf.

"Right? There was a whole other bed literally six feet away." The old anger flares briefly.

"Disrespectful." He's tracing patterns on my back now, soothing. We lie there, breathing each other's air, holding these truths between us. "When was this?"

"Seven years ago."

"And since then?" His hand pauses on my back, waiting.

"Work." I shrug against him. "It's easier to plan other people's happy endings than risk my own."

"That's…" He pauses, choosing his words carefully. "That actually makes sense."

"Thanks?" I'm not sure if I should be offended.

"I meant—" He sighs. "I get it. The control thing. If you're running the show, no one can hurt you."

"Exactly." Relief washes through me that he understands.

"Except then some chaos agent shows up with

a goat…" His voice lightens.

"And ruins everything," I finish.

"Or fixes it." He says it quietly, but I hear the hope underneath.

We're quiet for a minute—just breathing, existing. It's nice.

"Your turn," he says eventually, clearly done with heavy topics. "Little Poppy stories."

"I ran a wedding business at recess. Second grade." I grin into the darkness.

"Of course you did." He sounds delighted, his chest rumbling with laughter. "Please tell me you have photos."

"Somewhere. I had a whole setup behind the jungle gym. A dollar per ceremony. Two dollars for the deluxe package with flower petals—dandelions I picked from the soccer field."

"Entrepreneurial." He sounds impressed, fingers playing with my hair.

I nod, strangely proud. "I made bank until the principal shut me down."

"Why?" He sounds genuinely offended on eight-year-old me's behalf.

"Apparently, eight-year-olds can't legally marry people." I can still remember my indignation.

"Fascists." He says it so seriously that I snort.

"Right? I had a whole system. Color-coded certificates. A briefcase."

"Tell me it was pink." I can hear his grin.

"Hot pink. With Lisa Frank stickers—dolphins and rainbows everywhere."

"Perfect." He's playing with my hair now, his fingers gently working through the tangles from our earlier activities. "What else?"

I debate how much to share but realize we're already neck-deep in vulnerability. "I'm an only child and was desperate for siblings. I used to beg my parents for a brother or sister every birthday."

"What did they say?" His hand stills in my hair.

"That I was enough. It sounds sweet, but it felt like code for 'we can barely handle one.'" I laugh, though it's not really funny. "So I used to marry my Barbies to each other so they could have families."

"That's—" He starts, but I cut him off.

"Sad, I know," I interrupt before he can confirm what I've always thought.

"I was going to say sweet." He kisses my temple, so gentle it makes my chest ache. "You've always been building families."

Why does that make me want to cry? Maybe because no one has ever framed it that way before—not as something pathetic or lonely, but as something… purposeful.

"I guess I have," I manage, blinking hard against sudden tears.

"All those weddings, bringing people together, creating new families every weekend." His arms tighten around me. "That's a gift, Poppy."

"Even when I create chaos in the process?" My voice is small.

"Especially then. Perfect families are boring. The messy ones are the ones that last."

I melt into him a little more, feeling something settle in my chest.

"Hey, Poppy?"

I'm half asleep already, warm and safe. "Mm?"

"Today was perfect for me too."

I sigh a little, content. My hand finds his in the dark.

Yeah. Tomorrow can wait.

36

ALL IN

Dean

She's making coffee wrong.

Standing in the villa's kitchen wearing my shirt and nothing else, she grinds beans like it's a personal vendetta. Her hair is everywhere—long, unruly, and probably tangled from my hands. I got a little carried away last night.

But how could I not?

"You're staring," she says without turning around.

"You're murdering those beans."

"They deserve it." She glances over her shoulder. "Want some?"

"I want to talk."

The grinder stops and her gaze flicks over to mine. "That sounds ominous."

"Not ominous. Just…" I scrub a hand through my hair. "Necessary."

She turns fully now, leaning against the counter, crossing her arms. The gesture pushes my shirt up her thighs, and I lose my train of thought for a second.

"Okay," she says carefully. "Talk."

Right. The speech I practiced in the shower. While she was sleeping. While I was panicking about messing this up.

"I figure we have two options," I start.

Her eyebrow arches. "Only two?"

"Don't be cute."

"Can't help it." Her mouth lifts in a wry smile. "Poppy."

"Sorry." She's not sorry. "Continue with your PowerPoint."

I move closer. I need to be closer. "Option one: We date long distance. You go back to California; I go back to New York. We text, FaceTime, meet up when we can, and see where this goes."

"Hmm." She's doing that thing where she doesn't give away what she's thinking. And she's really damn good at it. "And option two?"

This is the hard part. The scary part. The part where I lay it all out and hope she doesn't run.

"Option two…" I take a breath. "We go all in."

"Define 'all in.'"

Another shallow breath. "You move to New York. Move in with me. We skip the whole dating-across-the-country thing and just… do this. Together. For real."

Silence.

She stares at me. I stare back. Somewhere outside, that damn goat is probably destroying more landscaping.

"That's…" She stops. Starts again. "Dean, that's insane."

"Is it?"

"Yes! We've known each other—"

"One week, six days, and approximately six-teen hours."

"You counted?"

"I'm a lawyer. I count everything." I close the distance between us, boxing her in against the counter. "And you know what? I don't care. I spent four days without you, and it was the worst four days of my life."

"Dean—"

"I haven't passed the bar in California, so I couldn't work as an attorney there," I continue, riding the momentum. "But you could build some-thing incredible in New York—if you're up for it. The wedding planning scene there is insane. The Hudson Valley alone could keep you booked for years. Rich people with country estates and too much money."

"You've thought about this."

"I've thought about nothing else." My hands find her waist. "The guest cottage becomes your office. You terrorize Manhattan's elite. I come home to chaos and goats—"

"Dean."

I frame her face, making her look at me. "I want option two. I want you in my house, in my bed, in my life. Every day. Starting now."

Her eyes are doing something complicated. Getting shiny. Shit.

"You can't just—" Her voice cracks. "You can't just offer me everything I want and expect me to be rational about it."

"I don't want you rational. I want you mine."

"I am yours, you possessive disaster." She's

definitely crying now. Happy tears, I think. Hope. "But this is crazy. Moving in together after two weeks—"

"I know," I admit. "It might sound crazy, but…"

"Shut up." But she's smiling through the tears. "My whole life is in California. My apartment. My clients. My—"

"Your what?" I challenge. "Your thriving social life? Your deep connections? Your fulfilling existence that definitely doesn't involve working yourself to death to avoid feeling lonely?"

Direct hit. She glares. "That's not fair."

"It's completely fair. We're the same, Poppy. Hiding behind work because it's easier than admitting we want more."

"And you think more is me moving across the country to live with a man who argues with goats?"

"I think more is us. Together. Figuring it out as we go." I thumb away a tear. "Unless you want option one. Unless you want to do this the safe way."

She laughs—tearful and disbelieving. "When have I ever done anything the safe way?"

"So…?"

"So you're insane. This whole idea is insane. Moving in together, starting over, building a business…" She stops and takes a shaky breath. "It's completely crazy."

My heart sinks. "But?"

"But…" She loops her arms around my neck. "I want option two."

The world stops.

"You—what?"

"Option two. All in. The whole disaster." She's

full-on crying now, but also smiling so bright it hurts to look at. "Is that crazy?"

"Completely." I kiss her, tasting salt and coffee and future. "Let's be crazy together."

She laughs against my mouth. "My mother's going to freak."

"She's going to love me."

"Dean!"

"What?" I lift her onto the counter. "Call her later. I'll talk to her if you want."

She gives me a look. "Yeah? And say what?"

I shrug. "I'll tell her that I found someone who makes me want things."

"Things?" She blinks.

"Noise. Chaos. A life that's more than billable hours."

"Stop saying perfect things." She wraps her legs around me. "I'm already saying yes."

"Say it again."

"Yes."

"Again."

"Yes, you controlling—"

I kiss her quiet. Then not quiet. Then we're definitely going to scandalize this kitchen again.

"Wait," she gasps. "We need to talk logistics. When do we—"

"Later."

"But—"

"Poppy." I pull back to look at her. "We just decided to blow up both our lives and see what happens. Logistics can wait an hour."

She studies me. This woman who crashed into my life with her lists and her chaos and her ability to see right through me.

"An hour?"

"Maybe two."

"Dean Whitaker." She grins. "Are you suggesting we celebrate our completely insane decision with more sex?"

"I'm suggesting we seal the deal. Legally binding and all that."

"You're ridiculous."

"You love it."

The words hang there. Love. Not quite said but absolutely felt.

"Yeah," she says softly. "I really do."

And then we're kissing again, and talking becomes impossible, and somewhere in Italy a goat is probably plotting our demise, but I don't care.

Because she said yes.

To option two.

To crazy.

To us.

• • •

"We're really doing this," she says.

We're back in bed. Exhausted. Sticky. Stupidly happy.

"We're really doing this."

"I need to give notice on my apartment."

"I need to clean out my closet. Make space."

"Dean?"

"Mm?"

"What if it doesn't work?"

I think about it. Really think about it. What if she hates New York? What if we drive each other crazy? What if this thing between us burns too hot and flames out?

"Then we'll figure that out too," I say finally. "But Poppy?"

"Yeah?"

"I don't think that's going to be a problem."

She props up on an elbow. "No?"

"No." I tuck her hair behind her ear. "Because you're it for me. Whatever that means, however that looks. You're it."

"You can't just say things like—"

"Watch me."

She kisses me. Soft and sure and full of promise.

"For the record," she says against my lips, "you're it for me too."

"Good." I pull her back down. "Now stop talking. We have a whole life to plan."

"I thought logistics could wait."

"Changed my mind. Tell me about your California clients."

And she does. Talks for an hour about her business, her dreams, her plans. I listen and plot and picture her taking over Manhattan one wedding at a time.

Option two.

Best decision I've ever made.

Completely crazy.

Absolutely perfect.

Just like us.

37

THE OFFER

Dean

"**W**e need to talk."

Four words that have never meant anything good in the history of practicing law.

Tom Feldstein doesn't do office visits. He summons. You go. You genuflect. You leave with either a promotion or a pink slip.

I follow him to the conference room—the one with a view that costs more per square foot than most people's salaries. He's got that look—the one that made him legendary in hostile takeovers.

"Sit."

I sit.

"You've been here eight years."

"Yes."

"You've made us a lot of money."

"That's the goal."

He stares at me over his reading glasses, a look that probably makes grown attorneys cry. "The partners have been discussing your future."

Here it comes. The thing I've been working toward since I graduated law school. The brass ring.

The validation that all those hundred-hour work weeks meant something.

"We want to make you partner."

The words land like a verdict I'm not sure I wanted.

"Oh."

His eyebrow twitches. "'Oh?' That's your response to partnership?"

"I mean—thank you. It's an honor. I'm just—"

"Surprised?"

Conflicted. Panicked. Thinking about a woman who's currently planning to move in with me.

"Processing," I say instead.

"Take your time." He leans back and studies me. "Though I should mention, we need an answer within the month. The announcement—"

"Actually." The word escapes before I can stop it. "I need to take some time off."

Both eyebrows now. "Time off."

"Two weeks. Maybe three."

"You haven't taken time off in—"

"Four years. I know."

"May I ask why now?"

Deep breath. "I need to drive to California to help my girlfriend move." It's the wrong word, "girlfriend," but it's all I've got for now.

The silence stretches. His face goes through several unreadable expressions.

"Your girlfriend," he repeats slowly, as if I just said, "my unicorn."

"Yes."

"You have a girlfriend."

"I do."

"Since when?"

Since I flew to Italy and blew up my carefully constructed life. Since a wedding planner with a chaotic goat showed me what I was missing.

"Recently," I settle on.

"And she's moving here. For you."

"With me. Yes."

He removes his glasses and cleans them. It's his thinking gesture. "Dean, can I be frank?"

"Always."

"When we discussed partnership two years ago, you weren't ready. Brilliant lawyer, yes. But you were…" He searches for words. "Rigid. Isolated. One of those partners who burns out at fifty and dies at his desk."

"Flattering."

"I'm not done." He puts his glasses back on. "Something's different now. You seem… what's the word?"

"Unhinged?"

"Human." His mouth twitches, almost a smile. "The firm's evolving, Dean. We need partners who understand work-life balance—who bring more than just billable hours."

"And you think I—"

"I think a man who takes three weeks off to help his girlfriend move across the country might be just the kind of partner we need."

I stare at him. "You're serious."

"Dead serious. Take your time. Drive to California. Help your…" He pauses. "What does she do?"

"Wedding planner."

"Of course she is." Now he's definitely smiling. "Bring her back, then give us your answer."

"That's… not what I expected."

"Leadership isn't about grinding yourself into dust, Dean. It's about knowing what matters." He stands. Meeting over. "Three weeks. Full pay. Don't check email."

"I don't know how to not check email."

"Learn."

He's at the door when I find my voice. "Tom?"

"Yes?"

"What if I say no? To the partnership?"

He turns and studies me again. "Then you say no. And we figure out what you actually want. Either way, take the time. She must be something special if she's got you volunteering for a cross-country move."

Special. That's one word for the force of nature currently disrupting my calm existence.

"Yeah," I say. "She really is."

38

PARTNER

Poppy

Dean's on the floor with Muffin, and I'm trying not to melt into a puddle of goo.

"Mommy's being mean," he tells the dog, who sprawls across his lap like she owns him—which, let's be honest, she does. "She won't let me hire movers. Says she wants to 'do it ourselves' like we're pioneers."

"I can hear you." I lean against the doorway, watching this ridiculous scene unfold.

"Good. Maybe you'll see reason." He looks up at me from the floor, his hair mussed from Muffin's pawing, tie loosened, and the first two buttons of his shirt undone. He looks nothing like the terrifying lawyer who just got offered partner at one of Manhattan's most prestigious firms. "Professional movers, Poppy. They have trucks, equipment, and insurance."

"We have a truck," I counter, crossing my arms stubbornly.

"We have a U-Haul reservation," he corrects.

"Same thing."

"It's not remotely the same thing." He turns

back to Muffin, scratching behind her ears. "Tell Mommy she's being stubborn."

My heart does something stupid at 'Mommy.' He's been doing it all week—casual references to Muffin being 'our' dog, to me being her mom, to us being her parents. Like we're already a family. Like this thing between us has moved past the 'what are we doing' phase into something involving joint custody of a clinically anxious dog.

Like this is real.

Like this is forever.

I'm trying not to be terrified that this will all blow up in my face, but honestly? I'm the happiest I've ever been.

"I want to road trip," I explain, joining them on the floor and folding my legs beneath me. "The full moving-across-the-country experience. See the landscape change, eat terrible gas station food, play horrible music you'll hate."

"I already hate your music." But there's no bite to his words.

"Liar. I caught you humming Taylor Swift yesterday." I poke his shoulder.

"Lies and slander." But he's smiling, that soft grin that crinkles his eyes and makes him look younger. "Three thousand miles, Poppy. In a U-Haul."

"With you." I say it simply, as if that settles everything.

He's quiet for a beat, absorbing that. "I don't do road trips."

"You don't do a lot of things." I crawl into his lap, displacing a disgruntled Muffin who shoots me a look of pure betrayal. "You didn't do goats, or weddings, or feelings, or Italian food that wasn't from that place on 48th. Look at you now."

His hands find my waist automatically, his thumbs brushing the strip of skin where my shirt has ridden up. "I'm going to regret this."

"Probably." I'm grinning now, knowing I've won.

"You're going to make us stop at every tourist trap." His voice carries a fond resignation.

"Definitely. World's largest ball of twine, here we come."

He lifts one brow, considering his fate. "We're going to fight about the music."

"Constantly. But the make-up sessions in sketchy motel rooms will be worth it." I trace the collar of his shirt, feeling his pulse quicken.

He groans, but his hands tighten on my hips. "Fine. But I'm driving."

"Control freak."

"Chaos agent." He shoots back without hesitation.

"Your chaos agent," I correct, watching his face do that thing—that soft, wondering expression that makes me forget why I ever thought moving across the country for a man I've known for only a month was crazy. That look that says he still can't quite believe this is happening, that I chose him, that we chose each other.

"Yeah," he says quietly, his voice rough with emotion. "Mine."

Muffin whines from her exile on the cold floor, pawing at Dean's leg with increasing desperation.

"Ours," I amend, reaching down to scratch her ears. "Right, baby? We're all yours. One big, dysfunctional family."

"She's not our baby." He says it automatically, but without conviction.

"She's absolutely our baby. Look at her little face." I gesture at Muffin, who's making her most pathetic expression.

"We're not those people." But I can see him wavering, looking at the dog with entirely too much affection.

"We're absolutely those people." I kiss his jaw, feeling the slight scratch of five o'clock shadow. "We're going to be those insufferable people who have professional photos taken with their dog. Matching Christmas sweaters. The whole nine yards. Deal with it, partner."

He freezes. Complete stillness, as if I've said something in a foreign language.

"About that."

I pull back to see his face properly, tension creeping into my shoulders. "You're taking it, right? Dean. It's partner. It's what you've worked for. It's what you've sacrificed everything for."

"Is it?" His voice is careful, searching.

"Isn't it?" I counter, studying his expression.

He's quiet for a long moment, his fingers tracing absent patterns on my hip—the same spot he always touches when he's thinking, grounding himself in the reality of us. "I don't know anymore. Everything I thought I wanted… it all made sense before."

"Before what?" Though I think I already know.

"You." The word lands between us, heavy with meaning. "Before someone made me realize there's more to life than billable hours and corner offices. Before I understood that success might look different than I planned."

Oh.

My heart is doing that thing where it tries to crawl out of my chest and throw itself at him.

"Dean—"

"I'm taking it," he says quickly, as if he needs to get the words out before he loses his nerve. "Probably. Most likely. I have three weeks to decide." He meets my eyes, and there's a vulnerability there that would have sent him running a month ago. "Is that okay? That I don't know? That I might want… different things now?"

I think about the Dean I met three weeks ago—so sure of everything, so rigidly in control, emotions locked down tighter than Fort Knox, with a five-year plan laminated and color-coded. Now, he's on the floor with a dog that sheds on his Armani, planning a road trip in a questionable vehicle, admitting he doesn't have all the answers.

"It's perfect," I tell him, meaning every word. "Not knowing is very human of you. I'm proud of your emotional growth."

"I'm working on it." He looks almost shy saying it.

"I can tell. You haven't made a Reddit post about this decision, have you?" I narrow my eyes at him suspiciously.

"…no." The pause is too long.

"Dean." I can't help but laugh.

"I made a very small pros and cons list. That's it." He's defensive now, which is adorable.

"Dean." I chuckle, shaking my head. "We're having a serious conversation about your future."

"We're having a conversation about our future," he corrects, and there go my internal organs again, liquefying at the casual way he says "our." "Which includes decisions about where we live, how we live, whether I want to keep working hundred-hour weeks or maybe… find balance."

"Balance?" I mock-gasp, pressing a hand to my chest. "Who are you and what have you done with Dean Whitaker?"

"Shut up." But he's fighting a smile.

"Make me."

He does. Thoroughly. His mouth claims mine with a certainty that makes my toes curl. When we break apart, Muffin has reclaimed his lap, glaring at me like I'm the other woman.

"For what it's worth, I think you'd be an amazing partner. But I also believe you'd excel at whatever you choose." I cup his face, making sure he hears me.

"Even if I chose to quit and become a stay-at-home dog dad?" There's real curiosity in his voice.

"Especially then." I nod seriously. "Muffin needs structure."

He smirks, looking down at the neurotic bundle of fur. "She needs therapy."

"We all need therapy." I'm not even joking.

He laughs, the sound warm and genuine, and stands, pulling me up with him in one smooth motion. "Come on. Let's go look at the plans for turning the cottage into your office again."

Muffin follows us to the kitchen, where my sketches are spread across the island: plans for the guest cottage office, ideas for the main house, dreams in architectural form.

"I still think we should knock out this wall," I say, pointing at the main support beam.

"That's load-bearing." He doesn't even look, just knows.

"You don't know that." I'm being difficult on purpose now.

"I literally had an engineer confirm it." He pulls out the report, proof of his over-preparedness.

"Engineers can be wrong." I'm grasping at straws, and we both know it.

"Poppy." Just my name, delivered with patient exasperation.

"Fine. But we're definitely painting the bedroom." I concede the wall battle to win the war.

"It's already painted." He looks at me like I've suggested burning the house down.

"Beige isn't a color. It's giving up." I wrinkle my nose at the thought.

He wraps his arms around me from behind, his chin resting on my shoulder. "What color then?"

"Blue. Deep blue. Like—"

"Like the water in Portofino?" He says it softly, close to my ear.

I turn in his arms, surprised. "You remember that?"

"I remember everything." His voice drops, intimate. "The dress you wore. How you laughed when I accidentally ordered six pizzas."

"You are so bad at Italian." I'm smiling at the memory.

"I was nervous." The admission comes quiet, almost shy.

"Dean Whitaker doesn't get nervous," I tease gently.

"Dean Whitaker wasn't in love before."

The words hang between us. It's the first time he's said it, just dropped it casually, like it's a fact. Like the sky is blue, water is wet, and Dean Whitaker is in love with me.

My breath catches, my heart hammering. "Dean—"

"I know. It's too much. Too fast. Too—" He's rambling now, clearly nervous.

"Perfect," I interrupt, pressing my fingers to his lips. "It's perfect. You're perfect. We're perfectly insane, and I love you too."

His face does something adorable—shock, joy, and relief all at once. "Yeah?"

"Yeah, you emotional disaster. I love you. Why else would I be moving three thousand miles?" I'm grinning so wide my face hurts.

"My sparkling personality? My excellent taste in dogs?" He's trying to sound casual but is failing completely.

"Muffin chose you, not the other way around." I poke his chest.

"Details." He kisses me. Soft. Then not soft. Then desperate, like he needs to prove this is real. "Say it again."

"I love you." The words come easier this time.

"Again." His hands are in my hair now, holding

me close.

"I love you, you controlling—"

He silences me in the best way. When we finally break apart, we're both breathing hard, and Muffin is judging us from her bed.

"Three weeks," he says against my lips. "Then you're here. In our house. In our bed. Planning weddings for people who aren't us."

"About that—" I start, but he cuts me off.

"No." His tone is firm and immediate.

"You don't even know what I was going to say." I pull back, feeling indignant.

"You were going to make a joke about our wedding. I'm not ready for jokes about our wedding." But his ears are turning pink.

"But you're ready to think about our wedding?" I latch onto that detail like a lifeline.

His ears grow even pinker. "Shut up."

"Oh my God. You've thought about it. Dean Whitaker has thought about marrying me." I'm delighted, practically bouncing.

"I'm leaving." He tries to step away, but I hold on.

"You live here." I tighten my grip on his shirt.

"Then you're leaving." But he's not trying very hard to escape.

"I live here too. Or I will soon enough." I grin at him, victorious. "Admit it. You've pictured it."

"I've pictured nothing." He's lying, and we both know it.

"Liar." I poke him again for good measure.

He sighs, defeated, his shoulders dropping. "Fine. Maybe once."

"Where?" I'm leaning in now, invested.

"Poppy—" He tries to dodge, but I'm relentless.

"Where was our hypothetical wedding that you definitely didn't think about?" I'm not letting this go.

He sighs again, longer this time. Defeated. "The courthouse. Simple. Just us and whatever witnesses we could grab. No fuss. No chaos. No goats."

"That's…" I pause, genuinely touched. "Actually really sweet."

"It's practical." He's trying to maintain his composure.

"It's perfect." I kiss his pink ears, feeling them heat under my lips. "But there would definitely be a big reception. Fairy lights. All our family and friends." I'm grinning now because I can actually picture it.

"We'll negotiate." He sounds resigned to his fate.

"We'll do no such thing." But he's smiling, and I know I've won.

I go back to my sketches, but I'm smiling too hard to focus. Three weeks. Cross-country road trip. New life. New city. New everything.

With a man who loves me, a dog who needs therapy, and a future that's completely uncertain.

I've never been happier.

Or more terrified.

But that's okay. We'll figure it out.

Together.

39

FOR BETTER OR WORSE
(BUT MOSTLY BETTER)

Poppy

ONE YEAR LATER

George is eating my veil.

"George. No. Bad goat. Drop the— GEORGE!"

He looks me dead in the eye and takes another bite. Two thousand dollars of French lace, and this asshole's treating it like an appetizer.

"I'm going to turn you into kebabs," I tell him.

He bleats. Victorious. A piece of tulle hanging from his mouth like a trophy.

"Everything okay in here?" CeCe pokes her head into the bridal suite, takes in the scene—me in my wedding dress wrestling a goat, George looking smug—and starts filming. "This is content gold."

"Help me!"

"Absolutely not. This is going viral." She zooms in on George. "Work it, baby. Give me drama."

"I hate you both."

The door flies open. Dean stands there in his

tux, looking like every dirty dream I've ever had, and freezes.

"You're not supposed to see me before—"

"Is that goat eating our wedding?"

"Just the veil."

"Just the—" He crosses the room in three strides, grabs George by the collar. "Listen, you terrorist. We had a deal. You behave, you get to be ring bearer. You act up, you become dinner."

George bleats. Drops the veil.

"Thank you," I breathe.

Dean hands George off to CeCe. "Take him. Now. Before I change my mind about the whole farm-to-table menu."

"You wouldn't."

"Try me," he growls. Protective Dean is hot.

CeCe disappears with George. Dean turns back to me, and his face does that thing. That soft, stupid thing that still makes my stomach flip after a year.

"Hi," he says.

"Hi."

"You look…"

"Like I just wrestled livestock?"

"Beautiful." He steps closer. "Completely devastating, actually."

"You can't be here. It's bad luck."

"Poppy." His hands find my waist. "We've had a goat destroy three separate events, a wedding where the groom fainted into the cake, and that incident with the flamingos. I think we've maxed out our bad luck quota."

"The flamingos weren't my fault."

"You specifically requested ambitious bird options.”

“I meant doves!”

“You got ambitious.” He tucks an escaped curl behind my ear. “Twenty minutes?”

“Nineteen.”

“You’re really going to make me wait nineteen more minutes?”

“Dean Michael Whitaker.” I poke his chest. “We’ve waited a year. You can handle nineteen minutes.”

“Fine.” He kisses me anyway. Quick. Possessive. Full of promise. “But I’m going on record that this is cruel and unusual.”

“Noted for the court.”

He grins. That real one that only I get. “See you at the altar, wife.”

“Not wife yet.”

“Semantics.” He backs toward the door. “Don’t let George eat anything else.”

“Don’t let Mason give a speech.”

“He’s my best man. He has to give a speech.”

“Tell him to keep it PG.”

“I told him to keep it legal. Best I could do.”

He disappears. I turn back to the mirror, assess the damage. The veil’s toast, but honestly?

Kind of perfect.

Nothing about us has ever been pristine. Why start now?

40

BIG WIFE ENERGY

Dean

Mason's crying.

"Dude," I say. "Pull it together."

"I can't help it." He dabs his eyes with Ivy's handkerchief. "You're getting married. You. Mr. 'I Don't Need Anyone.' Mr. 'Emotions Are For Weak People.'"

"I never said that."

"You implied it. Heavily. For years."

He's not wrong. This is quite the one-eighty for me.

Nate appears with shots. "Emotional support tequila?"

"It's two in the afternoon," I point out.

"It's your wedding day." He distributes glasses. "Normal rules don't apply."

"I'm not doing shots before—"

"To Dean," Mason interrupts, raising his glass. "Who finally pulled his head out of his ass."

"Poetic," I mutter.

"And to Poppy," Nate adds, "for being brave enough to take him on."

"Saint Poppy," Mason agrees. "Patron saint of

lost causes."

"I hate both of you."

"No you don't." Nate clinks his glass against mine. "You love us. Look at you, having feelings."

I do the shot and immediately regret it. "That's paint thinner."

"That's celebration juice." Nate checks his watch. "Fifteen minutes. You ready?"

Am I ready?

I think about the woman currently in the bridal suite. The one who crashed into my life with chaos and color and made me want things I'd given up on. Who moved across the country on a promise and a prayer. Who built a wedding empire in the Hudson Valley while simultaneously rebuilding me.

Twelve months of Sunday mornings, bickering over coffee strength. Of her reorganizing my bookshelves based on a whim. Of George's supervised visits that somehow became unsupervised. Of Muffin sleeping between us because Poppy's too soft to say no.

Twelve months of being happier than I knew was possible.

"Yeah," I say. "I'm ready."

"Good." Mason claps my shoulder. "Because I saw George heading for the cake earlier."

"He what?"

"Kidding." He grins. "Probably."

"I need you all to know," I say calmly, "that if that goat ruins one more thing, I'm moving to a state with loose livestock laws."

"You'd never leave Poppy," Mason says.

"I'd take her with me."

"She'd bring George."

Damn. He's right.

"Time to go," Nate announces. "Positions, gentlemen."

We file out. The venue's perfect—a barn on the Hoffman property, because of course Poppy charmed them into hosting after planning their daughter's wedding. Fairy lights everywhere. Wildflowers that "just happened" to coordinate with her color scheme. Guests murmuring, waiting.

And me, standing at the altar, trying not to fidget.

"Breathe," Mason mutters.

"I'm breathing."

"Breathe better."

The music starts. My heart does something stupid.

First down the aisle: Muffin, wearing a flower crown and looking personally offended by the whole situation. She waddles to her designated spot, flops down with a dramatic sigh and lets out a fart.

Then George, the rings tied to his collar with what I'm assured is an "indestructible" ribbon. He immediately veers left, investigating someone's purse.

"Get the goat," I hiss at Nate.

"Not my goat, not my problem."

Nadine—because somehow she's involved in this—lures George back with what appears to be a bagel. He follows, rings jingling.

Then CeCe appears, gorgeous in lavender, shooting me a look that says *hurt her and I'll end you*. Gloria follows, carrying wildflowers and judgment in equal measure.

The music changes.
Everyone stands.
And there she is.
Poppy Monroe.
Soon to be Poppy Monroe *Whitaker*.
My whole world.

41

HAPPINESS OVERLOAD

Poppy

He's crying.

Dean Whitaker, terror of the New York legal system, is standing at our altar with tears running down his stupid perfect face.

"You okay?" Dad whispers.

"No," I whisper back. "He's crying. I'm going to die."

"From happiness?"

"From complete emotional overload."

We start walking. Every step feels huge. Monumental. Like I'm walking toward the rest of my life.

Which, technically, I am.

Dean's not even trying to hide it. Just standing there in his perfect tux, watching me like I'm everything, tears tracking down his cheeks while his best friend Nate hands him tissues.

I lose it.

"Don't you dare," CeCe mouths from her bridesmaid spot.

Too late. I'm crying. Dad's crying. Pretty sure George is crying, though that might just be him eating something new.

We reach the altar. Dad kisses my cheek, hands me over to Dean with a "Take care of her" that's both threat and blessing.

"Hi," Dean says, taking my hands. His voice trembles a little and so do my knees.

"Hi."

"You made it."

"Did you doubt?"

"Never." He squeezes my fingers. "You look—"

"I know. You already said."

"Worth saying again." He leans closer, whispers, "Also, your veil's missing."

"George ate it."

"Of course he did." He's smiling through the tears. "Perfect. It's perfect."

Father Murphy clears his throat. "Shall we begin?"

"Wait," I say. Everyone freezes. "Dean's crying. I need to document this."

"Poppy—"

"CeCe, phone. Now."

"I'm the maid of honor, not the—"

"Phone!"

She passes it over. I snap approximately thirty photos of Dean's tear-stained face while he tries to look stern and fails completely.

"For the wedding album," I explain.

"I'm going to get you for this," he mutters.

"Promise?"

"Oh, I promise."

Father Murphy tries again. "Now may we begin?"

"Yes," we say together.

The ceremony's a blur. Traditional vows because Dean insisted, though I may have added "even when you argue with goats" to the "for better or worse" part. Dean definitely added "in chaos and in calm" to his.

"The rings?" Father Murphy asks.

George, miraculously, still has them. Nate retrieves them with minimal drama, which is possibly the most shocking part of the day.

"Poppy," Dean says, sliding the ring on my finger. "I promise to love you, protect you, and build a life with you that's messier and louder and infinitely better than anything I imagined. You're my chaos, my calm, my everything. Even when you reorganize my office. Especially then."

I'm sobbing. Elegant? No. But who cares?

"Dean," I manage. "I promise to love you, challenge you, and remind you every day that there's more to life than billable hours. You're my anchor, my adventure, my home. Even when you measure pasta water. Especially then."

He laughs. Squeezes my hands.

"By the power vested in me," Father Murphy says quickly, probably sensing we're about to go off script again, "I now pronounce you husband and wife. You may kiss—"

Dean doesn't let him finish.

Pulls me against him like he's been waiting his whole life for this moment. Kisses me like we're alone, like the hundred and fifty guests don't exist, like it's just us and this promise and the rest of our lives.

Someone whoops. Probably Mason.

Someone bleats. Definitely George.

Someone sobs. Could be anyone, honestly. We're all disasters here.

When we finally break apart, Dean's grinning. "Hi, wife."

"Hi, husband."

"Ready for forever?"

I think about our life. The house that's never quiet. The dog who needs CBD to make it through the day. The goat who's basically a felon. The thriving business. The partnership he took and transformed, bringing humanity to divorce law. The babies we're already talking about.

The beautiful, chaotic, perfect disaster we built together.

"Yeah," I say. "I'm ready."

We run back down the aisle, dodging rose petals and George's attempt to follow us. Behind us, our people cheer. Our weird, wonderful, chosen family who somehow all fit together.

"No regrets?" Dean asks as we burst into the sunlight.

"One."

His face falls. "What?"

"We should've eloped."

He laughs. Picks me up. Spins me around while photographers capture every ridiculous second.

"Next time," he promises.

"There's not going to be a next time."

"No," he agrees, setting me down, pulling me close. "There's not."

And then he kisses me again, and I know—

deep in my bones—that this is it.

My person. My home. My happily ever after.

Even if it comes with goats.

Especially if it comes with goats.

42

FOREVER STARTS NOW

Dean

The reception's in full swing when I finally get her alone.

I've pulled Poppy into the coat closet because apparently, I'm that guy now. The one who can't keep his hands off his wife at his own wedding.

"Someone's going to notice we're gone," she says, but she's already yanking my tie loose, fingers working the knot.

"Don't care." I'm already pressed against her, breathing her in.

"Very professional, counselor." Her voice is teasing, breathless.

"Screw professional." I press her against the wall, feeling her heart racing under my palms. "You're my wife."

"Say it again." Her hands are in my hair now, messing up what took the stylist an hour.

"Wife." Kiss her neck. "Wife." Her collarbone. "Wife."

"Okay, caveman, I get it—oh." The last word comes out strangled as I hit the spot behind her ear.

Yeah. Oh.

"Five minutes," I negotiate against her skin. "Give me five minutes."

"Dean—" She's already melting into me.

"Come on." I slide my hand up her thigh, find the garter I watched her put on this morning. "For luck."

"You're impossible." But she's not pushing me away.

"You love it." I nip at her jaw.

"I love you," she corrects, then gasps because I've found the spot that makes her forget arguments. "Damn it. Okay. Five minutes. But if someone—"

The door opens.

"OCCUPIED!" we yell together, jumping apart like teenagers.

"It's me, you degenerates." Ivy. Of course. "Your wedding planner's looking for you. Something about speeches?"

"Tell her we're dead," I suggest, not letting go of Poppy's waist.

"Tell her five minutes," Poppy counters, trying to smooth her dress.

"I'm not telling her anything. She scares me." Ivy's footsteps retreat. "But I'm standing guard. You've got three minutes before I let her in."

Poppy straightens my tie, fingers gentle now instead of urgent. "Come on. We have a lifetime for coat closet shenanigans."

"Promise?" I catch her hand, threading our fingers together.

"Promise." She kisses me. Quick. Perfect. "But

first, speeches. And cake. And that dance you've been secretly practicing."

"I haven't been—" I start to protest, but she's giving me that look.

"Mason sent me videos." She's smirking now, victorious.

"Traitor." I shake my head, already planning my revenge.

"You're going to be amazing." Another kiss. "My husband, the secret dancer."

My chest does that thing it's been doing all day. "Say that again."

"Which part?" She tilts her head, playing innocent.

"The husband part."

She smiles. The one that still stops my heart, even after everything. "My husband."

"Your husband," I agree, pulling her close one more time. "Forever."

"Forever." She says it like a vow, like she means it down to her bones.

• • •

We sneak back to the reception, her hand in mine, both of us trying not to look like we just made out in a coat closet. Take our seats. Listen to speeches that range from heartfelt (Mason) to hilarious (CeCe). Cut the cake without incident, though George definitely tries. Dance our first dance to a slow, romantic song because Poppy's a romantic and I'm a sucker for her.

"Not bad, counselor," she says as I spin her, her dress flaring out around us.

"I had a good teacher." I pull her back in, closer than before.

"YouTube?" Her eyes are sparkling with mischief.

"Mason, actually." I can't help but smile at the memory of my brother trying to teach me to waltz in his living room.

She laughs, the sound bubbling up. "Of course."

The song ends. Another begins. Our people join us on the dance floor. Nadine's doing something that might be the Electric Slide with Father Murphy. Gloria's teaching Nate to tango. George is… eating someone's centerpiece.

"Should we stop him?" Poppy asks, watching the goat with fond exasperation.

"Nah." I pull her closer, swaying with her. "Let him have his fun."

"You've gone soft." She's looking up at me with that expression I never get tired of.

"Your fault." I kiss her forehead.

"Guilty." She rests her head on my shoulder, fitting against me perfectly. "Hey Dean?"

"Mm?" I'm half-lost in the moment, the music, the feel of her.

"We did it."

"The wedding?" I pull back slightly to see her face.

"All of it. The whole thing. Built a life. Got married. Didn't kill each other."

"Yet." I can't resist.

She pinches me, right at my waist. "I'm being sentimental."

"Sorry. Continue." I rub the spot she pinched,

grinning.

"I'm just…" She looks up at me, eyes shining in the fairy lights. "I'm really happy."

Something cracks open in my chest. The last piece of armor I didn't know I was still wearing.

"Me too," I admit, voice rougher than I intend. "Terrifyingly happy."

"Good scared or bad scared?" Her hand comes up to touch my face, gentle.

"Good. Definitely good." I spin her again, just to see her smile, to watch her dress twirl. "Best thing that ever happened to me scared."

She laughs. Bright and real and mine.

"I love you," she says, squeezing my hand. "My disaster. My husband. My home."

"I love you too," I tell her, meaning every word. "My chaos. My wife. My everything."

The music swells. Our people dance. George bleats somewhere in the distance, probably destroying something expensive.

And for the first time in my extremely controlled life, everything's exactly as it should be.

Messy. Loud. Complicated. Real.

Perfect.

Absolutely freaking perfect.

• • •

Later, much later, when the guests have gone and we're sitting on the porch of our venue, watching the sun set over the Hudson Valley, Poppy leans into me.

"No regrets?" she asks.

I think about the boy who had it all figured out.

The plan. The trajectory. The carefully controlled life that made sense.

Then I look at what I have instead.

This woman who sees through my bullshit. This family we've built from scratch. This life that's nothing like I imagined and everything I never knew I needed.

"No regrets," I confirm. "You?"

"One." Her eyes meet mine.

"What?"

She grins. "We should've gotten two goats."

A deep chuckle falls from my lips. "Absolutely not."

"Three?"

"Poppy."

"Fine. But I want a peacock."

I use my stern lawyer voice. "We are not—"

She kisses me quiet. And yeah, okay.

Maybe one peacock.

But that's it.

Probably.

The End

(Just kidding. With these two? It's just the beginning.)

EPILOGUE

Dean

Posted to r/AmItheAsshole
username: RestingBriefFace

Final Update

About a year ago, I came here to complain about goat poop, fairy lights, a woman who reorganized my estate, and a very complicated earring situation.

Then I posted again—about if I should go after her in Italy. Your comments were… brutal, but fair.

So I just wanted to say: You were right.

About everything.

I said the words. (Out loud. With eye contact. No metaphors.)

She forgave me.

We spent a week in Italy, rarely leaving

the bed. And when we did, it was only to get coffee or eat pasta, or wander until we found gelato. It was the most perfect week of my life. I laughed more than I have in a decade.

I came home and married her as fast as she'd let me.

We're figuring it out—slowly, honestly, and together. She makes tea every morning. I learned how to roast vegetables. The goat still lives on the property. His name is George. We don't question it anymore.

Muffin now has her own Instagram account and more followers than I do. I'm fine with it.

(Mostly.)

Anyway, I wanted to say thank you.

For the advice. The snark. The unsolicited goat GIFs.

And for reminding me that sometimes, being vulnerable is worth the mess.

Especially when the mess wears linen dresses and sings to animals.

TL;DR:

She stayed. So did the goat. And for once in my life, I'm not looking for the exit.

gayunclesrevenge:

I KNEW IT. My enemies-to-lovers radar *never* fails. Proud of you, emotionally reformed legal bro.

goatgirl66:

GEORGE STAYS. WINNING!

CozyChaosQueen:

This is the best rom-com I've ever read.

MuffinStan92:

Please confirm if Muffin was flower dog at your wedding. The people NEED TO KNOW.

passiveaggressiveduck:

You've come a long way, my dude. I'm genuinely proud.

EPILOGUE II

FIVE YEARS LATER

She's crying again.

Not the angry, hungry cry, but the soft, hiccupy one that means bad dreams. I'm out of bed before my brain catches up, bare feet on the cold hardwood, muscle memory guiding me down the hall.

"Hey, sweet girl."

Emma's sitting up in her crib, tears on her cheeks, clutching the stuffed goat Nadine gave her. (Yes, a goat. Yes, I protested. Yes, I lost.)

"Dada."

One word. It wrecks me every time.

"Yeah, baby. Daddy's here." I scoop her up, and she melts into my chest. Eighteen months old, and she already has me wrapped around her tiny finger. "Bad dream?"

She nods against my shoulder, still sniffling, her breath warm against my neck.

"Want to tell me about it?"

"No." Firm. Decisive. She already knows what

she wants.

"Okay." I don't push. We have time for that later.

I carry her to the rocking chair Poppy insisted on. Said every nursery needs one. I argued about cost per use; she won by being pregnant.

Emma curls into me, thumb in mouth, breathing still shaky. I rock, hum something tuneless, and wait.

This is my favorite part of fatherhood. Not the fun stuff—though watching her chase George III (don't ask) around the yard is pretty great. But this: the weight of her trust, the way she fits perfectly in the crook of my arm, the absolute certainty that I'd burn the world down to keep her safe.

"Better?"

She nods but doesn't move, burrowing deeper. We've got time.

Through the window, I can see the guest cottage. The light's still on. Poppy's probably up planning the Summers wedding, the Dayton anniversary, or any of the dozen events that make up our beautifully chaotic life.

"Mama?" Emma asks, voice small and sleepy.

"Working. But she'll come kiss you soon." I adjust her weight, keeping her secure.

"'Kay." She accepts this easily, trusting.

She's getting heavy in that way that means sleep's winning. I should put her back in the crib. I should go back to bed. I should do a lot of things.

Instead, I keep rocking.

"Love you, Emmy girl."

"Wuv you, Dada."

And damn. There it is. The thing that breaks me every time.

Twenty minutes later, Poppy finds us. I hear her before I see her—bare feet on hardwood, that little sigh she makes when she sees us.

"Hey," she whispers, leaning against the door-frame.

"Hey yourself." I keep rocking, not wanting to disturb Emma.

She kneels beside the chair, running her fingers through Emma's curls with infinite gentleness. "She woke up?"

"Bad dream." I keep my voice low and sooth-ing.

She gives me that look. The one that says I've gone soft, but she loves me anyway.

"Come on." She eases Emma from my arms with practiced precision. Our girl doesn't even stir. "Bed. Both of you."

I watch Poppy tuck Emma in, smoothing the blanket, adjusting the goat just so, kissing her fore-head with such tenderness it makes my chest ache.

Back in our room, Poppy pulls me into bed, immediately curling into my side. Her spot. It has been since that first night in Italy when we decided to blow up our lives for each other.

"Missed you," she murmurs into my chest.

"You saw me three hours ago." But I'm already wrapping my arms around her.

"Still missed you." She presses closer, seeking warmth.

I pull her closer. She's cold—always is when she works late. I run my hands down her back, trying to warm her up.

"Dayton anniversary?" I guess, feeling her relax into me.

"Mm. They want doves." There's exhaustion in her voice.

"'Course they do." I kiss the top of her head.

"Told them we'd discuss alternatives." She yawns against my shoulder.

"Good girl."

She laughs softly, the sound vibrating through me. "Remember when you tried to ban all livestock from events?"

"Tried being the operative word." I'm smiling into the darkness.

We're quiet for a minute, just breathing together. These are my favorite moments—when the world stops and it's just us. No depositions. No timelines. No negotiations with terrorist toddlers.

Just us.

"Dean?"

"Yeah?" I'm already half-asleep, her warmth making me drowsy.

"What were you thinking about? In the chair with Emma?"

I consider lying, saying something flip. But it's almost midnight, and she's in my arms, and tomorrow isn't guaranteed.

"How I never thought I'd have this."

She props up on an elbow, looking down at me in the dim light. "This?"

"You. Her. The whole… thing." I gesture vaguely at the room, at our life. "Family. The real kind. Not the performance my parents put on."

"Dean—" She starts, but I need to finish.

"I was so scared when you were pregnant." The admission comes out rough, caught in my throat. "I kept thinking I'd mess it up. Be like my dad. Cold. Distant. More interested in winning than… than being there."

"But you're not." Her hand finds my chest, palm flat over my heart.

"Because of you." I cover her hand with mine.

"No." Her hand finds my face in the dark, cupping my cheek. "Because of you. Because you chose differently. Every day, you choose her. Choose us."

"Easy choice." The easiest I've ever made.

She kisses me—soft, sweet. My body notices.

"You need sleep," I tell her, even as I pull her closer.

"In a minute." She settles against me, fitting perfectly.

"Poppy—" I start to protest, but she cuts me off.

"Just… let me stay here a minute. With you. Like this."

So I do. I hold her while her breathing evens out, while the house settles around us, while our daughter dreams whatever perfect dreams toddlers have.

"Love you," she whispers, mostly asleep.

"Love you too, disaster."

"Your disaster." Her words are slurred with sleep.

"The only one I want."

She's out between one breath and the next. I

should sleep too. Big day tomorrow—deposition at nine, Emma's playdate at two, dinner with Mason and Ivy.

But for now, I just hold her—my wife, the mother of my child, the woman who crashed into my life with a goat and rebuilt me from the ground up.

Worth every sleepless night.

Worth everything.

• • •

Emma's awake.

Not crying. Just… talking. Full conversations with her goat about God knows what.

"Your turn," Poppy mumbles, face buried in her pillow.

"How's it my turn? I did three AM." I'm already sitting up, rubbing my eyes.

"Exactly. I do mornings after you do nights." She doesn't even open her eyes.

"That's not the system." But I'm already swinging my legs out of bed.

"It's exactly the system." She pulls the blanket over her head.

"Since when?" I'm standing now, looking for my sweatpants.

"Since I'm tired and you're whipped." I can hear the smile in her voice.

Can't argue with that logic. I crack a smile despite the hour.

I find Emma standing in her crib, goat in one hand, my reading glasses in the other. Her hair sticks up in a dozen wild directions, eyes bright as if she's already plotted half the day.

"Where did you—never mind." I lift her out, feeling her solid weight in my arms. "Morning, criminal."

"Hi, Dada!" Like the sun coming out. Every damn time.

"Hungry?" I carry her toward the kitchen.

"Uh-huh." She's already bouncing in my arms.

"What do we want? Pancakes? Eggs? The souls of our enemies?" I'm heading down the hall now.

She giggles, delighted by the routine. "'Nanas!"

"Bananas it is. But first, diaper." I set her on the changing table.

"No." Immediate. Decisive.

"Yes." I reach for a fresh diaper.

"No no no." She's already wiggling away.

"Emma Jane—" I use my warning voice.

She takes off running—in a diaper that definitely needs changing. Clutching my glasses and cackling like a tiny villain. Her feet slap the hardwood, goat bouncing at her side, my heart already bursting at the seams.

This is my life now—chasing a half-naked toddler who's apparently part track star, part goat, all Poppy.

I catch her by the kitchen. She shrieks with laughter as I swing her up.

"Gotcha." I'm breathless, which is embarrassing.

"Again!" She's beaming, hair even wilder now.

"After diaper." I hold her at arm's length, assessing the damage.

Her nose wrinkles in that way that's pure Poppy. "No diaper!"

"Yes diaper." I give her my best lawyer glare, which only makes her smirk wider.

"Negotiate!" She announces it proudly, like she's discovered fire.

I stop, blink. "What?"

She grins, pure mischief. "Nego-she-ate!"

"Who taught you—" I cut myself off. Stupid question. I can practically hear Poppy cackling from the bedroom. "Fine. Terms?"

"Two 'nanas." She holds up two fingers, confident.

"One banana." I hold up one, matching her energy.

Her tiny fist shoots into the air. "Two!"

"One and a half," I counter, already knowing I'm sunk.

She considers it, her tiny brow furrowed in concentration. "Deal."

I'm negotiating fruit portions with someone who can't tie shoes—and losing.

"Good job, baby. Now diaper." I carry her back to the changing table.

"Dada?" She's looking up at me with those eyes.

"Yeah?" I'm already melting, diaper in hand.

"Love you."

And there it is—the daily destruction of Dean Whitaker, Attorney at Law.

"Love you too, monster. More than all the bananas in the world." I kiss her forehead, breathing in her baby shampoo smell.

She pats my face with sticky hands. "Silly

Dada."

Yeah. The silliest.

And the happiest.

Who knew?

Acknowledgements

To my readers—thank you from the bottom of my heart. Your love for my books keeps me writing late into the night and waking up excited to dive back into these worlds. Every message, review, and preorder means more than I can say. You're the reason this book exists.

To my husband, John—thank you for being my rock and my biggest cheerleader. I couldn't do this without your patience, support, and endless encouragement. To my two amazing sons—you are my joy, my laughter, and the absolute best part of every day. I adore you both more than words.

To Karin Enders, who waved her editing magic wand over this book (and who I'm eternally grateful didn't run for the hills). This one was a royal mess, and wrangling Dean and Poppy onto the page was harder than herding cats. I blame George. Thank you for believing in me—and in them—even when they refused to behave.

Thank you also to Virginia Tesi-Carey for your proofreading magic! And to Alyssa Garcia for just being you. I'm so happy to have you on my team.

And to everyone who picked up this book—you've made my dream possible. Thank you, thank you, thank you.

About the Author

A *New York Times, Wall Street Journal*, and *USA Today* bestselling author of more than three dozen titles, Kendall Ryan has sold millions of books and they have been translated into several languages in countries around the world.

Her books have also appeared on the *New York Times* and *USA Today* bestseller lists more than 100 times. Ryan has been featured in such publications as *USA Today, Newsweek*, and *InTouch Magazine*.

She lives in Texas with her husband and two sons.

Other Titles by Kendall Ryan

For a complete list of Kendall's books, visit:
www.kendallryanbooks.com/books